2492

Attack Of The Ancient Cyborg

by

Eric Nixon

Dedication

This book is dedicated to my wife, Kari. Thank you for your constant support and encouragement through all of the years I worked to bring this story to life. This book exists because of you.

A Deadly Race

The warning klaxons shrilly stung her ears and echoed in tight confines of Bryn's spacesuit as she ran as fast as her enhanced body could manage down the narrow hallway – but the fireball was faster. The pressure wave lightened her steps as it buffeted and shoved on by; she grimaced, struggling to keep her eyes focused on the wide doors ten meters ahead while trying to ignore the flickering orange reflecting off the walls and her shadow lengthening on the brightening bare steel floor streaking underfoot. Red words on her faceplate display reminded how dire her chances of survival were.

A voice in her ear offered, "There's a narrow doorway ahead on your right. There will be a counter you'll have to jump over, but that should offer you enough protection." She appreciated the friendly tone but at the moment she would have preferred her home computer yelling in her ear, not being so nice.

"I, I don't think I can make it, Crane."

"You can…but just barely. Now!"

With near superhuman precision, she pivoted and pushed off the wall with her left foot, catapulting her through the opening, over the waist-high counter. Half a moment later, the whooshing wall of fire blew past, and briefly eddied in the entryway before quickly dissipating.

Bryn shook her head and checked the legs of her spacesuit to see how badly it was charred. She was surprised when everything was intact and gave herself a second to release a sigh of relief and said, "Thanks." The display in her visor showed a green smiley face.

"You're not safe yet. It's still out there, and you've got to get moving otherwise she will get to the controls first."

Ugh. She's going to be the death of me. Bryn hopped up to her feet and peered around the corner. Nothing. She turned right and raced to the wide doors, which slid open, letting her pass through to a large terrace that overlooked a fathomless drop-off into the sparsely-lit recesses of the massive space station. The far side of the expanse across from this towering building was another cliff-like building that culminated with a wide control platform. Encircling this portion of the station was a giant curving window dominated by a monstrous whirlpool-like stellar anomaly twisting uncomfortably close in nearby space.

Her faceplate lit up and zoomed in on an open-air tower on the building directly across. Her suit said, "That's it."

"Where is she?"

"Watching you from a lower terrace two floors down and 47 meters to your left."

Bryn turned to see a dark navy-colored spacesuit waive and fiddle with a small object.

"Shuck, she's going to get there first. What's the distance?"

A series of ghostly footprints appeared on her faceplate with an arrow showing her path to the other side. "You can do it with maybe a meter and a half to spare. Be aware that this will be one of the longest jumps you've attempted."

"Got it, thanks. How far is the drop?"

"Un-survivable."

With an eye-roll she muttered, "of course." Bryn backed up, rolled her shoulders, cracked her back, crouched, and sprinted. The edge blurred up to her and she pushed off with all her might, sending her sailing through the air, arcing toward the platform.

Her suit cautioned, "She threw an object in your direction, but it will miss." A small canister flew past and sprayed out a glittery gas. A now-familiar warning sounded as the display showing her chances of landing safely had dropped to zero. "Bryn, It was an air-thickening agent. Deploy your Tracelets."

As she passed into the sparkling air, her speed dropped rapidly and her trajectory nosedived toward the bottomless darkness below. Bryn's arms flailed uselessly in the direction of the platform's ledge.

To her peripheral left, a spacesuit sailed by, making the same jump Bryn had intended.

As she fell, Bryn snapped a wrist back and the Tracelet on her suit launched and latched a personal tractor beam onto the other spacesuit, yanking her back toward the ledge she just landed on.

In a desperate bid to avoid being pulled into the pit, the woman in the other spacesuit deployed her own Tracelets onto a far wall and pulled herself, and by default, Bryn, up and onto the top of the building.

Bryn rolled fast to avoid a foot aimed at her and responded with a kick of her own that knocked the other person down – inadvertently saving her as a blast of flame whooshed past. Bryn was barely aware of the other woman scrambling away as a fist-sized, fire-spraying drone zipped by. With a blue blur, the woman deftly avoided another volley of searing plasma bursts, rolled, sprung to her feet, and ran with the drone closing fast.

Great! She's occupied, so now I can get to the controls first. Bryn moved as quickly as she could. Thirty meters…twenty…

A brightness accompanied by a mildly explosive wave washed past, casting a quick shadow. She was about to turn when her suit exclaimed, "Don't turn around! You're almost there. Keep running!"

The control platform was perched atop a five-meter tower that overlooked the rest of the cavernous central core of the station. Without thinking or breaking her stride, Bryn effortlessly leapt into the air and aimed her legs forward to land at the controls.

For a fraction of a second, she was confused as the platform stopped moving up to greet her feet and she seemed to hang in mid-air. Amid the too-frequent warning chimes in her helmet, the sickening pull on her waist killed her inertia and pulled her violently backward as her arms uselessly lurched for the controls just out of reach.

Twisting to the side, Bryn saw the blue spacesuited woman was using her Tracelets to pull Bryn across the metal floor. She reached around, grabbed a molded handle attached to her belt, pressed a button and bided the four seconds of warm-up time until she would need to act. As she slid, she briefly noticed that the other woman had apparently rendered the fire-spitting drone into a charred lump of melted metal at the base of the window – but was more concerned with how terrifyingly close the anomaly was just outside. Taking up the entire span of the mammoth window, the swirling superheated elemental gases twisted in a hellish spiral to the fragmented magnetar that was somehow generating this spinning cosmic blender threatening to consume the station. *I don't have time for this. If I can't get to the controls, we're all dead.*

The other woman pulled Bryn toward her with the invisible tractor beams of her Tracelets.

"Now!" said Bryn suit.

She soled her feet flat on the floor in front of her and rose while still sliding. As Bryn passed, she unhooked the handle, squeezed it, and swung the burning fury of the sun sword's elongating blade at the woman in the blue spacesuit, who yelped as she tried to dodge the deadly slice. The tip seared through the blue suit, barely catching her flesh and leaving a puckering, bubbling, burning slash across her stomach.

The woman's movements to try and avoid the sun sword caused the Tracelets to toss Bryn aside and she smacked hard into the giant window.

Red lights furiously flashed as the station's alarm sounded. "DANGER," the station warned. "HULL BREACH. EVACUATE IMMEDIATELY."

As Bryn shook off the concussion, she saw, with horrified eyes, that the electric fire of her sun sword's blade was hilt-deep through the window and weakening the area around it.

Her suit offered a final positive thought, "Well, at least you tried."

"*Shuckkk…*"

The window softly blurped out into the void, like melted candle wax, spewing the two humans into space where they were instantly incinerated by the superheated jets of heavily irradiated gas and their carbon became indistinguishable from the other elements swirling past.

Life After Death

Bryn sighed and rolled her eyes at the large red blinking letters telling her: *YOU DIED!* She sat up, removed her helmet, and wacked it into the young woman in the blue spacesuit lying on the floor beside her. "Jerk."

Amory yanked off her helmet and hit her back. "Hey! Jerk yourself. I wasn't the one who felt the need to whip out a sun sword, of all things, and get all kinds of stabby on the window with it."

A life-like hologram of a person sitting in a puffy chair coalesced nearby. "Would you two like the run-down of this rather tragic training exercise?"

Floating screens opened on either side of the hologram figure. "Okay, let's review training 1,310, also known as Control Panel Race number 48." They pointed to the screen on the right. "On this side, we have Bryn Struse, who did wonderfully against the seven rooms set on auto-defend." They frowned slightly, "But, alas, she ran into some difficulty when faced with the small killer bot."

"That was so not fair." She turned to her friend and asked, "How did you do…"

The holographic figure interrupted, "Aht! We'll get to Amory in a moment. Anyway, you were not only nearly beaten by it but you allowed it to tear your suit."

"I wouldn't say 'allowed'."

The screen split and showed a clip of Bryn running determinedly down a hallway and screeching to a halt as a small orange, poof-like robot puppy with comically large eyes scampered into her path, made an adorable "waroof!"-sound while waiving a tiny paw at her.

"Nope, no need to show this. Turn it off!" Bryn tossed her helmet at the figure in the chair, which sailed harmlessly though them and rolled off to a corner of the projection room. "Come on, Crane, we don't need to see this."

Amory sat up with a huge smile on her face, "Oh, I think we really need to see this."

In the video, Bryn said, "YOU. ARE. SO. CUTE!" and scooped up the puppybot. "What are you doing here all by yourself? Well, I just can't leave you here. That'd just be wrong!" She snuggled it close to her, "I have a mission to do but afterwards, I'm going to take you home!" As she hugged it, its eyes turned red and its mouth opened, revealing rows of metal beartrap-like teeth.

"Woof! Waroof!" it squeaked in agreement as it lunged forward. The video froze."

"Oh, come on!" protested Amory.

Bryn asked, "Did Amory have to face the puppybot too?"

Crane replied, "Yes, but I have to caution that she handled it a little differently than you did." They gestured to the screen on their left. "Over here we have Amory Sutherland. She started the training at a different location in the station, but faced identical challenges. She also disabled the seven auto-defended rooms, but this is what she did when faced with an adorable killer puppybot."

In the video, Amory ran down a hallway and a small purple, poof-like puppy bounded out of a nearby room and looked up at her expectantly.

Without slowing down, or missing a beat, the spacesuited Amory hopped over the puppybot and kept running.

Bryn looked at Amory, "Wow. You're heartless. You didn't even glance at it. Actually, I'm kinda relieved, I thought you were going to kick it."

"I almost did!"

"Jerk."

Crane said, "Ah, but bypassing the adorable killer puppybot cost her some time later on. Watch."

The clip continued with Amory running down the hall and out of sight. The puppybot glared in her direction, levitated straight up into the air, and flew after her with its toothy mouth becoming a chompy blur.

Crane leaned back in their chair and said, "Her ignoring the situation ended up, literally, biting her in the ass later."

Bryn laughed.

"Yeah, yuk it up, Struse. At least I didn't cuddle a killer bot."

"I have to say that I would probably do it again. I mean, did you see it? It was SO cute!"

A hologram puppybot appeared next to Bryn.

"See? Come here little guy."

It hopped into her lap, curled up, and fell asleep.

Amory shook her head. "Don't come crying to me if it attacks you before we leave the projection room. Twice bitten, twice stupid."

Crane said to Amory, "It won't bite her, but in a minute it will drool all over her." To both of them, they said, "I'm going to skip ahead to the end bit."

"Yeah, what's up with that whole sun sword thing?"

Bryn looked up at Amory. "What? I think sun swords are really neat. We each got to pick one weapon or tool before the simulation started. You picked those air-thickeners, I picked a sun sword."

Crane commented, "Amory, nice use on the air-thickeners, by the way."

"Thanks."

They continued, "I know you two were competing this time when normally you work together, but in future training scenarios you might want to scale back on the risk-taking and focus more on self-preservation."

Amory asked, "Can you remove the sun sword from possible weapon choices?"

Bryn whispered at her, "Hey A, be quiet!"

Crane agreed, "Done." They said to Bryn, "It's not like you'll ever encounter one in real-life. The only people who have them belong to a tiny martial-based religious order that lives on a small moon orbiting an Outer Fringe planet. It may as well be a fictional item."

A chime sounded and Crane stood up. "Ah! Your lunch is ready in the kitchen. Anyway, it was a good, but not great, training exercise this morning. I'm sure you'll do better tomorrow!" And they vanished.

The girls got up and stretched. They reversed-pinched the air and a small screen appeared before each of them.

Amory said, "I'm sorry I got your favorite fictional weapon removed from the trainings."

As they quickly poked the screens and their spacesuits shimmered and transformed into their everyday casual clothing, Bryn replied, "Eh, it's no big deal. It seems like every time I've tried to use it, bad things happen." She glanced at a reflection of herself in her screen and ran a hand through her short red hair, trying to straighten it.

They slashed their index fingers across the screens, making them disappear.

Amory laughed, "Like that time you chopped your leg off."

The two of them exited the simulation room. "Yeah, and those times I accidentally killed you when we were working together."

"Good times."

They walked down the long main carpeted hallway of Bryn's house to the kitchen, grabbed plates of food from Crane, who was sporting a chef's outfit, and went around the corner to a table in the large, wider-than-tall, two-story living room. They sat facing the room-sized window, overlooking the looming tri-colored green, blue, and rusty red globe of Mars from a near-Deimos orbit, and ate their lunch.

Amory said, "On the plus side, it's not like we'll ever have to worry about getting into any kind of situation like this where we'd actually need to defend ourselves."

Bryn laughed, "You are so right."

The Table of Eight

The old man's fingers drummed impatiently on the highly polished wood of the boardroom table where his reflected fingers resembled a hyperactive dancing spider. His eyes, hiding under thick gray woolen eyebrows, spent time trying to avoid the centuries-old clock hanging on the wall to his left, so they instead locked onto an ancient painting on the right wall. He wasn't so much taking in the details of the art, but was instead staring through and using it as something to occupy his time while he tried not to think about the clock.

 The clock. As this thought took his mind, it also took his eyes for a ride toward the clock he did not want to look at. On the way, he saw the rest of the large room: walls adorned with other paintings and display cases featuring the greatest achievements of humankind throughout all stages of history. Portraits of great rulers were neighbors with shiny, jewel-encrusted scepters, swords, pistols, pens, and keyboards. It was a museum of greatness, which should have been meant for humanity, but instead was installed as a permanent private showing for the sole benefit of this boardroom with eight chairs.

He caught himself in time and averted his eyes away from the clock his gaze almost collided with, and down to his fingers tapping on the table. The luxurious metallic weave fabric of his patterned suit jacket moved noiselessly as he reached out and ran a finger along the edge of his quarter-meter-long, solid platinum, name sign that read, *Petr Pekar – Economy (Consultant)*.

Petr looked around the table, mindful to steer clear of the clock, at the career paths of the other seven platinum name signs that gleamed at equal intervals around the large round table: *Military*, *Technology*, *Entertainment*, *Religion*, *Information*, *Society*, and *Polistry*. He looked up from the last sign to see an oversized chair made from real antique leather, just like the one he was sitting in, only it was empty. As usual.

His eyes made a dash for the gold clock on the left wall. It told him that the meeting should have started twelve minutes ago. *Hmph*, he snorted and looked away until his sight landed on a large ornate frame. If he had looked harder he would have seen that it contained the original Magna Carta. Today was Petr's fifth meeting with this group, and each time Mr. Polistry had been late. *I'm sick of him always holding us up. Time is money, after all.*

Petr's fingers resumed their drumming as he glanced around the table at the other heads of their respective fields. Two people read from small holographic air-screens that hovered in front of their faces, while the others quietly talked among themselves. He looked at the woman sitting at the sign that read, *Bonna Neefe – Information*, and growled, "Can we start now?" The scowl on his face amplified the anger in his eyes.

The hushed conversations stopped as the collective attention of the room focused on Petr. Bonna touched a corner of her screen and swung it to one side. She replied with a calm and simple, "No." She gestured around the table, "As you can clearly see, we only have seven here. It's called the Table Of Eight for a reason. We'll wait until he shows."

The other five around the table nodded in agreement and returned to their conversations and diversions as if nothing had happened. Bonna slid the screen back in front of her and resumed reading.

Petr breathed heavily and stared glumly back at the thousand-year old painting on the wall of a king being crowned. He didn't much care for Bonna Neefe, the new head of the Table. Things, like tardiness, were viewed as trivial and unimportant to her. He thought, *If this were my company, this never would have been tolerated. Young people today have no respect for how things should be done. It's that damnable Basic mentality. It's creeping upward and infecting the upper classes.*

The more he stewed, the angrier he became. His mind wandered over the previous Table Of Eight meetings he sat in on. *They obviously greatly value my opinion, otherwise I wouldn't be here. I don't want to make waves so soon, but I will not stand for this much more. If they don't mention it, I'm going to make this man's tardiness a topic of concern.*

His sizeable forehead wrinkled further with thought, *What if they're testing me? Those around this table are the ones who run civilization. What if this is just their way of seeing what I'll tolerate?* He allowed a sideways glance at the gold clock. *If he's not here in a few minutes I'm going to say something.*

He got up from his chair, which caused the other members of the table to glance in his direction. Once they saw he wasn't leaving they shrugged and promptly ignored him again.

Petr thought to himself, *Would the rulers of society really tolerate this?* He stopped at the StruseCreator and tapped the "Coffee" pre-set default on the screen. The cover of the machine slid open to reveal a hot coffee, premixed with cream and sugar. He grabbed it and walked over to the only window in the room. From the space station's vantage point in an upper orbit, he looked down upon Earth, half bathed in blue, the other half shrouded by darkness. Almost on-level with his point of view was a line of ships entering and exiting the Solar Union Lightway above the planet. *This group controls all aspects of life, and has for millennia.* He took a sip of his coffee. *I'm going to force the issue.*

He sat heavily in his seat and glared at Bonna.

The others around the table noticed Petr's hardened gaze and their conversations quieted down as they traded sly smirks and eye-rollings with each other. Bonna continued reading from her screen and either didn't notice, or ignored the cause of, the now-noiseless room.

Petr surprised no one by breaking the silence again, his eyes still trained on Bonna, and pointing to the empty seat, "He's late. Again. He's been the last to arrive every meeting I've been to, so far, and has kept the rest of us waiting. It's not fair. We have more important things to be doing right now instead of waiting for some inconsiderate oaf to arrive."

Bonna slashed a finger diagonally through the screen, which rippled like liquid and vanished. She fixed him with her ice-cold eyes for what seemed like an eternity and didn't say a word. The deafening silence, added to the pressure of the others watching the wordless exchange, caused him to shift nervously and look down.

He cleared his throat and absent-mindedly fidgeted with his name sign.

After an uncomfortable period of time, she spoke. "Mr. Pekar." His body recoiled slightly as if slapped by her sharp tone, amplified by the extended silence. She continued, "Do you mean to tell us, that you actually have something more important than...*this?*" She gestured around at the table at the five other people staring at him.

His jowls shook as he sputtered, "Uh...well, you know, I'm just saying that it's, uh, awful that he's always holding up these meetings, which, of course, are v-very important, but we all have lives of our own and other things to do. And, I'd like to get home at a reasonable hour."

"I see." The coldness of her words indicated she saw much more, and was not happy.

Bonna touched her thumb and forefinger together, and separated them, causing a screen to shimmer open. She poked at it and screens popped up in front of each seat around the table.

The old man leaned forward and read the screen, which said, *Vote yes or no on the following: Dismissal and permanent removal of Petr Pekar from his consulting/candidacy position on the Table Of Eight. Majority rules.*

Petr roared, pounding his clenched fist on the table. "What! You can't do this! I'm powerful! Yes! A very powerful person, and I won't stand for it!"

The others ignored him and they each tapped their screens a single time and confidently looked Petr in the eye. Bonna looked at her screen and then at the people seated in front of her. "All but one of you in attendance has voted. If you have not voted, please do so now."

Petr shouted, "NO! This is preposterous! Why would I vote to remove myself? I will not participate in such foolishness! How dare you! You, yes YOU, should be removed for daring to suggest such a thing!"

All the screens disappeared except for Bonna's. Without emotion she said, "All votes have been counted. On the subject of dismissal and permanent removal of Petr Pekar from this body, we have six votes for removal, none against, one absentia, and…" she looked directly at the old man, "…one abstention. Petr Pekar is hereby dismissed. The Table Of Eight has spoken."

"You fools! You can't remove me! You *need* me! Do you know who I am? I'm too powerful! I'll have every one of you exposed for what you are and have you arrested, or killed! I will *destroy* each and every one of you! Mark my wor-gak--erp!"

His last word was cut off as his chair liquefied into a brownish metal, enveloped his body, and slid towards the door. His muffled screams stopped as the door closed behind him.

The other members nodded with amusement. One even patted his own chair. Bonna walked around the table, picked up the coffee cup and Petr's platinum nameplate, and dropped them into the Struse Recycler. Both items were instantly shredded by lasers, broken down with extreme temperatures, and separated by magnetically-pulsed centrifuges. The small screen above the Recycler showed the store of elements on-hand increased slightly for hydrogen and carbon, while the amount of platinum increased substantially.

Bonna spoke as she walked slowly around the table back to her seat, "Obviously Mr. Pekar took his potential position on the Table Of Eight for granted and lost sight of the monumental importance of the positions we hold. For thousands of years the Table Of Eight has been responsible with the arduous task of running civilization as we know it. This is not a social club, and we are not some minor civic-minded group to be trifled with, like how our departed former associate seemed to view it. We have been charged, since the beginning, to do what the lesser members of society are unable to do – ensure that humanity runs smoothly." Her fingers hooked quotation marks in the air, "'Elected' officials don't have the knowledge or experience that we do, nor are they able to fully grasp the broader implications of everything as a whole, like we can. We run everything so no one else has to think of it.

"I know you all know this, and I don't, for a second, doubt your dedication to the cause. I merely repeat it to drive home the point that we, the ones here in this room, are the true pillars of society. We are the Atlases of our respective fields. For one of us to treat what we do so casually, as Mr. Pekar did, is beyond reprehension. We can't, for a moment, allow ourselves to lose sight and waver from the commitment we made." She paused for a second shook her head and added, "Plus, I just could not stand the man."

Her last comment was greeted with laughter and general agreement.

The door slid open. A quick spike of fear caused everyone to turn and stare; afraid that somehow Pekar had come back to make good with his threat to kill them. There was relief and more laughter when it was the missing member.

"Hey. Sorry I'm late." He sat in the empty chair behind the *Polistry* sign. "I had some trouble with the new political director at Delm's Shipyard…but I'll save that for the 'new business' section of the meeting." He looked around and noticed someone missing…along with a chair. He jerked his thumb to the empty space on the table and asked, "What happened to the old guy?"

Bonna Neefe answered matter-of-factly, "His ship collided with an asteroid and he died."

"Hm. That's too bad. He was kind of a jerk, but still. Wait, does this mean we have to search for another member?"

Bonna said, "I'm afraid so."

"Wow, that's going to be awful."

She nodded in agreement, "It sure is, but sometimes it's unavoidable."

After a pause, she continued, "Ok, now that everyone's here, let's start the meeting. First thing on the agenda…status updates on our primary goal of the year: preventing Bryn Struse from reaching her eighteenth birthday…"

The Girl Who Hides

Amory, lounging on one of Bryn's couches, asked, "Hey Bryn, do you want to drop down there tonight."

"There, where?"

She pointed at the waxing crescent of Mars hanging hugely in the living room window. "There. It's Mars Day, you know."

"Sure. Where would we go? Ideally some place that's not too crowded."

Amory thumbed open a screen and a few seconds later said, "It looks like there's some nightlife going on in Fafa. We've never been there before."

"Isn't that a bad area?" Bryn asked.

"Parts are, but I've seen on the tubes that it's really up and coming. There's been a lot of new galleries and independent pattern makers setting up shops there.

Bryn rolled her eyes, hopped up and said, "Anything to support independent pattern makers. Let's go!"

The air beside Bryn shimmered and Crane appeared wearing a formal suit. "Going out?"

"There you are, yes! We're going to Fafa this evening."

Crane's face squinched up in a distasteful way. "Fafa? Are you sure? Don't you mean Farfu?"

Amory said, "Don't worry Crane, we'll be fine. We're just going to go and check out the nightlife."

"I'm just worried about you two checking out after the nightlife in Fafa checks you out. If you want something fun to do, I can arrange for the Opportunity Rover Museum to open and do a private showing for you. You haven't been there since…"

Bryn cut them off, "…since I was on a field trip when I was eight. It was boring then and I'm sure not a lot has changed. Are you really worried about us? Nothing's going to happen. I mean, you've seen us in the training simulations; we can handle ourselves just fine."

Crane shook their head, "I will always be worried about you. I've raised you since you were thirteen. As I've made you fully aware, you're no normal seventeen-year old. You're Bryn Struse…*thee* Bryn Struse. One of the most recognized people in all of the Solar Union. The daughter of Alva and Amelia Struse. The one person who will be inheriting humanity's largest corporation in a few months. You. There are plenty of reasons why people out there might want to do you wrong. Remember what happened at the Mars Day celebration two years ago when someone spotted you?"

She paused. "Well, yeah, that was a real pickle. I totally understand everything you're saying which is why I normally don't get out much. We're just going to go to see an area of the planet we haven't been to before, but don't worry. I'll wear the disguise and we'll even take the little shuttle and go cloaked and a long way to make sure no one sees or follows us."

Crane considered this and nodded, "That's fine. Just be careful."

Amory asked, "Hey, Crane, do you think anyone will want to do me wrong?"

They laughed, "As Bryn's best friend, maybe, but since she doesn't go out in public often, not a lot of people know who you are. I think you'll be safe. Unless your parents routinely annoy people at the embassy."

"The only person they annoy is me, so I think I'm good." She turned to Bryn, "Alright bestie, let's have an adventure!"

The girls walked past the kitchen, down the hall, through a large doorway into the shuttle bay, entered a small shuttle, and sat on the large curved couch. The ship silently lifted off, became invisible, and flew itself down a corridor and out of the asteroid the Struse's house was built upon. It flew toward the planet, banking around the bright patchwork of color that comprised the dayside of Mars. As it approached the horizon where night rotated into view, the shuttle entered the thin atmosphere and steeped down among the bright domes of the cities dotting the darkness. An opening appeared on a nearby dome and they soon touched down in the shiplot at the edge of Croppy Rock, the southern city that contained the neighborhood of Fafa.

Before leaving the ship, Bryn thumbed open a screen and hit a button. She grew slightly taller, her hair went from a red chin-length bob to long and brown, and the features of her face shifted along with rendering her glasses invisible and undetectable.

Amory was staring at a screen of her own and said, "There's a concert I just got tickets for. I think you're going to like it." She looked out the window and then turned to Bryn, "Oh good, we're here. Let's g…*ah!*" and slapped Bryn's arm. "Geez, Bryn, tell me before you change yourself. It always freaks me out!"

Bryn gave her an oversized smile and said, "Sorry! Also, who's Bryn? My name is Linna." She changed the subject, "So when does the concert start?"

Amory let out a little puff of exasperation and looked at her screen. "Well, *Linna*, It starts in two hours, so we've got some time to waste."

They left the shuttle and hopped on a nearby transport pod and a few minutes later arrived at the Croppy Rock neighborhood of Fafa. The area was made up of short, colorful buildings crowded together like a mouth brimming with too many teeth and managed to be equally enchanting and threatening.

The girls spent an hour walking around, taking in the sites and window-shopping. The streets teemed with life, and despite the increasingly late hour, everything was open. Amory said, "This is kind of weird to see actual stores," and quickly added, "Don't get me wrong, it's nice, but just weird to see so many. I thought your family's inventions ruined stuff like this."

"Yeah, it did. I know what you mean. It seems quaint in an olde-timey-fashioned kind of way."

Amory stopped and looked down an alleyway at a small banner hanging by a doorway that read: *Dione the Seer - Futures Foretold*. Under it was a small sandwich board that continued: *Find out what 2492 has in store for you.*

Bryn had continued down the street half a block before she looked around and realized that, apart from the people out on the street, she was alone. She spotted Amory behind her and double-backed to join her. "Something catch your eye?"

"Yeah, that," She said pointing at the sign down the alleyway. "Want to do it?"

Bryn let out a quick laugh of disbelief. "What? Go to a fortuneteller? Oh come on, it's just a waste of money."

Her eyes unwavering from the sign, Amory said, "I know, but it still sounds fun."

Bryn waffled, "Well, kind of..."

Amory hopped in the air with excitement. "Great! Let's do it."

As they entered the fortuneteller's shop, the girls glanced around and Amory summed it up: "Well, I wasn't sure what to expect, but this is pretty close to what I imagined."

Bryn asked, "Are you thinking of that movie that came out a couple of years ago called, *Fortune Teller*?"

"Yup. Right down to the smell."

"Me too. Totally."

They stopped and took it all in: it was mostly dark, with what little light there was coming from the dozens of faux-candles spread around the room. Faded tapestries with dusty gold fringe covered every wall and ceiling surface, which made it impossible to tell where one wall ended and another started. An incense-y aroma wafted about with a calming notation that beckoned the girls inside. The room seemed completely quiet at first, but then Bryn thought she could discern very faint music that was nearly imperceptible, but she still couldn't tell what style it was, much less who played it. To them, it seemed like something directly from a different century.

Bryn looked hard and used her glasses to scan the room. Disguised as Linna, Bryn didn't appear to be wearing glasses, but they were there, completely hidden beneath the tightly woven projection of Linna's face. She didn't need them for seeing; nobody did anymore. Glasses were heavily modified to include built-in screens, scanning devices of every kind, cameras to allow the user to see in all directions at once, and a whole host of other handy options. She looked for any kind of listening, monitoring, or recording devices that might help a supposed fortune teller learn about potential clients in advance so they can wow and surprise walk-ins by knowing so much about them. Despite all of her scanning, she found nothing.

Amory whispered, "I wonder if anyone's..."

"And how can I help you tonight?" Bryn and Amory jumped back in surprise as a voice came from one side of the room.

The older woman, blended in so well with her surroundings that she seemed to melt right out from the wall. She gave Bryn and Amory a penetrating look-over that made them feel that she were somehow doing a better job of scanning them than Bryn had done of the shop with all of her gadgets. The woman's demeanor lightened as she gave the two girls a slightly approving look accompanied by a light nod and a faint, "Hm."

When they had gotten over the mild shock of the shopkeeper spooking them, Amory managed, "Uh, we'd, um, like our fortunes read."

The older woman smiled and sat down. "Well, you've come to the right place, my children. Have a seat," as she patted the table with the many bracelets around her wrists jingling and clanking like a wind chime telling of an approaching storm.

The girls sat down at the round wooden table. The woman said, "Welcome, my name is Miss Dione." She looked at Amory and said, "Now...Am'ree, would you like to go first?"

Both girls were surprised and looked at each other. Amory replied, "Err, no, I think she would, though."

Dione gave a look of bemused resignation, shook her head and pointed at Bryn, "You're going to be an interesting one, that I can tell already, so I'm saving you for last."

Amory protested, "Hey!"

The fortune teller laughed and spoke to Amory without taking her eyes off Bryn, "I'm not saying that you're not interesting, but I can already tell that hers is going to be more so. Oh yes."

Bryn looked at Amory with a big smile on her face and thought through their shared nano connection, *Aw yeah, she said I'm super interesting.*

Dione reached out and cupped Amory's hand, closed her eyes and all was silent. Amory looked at Bryn with a questioning look, and Bryn shrugged her shoulders in an uncertain reply and thought, *I dunno, just go with it.*

Dione spoke as eyes remained closed. "You have an opportunity with a new job...travel...that job would have you traveling great distances...more so than most normal people travel these days...great distances...the traveling part of your life seems to be...within your job, so I think that your job is what will cause you to be traveling so far. But, it's not your future, it's someone else's chosen for you so you choose not to."

Amory checked to make sure the old woman's eyes were still closed and turned to Bryn to give a nodding look that conveyed her being impressed.

The seer continued, "With your personal life...many friends…much happiness but no love on the horizon. Fear. Spikes of fear...several of them are there with strong links back to your friend who shines most brightly...the one who hides...behind masks..." Bryn's skin puckered with a strong chill. Miss Dione continued, "...the masked one will cause great concern and fear many times this year, for her…and yourself. If you do not die, I see a path you head down starting this year will lead to...something."

Amory rose up in her seat slightly. "Uh, *if I don't die?* What? Also, it will lead to 'Something'?" That's all a little vague, don't you think?"

Dione opened her eyes and looked at Amory. "Child, death is always a possibility for each one of us. I am only telling what I see for this year, 2492. Things get fuzzy when I look further out. Come back next year and I'll be able to see more clearly."

Amory, quipped, "If I don't *die*, that is. Geez!"

Bryn said, "Actually, apart from the ending, it was pretty right on."

The seer turned toward Bryn, took her hand, and closed her eyes, "Now for the girl who hides."

Bryn almost thought, *How does she know? It's impossible to tell if someone is wearing a Masker device*, to Amory, but was afraid that Miss Dione would be able to read her thoughts so she blanked her mind.

The old woman tensed up and began to speak quickly. "Sadness...the burden of sadness you carry weighs heavier on your heart and body...this will start soon...earlier than you anticipated....in a matter of minutes...caution, girl, be cautious...you are prepared and will get through it...those you miss...you will be compelled to look for those who have been absent from your life...many eyes will be on you...more so than usual...some will be angry eyes filled with fire...powerful hands with evil intentions reaching from all directions...attempting to take things from you, and take you from life...you'll give up the mask...duty...and fulfill your duty...and whatever you do, don't go to Eris."

Bryn cocked an incredulous eye towards Dione. "What? Why would I want to go to Eris?"

"I do not know, but I would strongly advise against it."

Bryn asked, "Can I expect anything positive this year? All of this sounds pretty negative."

"You will have periods of scattered happiness, intermixed with monotony, and a long stretch of sorrow."

Amory giggled, "That sounds more like a weather report."

Bryn frowned. "Oh. I was hoping for more prolonged happiness in my life."

Miss Dione looked at Bryn in the eye. "It is not my place to tell you merely what you want to hear. I'm here to tell you what will happen so you may prepare and be ready for what awaits. No, your outlook is not filled with joy, but it will be an important year, which will impact the rest of your life. This year is something you need to live through because the rewards will be beyond measure."

Bryn cocked her head to one side. "I thought you said you couldn't see more than a year in the future?"

Dione shrugged, "Usually I can't as my abilities are dimmed by time, but your path is quite bright."

"And, that path leads to...where?"

Miss Dione said, "Come back next year and I'll tell you. You're not ready to see what I see now." She gently tapped her hand on the table twice, once again clanging her bracelets, and said, "Fifty credits, please."

Back on the street, Amory and Bryn glanced at each other, then at the Dione's sign in the alleyway, and back. Bryn broke the silence first, "Wow. That, uh, wasn't quite what I was expecting."

Amory agreed. "Um, yeah. I will say that if she's even sort of accurate on anything, I'm coming back next year. If I make it, that is." She laughed and they started walking again.

"Ugh. I don't know if I will," Bryn said. "That was really negative." She looked around and saw there were noticeably fewer people out now.

Amory perked up, "The concert! That'll cheer us, well, especially you, up!"

"Yes!" Bryn perked. "That sounds great!"

They arrived at an intersection and Amory pointed down a street that veered off to the right. "The club's that way."

Stage

As the girls walked, the colorful charm of the neighborhood seemed to fade as the buildings grew taller, more crowded, and dingy. What stores lay out here were mostly closed, and it was nearly impossible to tell what was for sale in the scant few shops that were open.

After a few minutes of walking down noticeably sparser and darker streets Bryn seemed uneasy, "Ehh, are you sure it's this way? Maybe we should go back. This is starting to look like a NoGo area on Earth."

Amory agreed, "Yeah, but that's part of its charm. Don't worry, it's just ahead." They turned one more corner and saw a large building in the distance teeming with life, lights, and music. "See, there we go." They bee-lined for the lively building like moths to a backyard bug zapper.

The sign on the roof proclaimed it as *The Tower of Fafa*. Wrapped around each floor was the name of the floor and the scrolling marquee for that evening's entertainment.

Bryn scoffed, "Not much of a 'tower,' it's only eight floors. Oh wait! Eeeee! Look, there it is!" She pointed to the fourth floor, called Stage, which scrolled by with the times and band names, "...1am - Senõr Pueblo..."

Amory said, "Shoot, they've already started. Let's get up there.

A minute later, they showed their ticket screens, and entered a large, loud, poorly lit room crowded with a few hundred people, half of which were shimmering slightly. Bryn surveyed the crowd and shook her head and thought to Amory, *These guys are awesome. Why would so many people choose to tube in instead of actually being here in person? EEEEEEE! My favorite song of theirs!*

Amory motioned for them to work their way up closer to the stage.

The band jumped around the stage, bathed in smoke and multi-patterned light, while hammering on their instruments.

> *...it looks like all is well-hel-el*
> *Except my town's been blown to hell!*
>
> *Oh no, I'm hit*
> *Hurts-a, wee bit*
> *So cold, bright lights*
> *Grandpa, says hi*
> *Oh no, what's this*
> *Rigor mortis*
> *Big guy, upstairs*
> *How did I get up here*
> *Yeaahhhhh, well I fought and died*
> *Guarding the coast of Wyoming*
> *Yeaahhhhh, well I fought and died*
> *Guarding the coast of Wyoming*

2492: Attack Of The Ancient Cyborg

Do you think it's right
That my mouth is still foaming
Yeaahhhhh, well I fought and died
Guarding the coast of Wyoming

Bryn and Amory jumped in place and sang their hearts out to every word, with the joy and excitement of the show having made the fortuneteller's words of warning long-forgotten memory.

Sanctuary

After the show, the crowd entered the Stage's lobby, where holographic signs tried their best to grab peoples' attention to divert them to more entertainment options on other floors. Looking at the list, Amory asked, "What about the top floor?"

"Huh?" Bryn eloquently replied.

Amory pointed, "These signs only list options on the first seven floors. There are eight floors in the building."

Bryn shrugged, "So. Maybe the top floor is made up of offices."

"No, it looks like a bar of some kind. Here, look at this capture I got of it when we first saw the place." Amory thumbed open a screen and zoomed in on the top floor. Behind the tinted windows was clearly the look of a dimly-lit bar. "Wanna check it out?"

Bryn was conflicted. On one hand, she didn't really care to go to the bar. The super-enhanced nanos in her body that her inventor parents gave her and Amory saw to it that alcohol had no effect on them, so the whole mystique in going to a bar just wasn't there. Then again, she was having a great night, and didn't want it to end just yet.

Amory leaned over and said, "I just looked it up and found their menu. They've got Wums."

That's all the convincing Bryn needed. "I'm game. Where do we find this mysterious top floor?"

They stepped onto a nearby lift and the floor options only showed the first seven. The top floor wasn't listed.

Amory told the lift, "Level eight, please."

An empty slot on the lift's panel illuminated with the single red word *Sanctuary* and they were whisked upward.

The door opened, they stepped off the lift and froze. The dimly-lit room was large, extending off to the right and left, and a long bar dominated the back wall. About fifty or so tables, half with patrons, were ahead and to the right. A few more tables were to the left, abutting a railing, which overlooked the eight-story atrium into the entertainment complex below. Flashing lights and thumping music spewed up from the lower floors into the large circular opening, but the lighting and music in this area was subdued and quite opposite from the multi-tiered partying churning below. A long-since deactivated robot at the doorway was slumped over the host station with a sword sticking through its back. The hand-scrawled note read, *Sanctuary. Seat yourself.*

Amory nodded and smiled, "Now that's some clever marketing there."

Bryn agreed, "Yeah, it really sets the mood as well."

The girls looked and saw that the tables to their left, by the atrium, were empty, whereas most of the occupied tables were on the darker side of the room. The people on the right had that sketchy quality that allows them to blend effortlessly into dank, dark places with considerable ease, like it was their element. If the setting were changed to a sunny, flower-filled park, these people wouldn't be more out of place. Some wore masks, and most everyone had hats on, casting shadows across their faces. No one wore any clothes of distinction; in fact, they all seemed to be similar oversized outfits of muted browns, grays, and blacks. Despite their similar appearance, each patron was either sitting alone, or in pairs, drinking and talking quietly.

Bryn thought to Amory, *I don't know about you, but I'd rather sit over the by atrium. Those people look kinda scary. Look, that guy over there with the hat has a gun on his belt.*

Amory thought back, *Which one? They all have hats and guns. Oh wait, I see him now. Scary indeed.* She took one last glance at the dead host bot at the door and chose a table to the left, by the edge.

Amory peered over the railing, down at the hundreds of people, bathed in light, dancing to the pumping music, and said, "Hey, it looks fun down there. I think there's dancing on the lower two floors and the floor below us as well. I'm guessing virtual reenactment-type rooms are on other floors, but I can't really tell from here."

"Great, it should be a good time," Bryn responded while poking through the screen in the console in the middle of the table. "Where are those Wums you saw on the menu? I can't seem to find them."

Amory pretended not to notice and exclaimed, "Oh! I like the song they're playing on the next floor."

2492: Attack Of The Ancient Cyborg

Bryn frowned and continued to check out the menu. "Um, problem here. Wums don't seem to be on the menu."

Amory turned around and sat in her chair. "Drat. Too bad I totally lied about that. I've had a hankering for Wums all day."

"You always have a hankering for Wums, wait, what? You *lied* about them?"

"Yes, but only to convince you to come up here because it looked interesting. Back to the more important topic, Wums are totally 'Wum-tastic.' They are, you know."

Bryn shook her head with a look of bemused resignation. "Tricky, tricky Amory. Now I've got to find something else on the menu. By the way, have you ever thought of being a pitch-person for Wums? You know, since you're ditching out on the whole ambassador thing. I think you'd be great at it. Plus, the fortune teller said you weren't going to…"

Bryn

Bryn thought back, *Don't forget, while I'm in disguise, I'm Linna, not Bryn and*…Bryn looked at her friend and noticed that her demeanor dropped several notches in the serious direction. *What's up?*

Amory thought back, *I know your back is to the rest of the place, but I just noticed the people are unusually freaky-looking. Like the kinds of people you'd find at some kind of bounty hunter bar or something.*

Bryn replied, *Bounty hunter bar? P-shaw! That's the kind of thing you see on the tubes, not in real life.*

I don't know, maybe. I've read about them, but I didn't think they were real. All I'm saying is there is a whole new level of scary people hanging out at the other side of this place.

Bryn asked, *Are they looking at us? Or, more importantly, are they winking at you? Because if they are,*

I'd be happy to leave you alone with those attempting to woo your tender heart. I know Miss Dione said you wouldn't find love, but maybe we can prove her wrong.

Amory giggled, *Woo you, Struse. No, they're just talking quietly, drinking, and being generally sketchy but they're definitely spending a bit too much time looking at us. I'll let you know when they start winking so I can send you over to them.*

Bryn said aloud, "Great! Now let's get some food."

Management

The manager of the entertainment complex was sitting in his office reviewing a screen of financial data when the building said, "Hamor, I think you'll be interested in this."

Half annoyed by the intrusion, Hamor was also thankful for a break to get away from the endless list of numbers. He perked up, "Hey, Slim, what'cha got?" The screen in front of him split to show a close-up of a girl with brown hair sitting at a table in Sanctuary. He casually looked over at her face and made a shrug, "Yeah? So who'm I lookin' at? Is there a warrant out for her that we can collect on or somethin'?"

Slim, the building's computer, sounded pleased with itself and spoke with a certain smugness, "Even better. Her name is Amory Sutherland," and waited for a spark of realization to come over Hamor, but none came.

42

He shrugged again, "Yeah? So what? Am I supposed to know this girl?"

Slim let out the faintest, barely audible exasperated sigh and said, "If you're not into the celebrity gossip news stories, then no, you won't know her…"

Hamor was starting to see where Slim was coming from, "Wait...is this girl famous?" and added with a sneery smile, "Hold on a nan'…you're into celebrity gossip? Oh that's rich! I can't wait to tell everyone…"

Slim cut him off. "Yeah, you do that and I'll be sure to send the Boss footage of you stealing elements from the StruseCabinet."

The smile was whisked away from his face and he was instantly all business. "So, who's she again?"

"Amory Sutherland."

Hamor shook his head. "I dunno her."

The computer went on, "She's not famous in her own right, but her best friend is. You might have heard of her. Bryn Struse."

A moment later, the light flicked on above Hamor's head. "You mean Bryn Struse, *the* Bryn Struse, as in StruseCorp?" He pointed to the Recycler/StruseCreator machine in the corner for effect.

Slim smiled. "Yup. That's her."

Hamor's eyes got big. "Holy shuck. She's gotta be one of the richest people in the whole Solar Union…" He trailed off for a moment. A few seconds of silence later, he seemed to be filled with a new direction, "I've got to tell the Boss about this."

The computer agreed. "That's exactly what I thought you would say."

Hamor panned out the screen with Amory, revealing another girl with brown hair. "Who's the other girl with'er?"

Slim replied, "No one important. A nobody Basic from Pavonis named Linna Meekins. I just reviewed nearly all recorded public appearances of Bryn Struse and this other girl hasn't been with her before, so I'm speculating that she's just a friend of Amory Sutherland."

"It doesn't matter. She's inconsequential. We'll just get rid of 'er." Hamor grinned large. "View me in with the Boss."

"Already done," the computer responded.

The air in front of Hamor's face shimmered and a blue light arced around, forming the edge, which filled in with the rest of the screen. A crystal clear picture showed the top of an ornate wooden desk, with bookcases comprising the background, filled with expensive things. Hamor was always deeply impressed whenever he saw these rare glimpses of the Boss' life. *Wow. And I bet that's real wood too.* The muffled sounds of a party deep in full-swing thumped, laughed, and blared in the background for a moment and then resumed a level of stifled quietness as an out-of-view door opened and closed.

A handsome man entered the view, wearing rich-looking party clothes, as he came around his desk and sat down. The expression he wore on his direct and unblinking dark eyes was that of divine discontent. "Mr. Hamor, What could be so important that it required you to interrupt my social time?"

Confident as all get-out, Hamor leaned back in his seat and said, "Mister Fenter, sir. How 'bout a ransom to make your fortune look like chump change."

The Stranger

The ancient cyborg had followed the two girls all night and was able to enter Sanctuary without catching their attention. Patrons seated at nearby tables quieted when the half-human, half-robot, half-finished monstrosity walked in and headed toward the darkest corner of the room.

Standing at nearly three meters in height, the cyborg was, at the very least, imposing. It wore a wide-brimmed hat that cast a dark shadow over its face, causing its eyes to stand out in the darkness; the right eye crackled with the haunting blueish white of electricity, while the left burned with a single red intense light. The lower half of the face not shrouded in shadow seemed to be almost human with exposed muscle tissue that someone forgot, or was unable, to cover with skin. The long brown trench coat was open, flowing as it walked, giving those in its way a glimpse of the metal exoskeleton with raw, exposed muscle tissue interspersed with wires, cables, and tubes.

The man this thing was made from must have been massive.

On its uncovered hip sat a holster with a ridiculously huge blaster. Even the biggest, meanest patrons who could see the cyborg face-on were immediately rendered uneasy and afraid, and those with a heightened sense of self-preservation quickly moved to other tables further away. It was well-known that the last cyborg was made over two hundred years ago, and this one appeared to have left the factory before it was finished.

The cyborg sat down and watched the two girls at the far side of the cavernous room. It heard the whispers of every person in the room as they stared at and speculated about the newcomer, but they caused it no concern. This place had a reputation for being a safe haven for the criminally inclined, and attracted all sorts of dealers, schemers, mobsters, and hunters. All humans feared something, and for those seated nearby, this battle-scarred cyborg was something, indeed.

It took a fraction of a moment to identify the patrons, scan for weapons, and ascertain the building's security measures before settling its gaze upon the table by the atrium. The girls were its primary target. Everything else was expendable.

A screen that just appeared on all the tables was troubling to the cyborg. It was from Hamor, the manager of Sanctuary, offering a 100,000-credit reward for the capture of the girl named Amory, sitting closest to the railing. As for the other girl, there was not a reward. It went on to say that if you wanted to avoid a potentially dangerous situation, now would be a good time to settle up and leave.

The cyborg considered taking control of the setting before anyone else could react, but then did something rare: it reconsidered. It had been provided information that the girls were frequently active in some type of combat simulation training, but to what extent, it did not know. It chose to observe as the girls were about to be tested by the decent range of small-time thugs and well-experienced bounty hunters present.

The new plan was to sit back, watch, and assess their abilities.

Trouble

Bryn and Amory were happily feasting on their plates of Swacky, when Amory glanced over Bryn's shoulder. Her eyes got large and in mid-chew thought to Bryn, *Hey, you wanted to know when people were wooing, well, I'm going to send them all your way because everyone in here is staring at us.*

Bryn's eyes darted around the screen of her glasses, which split the view to show the room behind her. She put another triangle of Swacky in her mouth and thought back to Amory, *Look, there's a screen up on everyone's table but ours.*

Amory watched the sketchy people look at the screens, then over at the two of them, and back again to the screens. A few hurriedly scuttled out the door. Many reached for something at their sides. *That's kind of rude. At least they could pretend to be secretive about it. Yup, I see the screen. I think we're going to need to leave somewhat soon...that, or we're going to have to put all of that special training Crane insisted we do to use, for once.*

Bryn shook her head. *I think he was just overly paranoid that someone would want to attack me and/or you, for some reason. I don't think we'll need to actually use that stuff. Maybe these people think we're super pretty, or something.*

Amory ate another triangle of Swacky and disagreed, *I don't know about that. I mean, me, yeah, I can see where they'd find me pretty and all, but you, oh, I mean Linna, no way. Shug-lee. Oops, we're about to find out what's going on because our first suitor is coming this way. Can you record this?*

Bryn thought back, *I see him, and I'm recording.*

Amory smiled, *Oh wow, he's totally your type...and watch out, he's got something in his hand.*

Bryn watched the corner of the screen in her glasses showing a big galootish man lumbering toward them. With her eyes, she rotated the screen to quickly scan the rest of the room. It looked as if the other patrons were watching to see what Mr. Galoot could accomplish. Bryn responded, *Yup, coming up on my right. I got him.*

As the man approached their table, he stuck a short metal stick against Bryn's arm, and, with an electric crackle, she went rigid and tipped off her chair onto the floor. Amory gasped as she looked at the empty chair where Bryn had been just sitting, to the big galooty guy. *Yeah, great job Bryn. You 'got him' alright.*

"Now tat I haf yur attenshun, Am'ree, yuh need tuh come with me."

Hm. Amory thought. *He doesn't seem too bright either.*

Hey! Bryn interjected from the floor as she pretended to be unconscious. *This lump just shocked me and you're commenting on how he looks instead of doing something. Geez! What kind of friend are you?*

Amory thought back, *An awesome one, of course.* Then, to the thug in a shrilly terrified voice, "Oh no! You zapped my friend! Someone help! HELP!"

He was reaching for her, but hesitated for a moment and looked back around the room as he suddenly felt awkward about trying to kidnap this girl. He turned back to the table quickly, almost as if he sensed something was wrong, but Amory had been in motion since he first hesitated. Her speed and strength surprised him as she grabbed his hand holding the stun stick, twisted it back, jabbed it into his stomach, and flicked it on. He went rigid, convulsed a few times, and fell backward.

A war-like roar preceded the chorusing of chairs scraping on the floor as the people seated on the other side of the bar got up and rushed at the girls.

Even before the galoot hit the floor, Bryn had used her wrist Tracelets to flip the three nearest tables up on edge as a protective shield. Amory crouched behind a table and shot off a few Tracelet repulser blasts flinging several rushing thugs back through the air and crashing down on others. Bryn used this chance to scramble over their table and set up a position by Amory. They both crouched down as bottles smashed against the table. "What the shuck did we do?" Bryn yelled to Amory.

"I don't know, maybe we got the last of the Swacky? There's a lot of them. Maybe twenty or so." Amory tensed up and looked ready for anything. "Aw, come on Bryn, we could easily take them." A chair crashed into the upended table and the splintered pieces flew over them and down into the atrium below.

Bryn shook her head. "No way. Doing this type of thing in a simulator is one thing, but this is for real.

People could get hurt, or even killed. I vote for us getting out of here."

Amory was about to ask how, but quickly took in the situation. The elevator door was blocked and the sketchy crowd of people was closing in. The two of them turned, looked through the railing behind them, and down the seven stories to the club floor below. She gave a shruggy nod and said, "Well, sure, we can do that..."

Wwwuuuhhnnnnnn. Wwhhuunnn. Wwhhuuunnnn. Three waves of energy from stunner guns slammed their barrier hard.

They shared a panicked look. Amory said, "Yikes! That sounded serious! I'm turning on my energy absorber."

Bryn nodded quickly, and the girls each thumbed open a screen, hit buttons, and were surrounded by barely visible, ever-so-shimmering fields.

The sound of unusual silence gave the girls pause and they looked at each other while trying to listen...

The long green flaming blade of a sun sword sliced the upended protective table in half and singed the floor directly between them. They screamed in unison, leapt away in different directions, and each hid behind another upturned table. Bryn was close to one end of the long bar, and reached out with her Tracelets to snag the first thing she saw, and swung it towards the woman with the sun sword who was bearing down on her.

The large bottle arced through the air. The attacker with the deadly blade instinctively raised and swung out at the object hurtling at her.

The sun sword connected with the bottle, effortlessly melted through the glass, causing the highly flammable alcohol inside to erupt into an intense fireball engulfing the attacker and sending her flying backwards. Bryn stared in wide-eyed horror at what just happened, but quickly snapped back to reality as the fire suppression foam poured from the ceiling. Movement caught her eye and she saw Amory using her Tracelets to launch chairs at other attackers with impressive accuracy. Each time a chair shot out, it knocked down an advancing person, although, it was getting harder to see with the sea of foam pouring down between them and the rest of the ornery bar patrons.

WHUM WHUM WHUM. Three stunner shots hit the corner of the bar where Bryn was in rapid succession from various sides of the room. The solid metal bar took most of the energy, and her protective field absorbed the remainder, but it still forcibly knocked Bryn to the ground.

Amory yelled out in her mind, *Bryn! Are you OK?*

Ow. I'm still conscious so I think I'm fine. Um, I don't know about you, but I'm ready to leave.

Ok, over the railing, now!

Just as Bryn was about to get up, she noticed the inactivated sun sword hilt lying nearby on the foamy floor. She pointed an open hand, pulled it to her with a Tracelet, and ran for the railing. The mad rush of people towards her and Amory had degenerated into a flailing heap slipping and falling in the fire foam.

Amory reached the atrium first, turned to face the bar patrons, waived and yelled, "Thanks!" before vaulting effortlessly over the railing.

Bryn thought, *Oh, this is easy!* and followed her friend's lead…*WHUM*…a stunner shot's blast of energy slammed solidly into her causing her to body to freeze up and awkwardly tumble over the edge.

"Wooo!" Amory yelled. "This is just like the training simulations!" As the ground floor blurred up to greet them, Amory fired off her Tracelets' repulsor beams to push against the floor and soften her landing. She had to act quickly to snag Bryn and keep her from splatting onto the floor. Amory landed on her feet, Bryn smacked a little too hard on her side in the middle of a throng of young people partying. The crowd stopped dancing long enough to shower them with hooting, applause, and whistling.

Bryn, are you ok?

My left arm is completely numb. I got shot by...

WHUM, WHUM. Two of the nearby dancing kids were thrown back into a wall like discarded dolls. Without hesitation, the two girls ran out the door.

"Look, a taxi!" Amory yelled.

"We have to wait for our shuttle!" Bryn scanned the night sky, "Crane's sending it..."

"No time! Go!"

They jumped in the back seat, slammed the door and looked nervously at the people exiting the club behind them.

"Where to?" the Happy Taxi asked.

"Uh...uh.." sputtered Bryn as she tried to think of where their ship was.

"Anywhere, just go!" yelled Amory.

"Got it. Off we go!" and the taxi leapt up into the air and away from the erupting chaos of the club.

Escape

The girls turned around and knelt backwards on the yellow bench seat and watched out the back window as the crowd from the building spilled out into the street, shrank into tiny dots, and was gone. With big smiles, they sat and relaxed with a synchronized sigh of relief.

Bryn said, "Wow and ow."

"Yeah, you can say that again," Amory agreed.

"Hmm. I think I will, thanks. Wow and ow."

"How's your arm?"

Bryn tried to move it, "It stings like crazy. It's not completely numb anymore, but wow, it does not feel good. I want to avoid getting hit with that again."

"Was your absorber on?"

"Yeah, that's the really bad thing. I'm afraid to think what would have happened if it wasn't on."

Amory said, "Yikes. It was kind of like doing a training in the simulator, only with more adrenaline."

"Probably because we knew it was real instead of just a training program. This…this was scary."

"Yeah it was. Not at first. When it started going down, I was all kinds of like, 'Oh, we've got this, easy peasy,' but then it turned ugly." Amory thought for a second as she watched the lights of the city pass by below. She perked up and asked, "Oh, can you give me a copy of the footage you recorded?"

Bryn said, "Sure thing." Both girls thumbed open screens, Bryn pulled it up on hers, touched a finger to the clip and dragged it over to Amory's screen.

"Thanks." Then, Amory asked the cab, "Hi, taxi? Did we ever tell you where to go?"

The Happy Taxi cheerfully replied, "I believe you said…," and then it replayed her yelling, "Anywhere, just go!"

Amory turned to Bryn, "Hey, where is your ship parked?"

"It's just getting out of the shiplot now." She then looked at the city map that was scrolling under the taxi's icon on the panel in front of them. "Please drop us off at Maddox Park. It's just ahead."

"Can do!" The taxi cheerfully responded and began its descent.

One Of Ours

Several of the less-injured thugs clambered out of the bar in an attempt to try and stop the girls, but they were in the safety of the taxi and lifting off before anyone could get far from the door. One of the smarter bounty hunters nonchalantly snapped a picture of the cab's number and walked back inside.

Most of the crowd from Sanctuary was outside and watching the taxi disappear into the night. No one seemed to notice the rough, unfinished-looking cyborg walk out and join them in watching the taxi leave. It observed the shrinking cab for a moment, emotionless apart from its glowing and crackling eyes, and then, without a word, headed the other way down the street, disappearing into the welcoming shadowy darkness.

The picture-clicking bounty hunter walked through the cafe, ignoring the scene of extensive damage that lay strewn about. She walked up to Hamor, who, standing in the middle of the room surveying things, seemed a lot more concerned about the condition of his bar. She said, "Here's the cab's info. They just left, so you've probably got time to catch them."

Hamor looked at the floating screen showing a looping vid of the bright yellow taxi lifting off and smiled. To the woman, he said, "Thank you." He turned and barked, "Slim, this is one of ours. Get it back here now with the passengers intact. They're gonna pay for this."

The bar's sentient computer system replied, "I'm on it."

The bounty hunter asked, "You need anything else?"

Hamor looked at her and said in a moment of real sincerity, "You know, I just might. Because of your quick thinking, we're gonna to be able to catch these punks. If you hang out for a minute, I'll get you the reward."

"That'd be great, thanks," she smiled.

Recalled

"We're almost there," Bryn said as she looked at the location screen. "I don't know about you, but I'm exhausted."

"This, coming from someone who hid behind an upturned table? Uh, who was the one slowing them down with a wall of flying chairs?"

Bryn glared at Amory.

"What? I'll give you a hint to the answer to this trivia question is…me!"

Bryn continued to glare at Amory.

"Eh? Eh? Me? The one who should be tired, but isn't? Eh?" She posed an extremely exaggerated fake smile, and was inversely mirrored by Bryn's furrowed brow. "Hey! How's your arm do-"

The taxi made a hard bank to the right and the girls took a tumble and hit against the side door with a loud "Oof!"-ing chorus.

"What's going on?" Bryn yelled, squished against the door by Amory.

"Taxi! What are you doing?" Bryn yelled as she was trying to pull herself up, but ended up stepping on Amory in the process.

"Ow! You did that on purpose!"

The taxi cheerfully responded as it leveled off, "I've been informed that the landing area of Maddox Park you chose is not safe at this time."

The girls clambered to get back to their seats. Amory shot Bryn a dirty look and punched her arm.

"Ow!"

"I feel better now, thanks." Amory turned to the taxi, "Great. Just put us down here, thank you. We'll manage the rest of the way ourselves."

The taxi brightly replied, "I'm afraid I can't do that. You see, I've been told that the only safe place is to return you back to the location I picked you up at."

A heavy sinking feeling dropped deep in the girls. Bryn spoke up, "Um, who is telling you this?"

"My dispatching company. I apologize for any inconvenience, but remember, it's better to take the safe route to your destination. There will be no additional charge for this unexpected deviation in our route."

Bryn turned to Amory, "I really don't want to go back there. I've had far too much excitement for today."

"I completely agree. Although, in a way, it's just like doing two simulations back to back."

Bryn said, "Yeah, but the simulators don't hurt…much. Plus, simulations end when you want them to. This is like one that's restarting."

"You're right," Amory agreed. I'd rather not face a bar full of angry people with guns and time to get ready for us."

"How do we get out of here?"

"Hm," Amory thought. "Hey, is that a sun sword?"

She handed it to Amory, "Yeah, I grabbed it from that woman after I accidentally set her on fire."

"Perfect. Hold on!" and flicked it on.

The interior of the taxi was spacious, but the burning electric blade of the sword sprung out and effortlessly pierced the roof. Ignoring the alarms and warnings the taxi shouted, Amory forced the humming flaming blade down and around. Once a full hole had been cut, she kicked hard and a large part of the roof and side of the taxi creaked, leaned out, and fell free from the craft.

"I'm not feeling good about this…Amory!" Bryn yelled over the strong cold wind that filled the cabin.

Amory shut off the sun sword. "Let's go!" she yelled back as she tried to jump out of the hole. The taxi was faster and quickly rotated sideways so it was flying level, keeping the hole as inaccessible as possible. The floor rotated with the ship and whacked Amory in the face, causing her to tumble down on top of Bryn.

"OW!" Yelled Bryn.

Amory shook her head for a second, looked up at the hole she just carved a couple of meters above her and was trying to figure out how to get out when she looked down at her best friend underneath her. "Ha! Now you know how it feels!"

The happy taxi said, "I'm afraid I cannot let you exit the taxi until we have come to a full landing in a safe area. Safety is Happy Taxi's number once concern. Please note the damage to the taxi has been added to your fare." The small green glowing number on the fare screen increased by several digits.

"Great. Now let's really get out of here." Amory flicked on the sun sword again, jammed it through the back of the seat, and into the engine compartment behind them. A small explosion rocked the taxi hard and it began to level off. Amory shut off the sun sword.

"Yes!" Bryn cheered.

Damaged, the taxi listed the opposite way, causing the girls to lose their balance. Bryn, followed by Amory slid towards the gaping hole and the girls scrambled to keep from falling out.

Amory grabbed and held onto an armrest, and watched helplessly as Bryn slid down the seat, through the hole, and into the darkness of night below.

Ready To Receive

Hamor paced in his office. He knew the taxi would simply turn around and bring them back, and things would be good. Very good. He stopped in front of the large one-way mirror that overlooked the wreckage-strewn floor of Sanctuary that was currently being used to tend to the few injured patrons. *That medicbot was a great investment after all. If all these injured patrons showed up at the local hospital all saying they got injured in a melee at my bar, the police would be arrivin' n' askin' all sorts of questions and lookin' at things I don't want them to see. At least I can get everyone fixed up as good as new, and wipe their short-term memories before they leave so I can be assured no one'll be sniffing around.*

He looked at some of his injured employees. "Troops" was too strong of a word, and "henchmen" conjured images of some kind of evil-doer with uniformed heavies. Whatever they were, they were bested by two little girls. If word got out about this, he'd be in an awful situation. Not only would everyone in the area lose respect for him and his organization, but the element of fear would be erased, and only way he'd get it back would be to go on a terror spree of some kind, and that would entail a lot of work and overtime for his crew. It was incredibly difficult and expensive to exist in the faint sliver of questionable business practices these days and even the smallest unplanned hiccup could cause a business like this to collapse.

He kicked the leg of his desk. *Shuck! I've worked so hard to get where I am, I ain't going to lose it because of some kids, no matter how tough they are.* This got him thinking about how the girls caught his people totally off guard. *I mean, shuck, it's a mid-week night. I would be caught off guard too if someone came in busting heads while I was relaxin' on a night off.* He kicked his desk again, harder this time. *Still though, while they might have been surprised, when things got rough they should've taken care of these two with two shots. Bam. Bam. Done.*

The screen floating at the edge of his vision that he had been ignoring swung around to face him. Hamor yelled, "Tant!"

A surprised looking young guy with dark hair popped up on the screen, "Tant here, sir."

"When that taxi arrives, you had better be ready for them. Do not let them make a fool outta you like they did earlier. Remember, they're just kids and you guys are experienced professionals. Also keep in mind that Amory is the key to endless riches for us, so do not mess this up. Understood?"

"Completely, sir." He then noticed that Hamor seemed distracted all of a sudden. "Hamor?"

After a few moments, he looked back at Tant and said, "I was just watchin' footage from inside the taxi that's coming back to you. I saw a sun sword flash before the camera was destroyed, so be ready, they're frisky."

Tant nodded confidently, "We'll get 'em. Don't worry."

"Oh, I'm not…but you should be. Don't fail." With that, he ended the connection.

Dropping In

"NOOOO…" Amory shouted at seeing her best friend falling to her doom…and began to scream out of pure surprise when a tractor beam latched onto her legs and yanked her hard out the hole. "…OOOOHHHHHH!!"

With the cold air rushing by and the rooftops absurdly close, both Bryn and Amory yelled in unison, "SHUUUUUCCK!"

With her right hand, Bryn shot out a Tracelet beam in an attempt to grab ahold of a spire from the closest building shooting up at them. It pulled her close to the building but she was falling too fast and ended up bouncing wildly off the side.

Amory tucked in her arms and accelerated quickly, catching up to Bryn. The two grabbed each other and held tightly. Immediately below them was a crowded rooftop.

Shuck we're going to hit…

NOOOOOOO!

A solid buffering surrounded and supported their bodies and became more pronounced as they slowed toward the rooftop.

Amory asked, "Wha-what's happening?"

"It's the building!" Bryn shouted. "The building sensed us about to hit it so it slowed us down!"

"Oh my gosh, I'm going to give a big wet sloppy kiss to whomever invented that."

They slowed down to nearly nothing and were able to gently step down on the well-appointed rooftop – and found themselves in the midst of a small party of people. Amory held tight to the hilt of the sword, looking from person to person…to the grill…to an astonished person…to the beverage dispenser…to the faux torch lights…to the terrified person…and the festive "Happy Birthday!" signs. Her grip on the sword handle loosened, as she smiled and gave a sheepishly friendly, "Uh, hi there."

All the party-goers stared wide-eyed at the two people who dropped from the flaming ship they saw streak by, fell hundreds of feet, and landed softly on their rooftop deck. Finally someone broke the astonished and awkward silence by saying, "Hey…um, are you two ok?"

Another person said, "You hit that building really hard."

"Oh yeah, we're fine," but then quickly looked back at Bryn and asked, "Wait, are you fine?"

"I think I've got a broken wrist, but it's healing nicely thanks to my nanos. I should be perfect in about ten minutes."

Amory turned back to the one who had spoken to them, "Yup yup, we're good."

"Um, are you sure? It looks like you fell a from a burning ship, without a rocket, chute, or anything." The staring eyes and silent tension was getting to be overbearing.

Bryn piped up: "Yeah, we sure did. We took a taxi and asked 'Can you drop us off here,' and wow, they really did. That's the last I ride in a Literal Cab. Next time I'm going to call Figurative Taxi."

Everyone laughed, which did a lot to ease the tension.

"Do you two want a drink or something?"

With a big nod, Bryn agreed, "Yeah, a Thirsti would be perfect, thanks."

Empty Cab

A screen popped up and alerted Tant that the taxi was approaching. The dispatcher had instructed it to land in the private lot behind Sanctuary, so prying eyes would be limited. He signaled his people and they encircled the landing site with an array of weaponry aimed at the growing light coming towards them. *Wait, what's that extra light…is it on fire?*

The more Tant saw of the ship as it came into view, the greater the worry bubbled up within him. *I've got a bad feeling about this.* The taxi swooped up and slowly descended above the landing spot. He didn't need to see anymore to know what happened. His mind started churning to think of what to say to Hamor.

It landed, and the group of mercenaries stared at what was left of the empty twisted, charred mess that vaguely resembled a taxi. Voices began to arise…

"What happened to it?"

"Did someone else get to it first?"

"Maybe it was a bomb of some kind?"

"Tant, sir, what do we do?"

Shuck, shuck, SHUCK! "Get to the air and find them! They were probably going to meet up with their ship. Search everything between here and Maddox Park! Don't come back until you find them." Tant turned away from the taxi and screened in Hamor. There was no way he could make up a story to cover for this. "Sir, they escaped long before it got here."

Hamor's expression was emotionless. He knew they had only escaped a few minutes ago, but also was aware that there was nothing Tant could have done in the meantime. He asked, "So, what are you doing to fix the situation?"

"My people are taking to the air as we speak to look for them. Hopefully they can cut them off before they reach their ship."

Hamor said, "Good. Keep me informed of your progress," and the screen went dark.

Rooftop Party

At the rooftop party pad, Bryn and Amory stood with cool bubbly beverages in hand and had begun to mingle with the dozen or so people at the party. The guy who first spoke to them when they landed, Aver, continued talking to Bryn. From a distance, Amory could see that while Bryn had only known him for a few minutes, she was doing that short of shy and blushy thing she did when she was smitten with someone. Amory could see why. He was a handsome guy, with short dark brown hair with a pleasant personality that exuded some qualities such as being smart, charming, witty, and funny in correct amounts without overdoing it. All-in-all, a good person.

Amory excused herself for a moment and went to a quiet corner of the large rooftop deck. If she leaned a little to the left, and looked up, up, up, up, there was a great view of Mount Olympus. The sheer size of the mountain, the tallest in the entire solar system, always wowed her. After looking at it for a second, she got to work.

Amory thumbed opened a screen and contacted the Fafa police department. After speaking with the holographic attendant, she forwarded a copy of the vid showing what happened in the bar. The attendant thanked her for reporting the incident, said they were in the clear, and advised them to go home. They would take care of it.

Amory thanked them, slashed out the screen with her finger and rejoined the party.

Amory spotted Bryn across the party in a cozy corner still talking to Aver. As she approached the people and took a drink form her glass, a bright, low-flying light to the right caught her eye. She turned and saw several small ships skimming along the rooftops across the street slowly and purposefully. *Oh, that's bad, bad, bad. I bet it's those guys from the bar out looking for us. It's probably time to leave.* She deflated a little and sighed. *It figures. As soon as I'm about to join a party and be sociable, I've got to go.*

Amory focused her thoughts and yelled, *BRYN!* in her mind.

Across the rooftop, in the cozy corner, Bryn visibly jumped and looked around quickly for Amory. To Amory, it looked like the guy was asking her if she was ok.

WHAT? Bryn hissed back in her mind. *Geez, that was LOUD! Sometimes I wish our nanos weren't thought-linked to one another.* She turned back to Aver and said, "Oh, nothing. I thought I heard something."

Amory thought, *Sorry to say this, but we've got to go. NOW.*

Bryn shook her head slightly. *No way. We just got here, and I'm making a new friend. Do you have any idea how hard it is for me to make new friends? And he's cute to boot!*

A. That last part is weird to hear from you, of all people. B. He is cute and I will be happy to let you know more about him after you make proper introductions. C. Trust me, I don't want to leave either, but, well, look behind you.

Bryn turned around and saw several small ships scouting slowly around the building across the street. She looked deeper and her glasses magnified her vision enough to see a rider in one of the crafts. *Hey, that's a guy you knocked out with a chair back at the bar!*

Yeah, and I bet he and his buddies would love to thank us for that...which is why we need to go. During their silent conversation, Amory had threaded her way through the party and was now standing besides Bryn. "Hey Linna, I've got to get going now or I'll miss my connection back to Europa."

Aver looked surprised. "Wow, you live on Europa? What's it like there?"

Amory said, "Oh no, I don't live there but some of my family do. It's cold and full of icy goodness. Anyway, it was super nice to meet you. Thanks for inviting us."

They all laughed. Aver said, "You two can drop in anytime. Figuratively, or literally. If you want, I can let you know when I'm going to have another get-together."

"That'd be great, thanks," said Bryn. "Here's my contact info." With her left thumb and index finger, she made a little box-type motion, opening a screen, hit a button, which called up her contact card, and gave it a solid poke with her middle and index fingers. Her card floated between them, and Aver thumbed open his own screen, which caught the card and then slashed out the screen.

"It was very nice meeting you both," and gave an extra large smile to Bryn.

Bryn smiled back, they waived goodbye, and walked towards the ledge.

From Aver's perspective it seemed like they were having an animated discussion, but they weren't talking.

Aver called after them, "Uh, Linna? The door is back this way. Inside."

"You're sweet, thanks, but our door is right here, silly." With that, a small starship rose up along side the building and a walkway extended from the hatch and landed in front of the girls. Everyone at the party stopped talking and stared. The average person used public transportation to get places. While it wasn't unheard of for people to own ships, they tended to be smaller ships capable of short trips. Most people didn't own actual starships, capable of interstellar travel, and the average person would be hard pressed to name anyone they knew who owned such a ship. Everyone at the party waved goodbye. As soon as the ship lifted up and sped off, they immediately began talking about the two mysterious drop-in girls.

Aver, however didn't pay them any attention. He stared at the ship as it disappeared down the street with a smile that seemed to be hopelessly stuck there on his face.

He also failed to notice the half dozen ships which had passed slowly by a few minutes ago had turned around and were now in pursuit of the girls' ship.

A Bit Of Luck

What a night. Tant had been searching tirelessly with his people for the Amory girl and her friend. The only thing…*well, two things* he thought, that kept him going was the possible ransom money they would get for the best friend of Bryn Struse (*wow!*)…and what Hamor would do to him if he failed in finding her (*ugh!*).

He was alerted by one of his scout ships that there were two people hiding out near a small structure behind an apartment complex. He landed his ship nearby and snuck back to the location given to him, only to spy two muggers who were counting their loot. Hidden in the shadows, Tant squeezed a black rod which sent out a dull blue pulse, rendering the muggers unconscious. He was in the process of taking their stolen money when one of his more trusted co-workers, Nutara, popped up on a screen in front of him along with a picture of a starship.

"Sir, we're discovered their ship. It landed in Maddox park a few minutes ago and just started to move."

This is good news, Tant thought. He asked, "Wow, a starship. Are they inside?"

"No, we've been keeping an eye on it and no one has approached. Judging by how low and slow it's flying, I think they've called it to pick them up."

Tant admired Nutara. She was one of the few of his mercenaries with a good head on her shoulders. "Finally! We got a bit of luck tonight! Stay on them and do whatever you need to do to prevent them from leaving the area. If it takes off, we might not be able to catch it. I'm on my way."

He finished stashing the money into a pocket and trotted back to his ship. *Perfect! Maybe my night isn't going as badly as I was thinking. I might be able to salvage things after all.* A moment later, he got in, and lifted off in the direction of the others.

No Worries

"Welcome aboard!" Bryn's ship greeted.

"Thanks, George," she replied to the ship. Let's go home."

Amory asked, "Wait. Can you go past the Tower Of Fafa first?"

Bryn showed a surprised look that was tightly intertwined with a frown.

Amory said defensively, "What? I just want to see something."

Bryn's surprised look melted into a full-on doubtful expression.

"No, really. This should be spiffy. I promise," pleaded Amory.

Bryn conceded, "Well, only if you promise. Ok, let's go."

The ship chimed in, "Just to let you know, we're being followed by five small ships. Correction, five small attack ships."

"How do you know they're attack shi-" and their ship was rocked by an exploding energy wave hitting the hull.

"Just a hunch," George replied. "Are these fine folks friends of yours?"

"Sparring partners, actually," Amory added.

"Yeah, this is what just happened to us." Bryn thumbed open a screen of the fight in the bar and sent the clip to the ship.

George said, "Wow, no wonder they're after you. It'll be over in a second though. Look ahead."

The explosion on Bryn's ship caught the curiosity of the large police battalion that had enveloped The Tower Of Fafa complex. Bryn's ship did a quick climb, and scores of police ships zoomed under and forced down the attacking ships with a barrage of tractor beams and energy-absorbing foam.

"Wow! Look at all those police! How do you think they knew to come?" Bryn asked to no one in particular.

Amory responded, "Oh, that was probably me. I called them when we got to the party and let them know about our little run-in."

George seemed impressed. "That's a lot of police. I don't think you'll need to worry about them chasing you any more."

"Great," Bryn said. Let's go home."

With that, the ship shot upwards, piercing the twinkly-spattered night sky, and into the deeper darkness of space beyond.

New Plans

Tant was catching up to the other ships, but from his lower, street-level vantage point, he saw the fleet of police long before the others did. This gave him enough time to override the ship's flight computer, slam on the stopper, bank hard to the left, and skillfully swing into the basement garage of a nearby apartment complex. He maneuvered to the lowest level, killed the engine, and ran into the building.

Half a minute later he was up on the observation deck, which offered a great view of the swarming police taking down his people several blocks away.

Shuck!

His eyes looked further down the street and saw that the entire area around Sanctuary was crawling with police ships and robots.

Double shuck!

Tant paced quickly for a minute while he chewed on his fingernail. He sat down heavily on a bench by the edge, stared up, past the visual cacophony of blinking blue strobes, at the looming giant mountain; bathed with a pale white light while dotted with millions of small bright yellow specks. He closed his eyes and breathed deeply. *Relax. This is not a time to react irrationally. I need to think this through before I act. Everything happens for a reason.* With one last deep breath, he opened his eyes, making sure to look far enough up the mountain to keep the police lights out of view. He thought, *I wonder how they light up all of Olympus like that? It really is beautiful. I've always meant to go on an Olympus tour, but I've always been too busy with work.* He stared for a while longer and came to the realization that with his boss most likely arrested, and his place of employment probably closed down, he was now facing an unexpected, yet well-deserved, vacation.

A few minutes later, he looked down and saw that his cohorts in the small attack ships had been taken away. The only area of blinky-light activity was in front of the bar, and even that was beginning to diminish. He looked up again at the view and reviewed his options.

Ten minutes later, Tant now had a vague plan of what to do next. *Everything will turn out as it should.* He took one last look at Mount Olympus, thought, *Thank you*, turned, headed back towards the parking deck, and to his ship.

Home

Bryn's ship cleared the atmosphere of Mars and glided silently through the seemingly endless darkness ahead. If George had opened a screen showing what was behind them, they would have seen a brilliant view of Mars as it slowly shrunk away. Bryn thought about doing just that, and would have if she were alone. She wanted to make the most of her and her best friend's time together since Amory still hadn't fully made up her mind yet on whether or not she was going away for more training with the Off-World Ambassador program. If she did go, she would be gone for months.

Bryn said, "Wow, that was an interesting night."

Amory agreed. "Yeah, it was. That was such a good concert, and also the walking around Fafa was neat."

"And that fortune teller. She was a hoot." Bryn said.

Amory looked oddly at Bryn. "You think she was a hoot? I thought she was strangely accurate with some stuff about us, but wow, if even part of what she said about you comes true then man, you're going to have a bad year."

Bryn poo-pooed her. "P'shaw. Everything's going to be great, as long as you don't die." They both laughed. "I mean, hey, I've already had my family disappear, so I think I've been through the worst of what life can throw at me."

"Good point." Amory knew that while this happened years ago, and Bryn had dealt with it and mostly moved on, it was still a subject that was best not to dwell on, so she changed it. "So, why do you think those people attacked us in that bar?"

"I don't know." Bryn said. "They seemed more interested in you than me...oops, that reminds me." She thumbed open a screen hit a few buttons and Linna morphed back into Bryn.

Amory said, "Thanks. I was going to say something, but I figured you'd change back sooner or later."

Bryn continued, "Yeah, sometimes I forget I'm wearing her. Oh, so anyway, it seemed like that first guy who came up to the table was only interested in you."

"That's weird. I mean, who would be interested in me?"

George interrupted, "If I may?"

Bryn said, "Sure, all theories are welcome."

The ship asked, "What if someone recognized Amory?"

Amory wondered, "From where? It's not like I'm famous, or rich, or anything."

George continued, "Yes, that is true, but if someone is a follower of all things related to Bryn, they would know that you're her best friend."

"Yeah, but why would someone want to attack me?"

George said, "What if he was trying to kidnap you?"

"Oh. I don't think I like that."

Bryn said, "That makes sense. If you were kidnapped, they could then try and ransom you, knowing that I'd pay at least a few dozen credits for your prompt release."

Amory smiled. "Wow, a few dozen. I must mean a lot to you."

"Yup. Maybe even four dozen." Bryn added, "Less, of course, if they gave you back missing limbs. If I'm going to pay a few dozen credits for an Amory Sutherland, then you need to be in one piece."

Amory gushed with fake gratitude, "Gosh, Bryn. You're the bestest."

George said, "Approaching Deimos."

Bryn cheered, "Yay! Almost home!"

Ahead in the forward view and to the left, grew the large, lopsided crater-laden moon of Deimos. The bright surface formed a jutting wall of rock, covered with thousands of tiny lights of the housing complexes that littered the surface and interior of the asteroid-like moon. It slipped past leaving a view filled with darkness ahead. A few moments later, a mid-sized asteroid with a home perched atop grew into view. A section of the closer side of the house opened, the ship slid in sideways, the girls felt a brief sickening tug at their stomachs, and the ship locked into place with the slightest of shudders.

"I trust you had a good flight. Have a good night," wished the ship.

"Thanks, George. You too," replied Amory.

The girls walked down a hallway in the ship and out though a wide door that opened to the welcome room inside Bryn's house. "Happy early morning!" the house's sentient computer's hologram greeted.

Bryn smiled at the figure of the house. "Thanks, Crane. Happy a happy day to you, too!"

Amory waived, "Hey, Crane! How was your evening?"

"Crazy-rambunctious, as always, Amory." They leaned in closer to Amory and lowered their voice, "Actually, it was really nice having Bryn gone for a few hours. You wouldn't believe how messy she is."

"Hey! I heard that!"

Amory said, "No, they said 'you wouldn't believe how pretty she is.' They were giving you a compliment."

Bryn's glare shifted from the smiling Amory to the smiling Crane and back again. "I'm keeping my eyes on both of you. You, and you." She turned and stepped through the door to the rest of the house, making sure to look behind her in the screens in her glasses. She saw Amory and Crane give each other a high-five and giggle.

When Bryn entered the hallway she smiled upon hearing the familiar, hurried *clickity-clickity-clickity* sound on the shiny floor, and saw her mini-dachshund, Dr. Waggles, excitedly running toward her at top speed. He skidded to stop and slid on the smooth floor into Bryn's ankles. With a crazy-happy look, Dr. Waggles stood on his hind legs and waved his little paws in the air at Bryn, as if to say, "Hello! Missed you! Love! Love! Love! Pick me up!" all at once.

Bryn cooed, "Oh, Dr. Waggles! You must have been the one Amory and Crane were talking about, because you're so pretty. Yes you are! Yes you are! You're one dapper, dappled treat that I want to eat up, nom, nom, nom! Look at you stand like a li'l person. Oh you come here," as Bryn scooped up the mini-dachshund and hugged him close. Dr. Waggles licked her face while his small tail wagged back and forth. She kissed him one more time and put him down on the floor.

Amory bent down and waived her hands back at the dog. "Who's a puppy? Who's a puppy?" Dr. Waggles decided he was a puppy and got all kinds of crazy running around and standing up, only to lose his balance and tip over in excitement.

"Good boy Waggles." Said Amory as she scratched his head.

They went into the first doorway on the right, to the open kitchen. Bryn asked, "Hey, Crane, can I have a water?"

Amory added, "Oh, that's a good idea, can I have one too?"

"Sure," Crane said as a glass of cold water appeared in front of the girls. Bryn sat on a stool while Amory leaned against the counter. "So, how was your night?" Crane asked.

"Pretty good." Amory said. "Kinda quiet."

Bryn agreed, "Yeah, it was nice hanging out with Amory."

"That's interesting. Oh, is that a sun sword?" Crane said to Amory, pointing to the sword handle attached to her belt.

"Yes. Yes it is." She handed it to Bryn, "I think this is yours."

"Thanks."

Crane continued, "Speaking of that, I spent the last hour or so watching some exciting stuff. Check this out, you're going to love it."

A large screen appeared in mid-air. The vid showed the inside of Sanctuary with Amory hiding behind an upended table, flinging chairs at oncoming thugs.

"Oh, *that*." Bryn said.

Crane held up a hand and shushed her. "No, no, wait. This is my second-favorite part." The scene skipped and someone from the other side of the bar stood up, and fired a stun blaster at Bryn, mostly hitting the bar, but the last shot knocked Bryn down. "Here's the best bit." It skipped again and Amory vaulted gracefully over the edge. Crane leaned over and whispered, "Nice move." Amory smiled back. Next Bryn was climbing up on the railing, but was hit with a stun shot, lost her balance, and was knocked over the edge with arms flailing. The screen vanished.

"Hey, now. That's not fair." Bryn said. "I ended up making it out just fine."

Crane said, "Yes, you did. But...you let yourself get shot twice with a stun gun. You've been through thousands of training simulations over the past few years and by watching you tonight I could see you have a lot to learn. You were careless and sloppy. What if it wasn't just a stun gun...set on the lowest setting, mind you. What if they were shooting a blaster, a sizzler, a rail gun, or a gravity imploder? You would have been splattered all over that place."

Bryn was serious and quiet. She mustered up a faint, "I'm sorry."

"Don't be sorry. Someday, there might not be an opportunity for you to say that because you'll have been captured or killed. Why did you even go there in the first place? Even if you didn't know that Sanctuary is a known hangout for bounty hunters and dastardly types from the Fringe, you still should have opened a screen and asked me what I thought when you saw the sketchy clientele. After all, I do know everything."

"I know. I'm sorry..." and quickly added, "I'll do better next time."

"Well, you're lucky there will be a next time. Those creepy creeps were all rounded up, thanks to Amory's quick-thinking call. Let this be a lesson for you two. The manager of the club had sent a message to the tables there that he would pay a 100,000 credit bounty to whomever could bring him Amory."

Bryn said, "Hey, that's what we suspected! What kind of bounty did they offer for me?"

"Nothing," Crane responded. "They didn't recognize you in your Linna disguise." Bryn frowned and Crane went on. "The important thing is that now both of you need to be extra careful. No one has ever made an attempt on Amory before, but that doesn't mean this will be the last time. As awful as it is to think this way, you both are targets to a whole lot of people. And, as a result of tonight's festivities, I'm going to make the trainings a whole lot more difficult. No more of the 'Special Forces' level you're used to training at. It's going up to 'Very Special Forces' level from now on."

Bryn protested, "Wait, there's no such thing!"

"There is now. I can't keep a force field around you all your life, so I need to make sure you're prepared for anything," and he turned to Amory, "and that means you as well." Anyway, I'm glad you had a great night, but I'm going to leave you alone while I do more important things...like rescue a helper bot from Dr. Waggles' evil clutches. He's wrecked three of them this evening since you left."

"Goodnight, Crane," Amory said.

"Goodnight," Bryn said, and added, "Thank you."

They nodded, "You're welcome. Goodnight!" and disappeared in a flourish of confetti, which vanished when it touched the floor.

The two girls stood and sat there for a minute, mulling over Crane's words. Neither said anything, instead letting their silence act as a solemn agreement of their realization that Crane was right.

Amory broke the silence first with slapping her palms on the counter and stretching her back. "I had a great night as always, Miss Bryn, but I'm beat and heading to bed."

"I had a great time as well, Miss Amory, and I'm heading to bed as well. G'night, A."

Amory started to walk down the hallway. "G'night, B."

Dr. Waggles ran past Amory in the hallway, carrying the leg of a helper bot in his mouth. Amory smiled, and briefly thought about how much she'd love to have her own Dr. Waggles, but dismissed the idea as impractical with her new job and all. *If I'm going to go ahead with it. Ugh, it's such a huge decision.* She turned at the second doorway on the left into her room. It wasn't really her room, but since the two of them had been best friends their whole lives, the Struse family had always kept a bedroom for Amory. She was practically part of the family.

Amory always loved Bryn's house. The Struses were the wealthiest family in history but, as big houses go, this one wasn't outlandishly huge or garish as what tends to happen when rich people have tons of money and nothing practical to spend it on. Size-wise, she thought it was on-par with something a minor celebrity might have, but this is not the kind of place that one would expect someone of their fortune would call home. It was warm, comfortable, and just right.

Amory changed into her nightclothes, got into bed, and relaxed. The bed immediately noticed the tense areas on her back and lightly massaged them. She smiled as her eyes slid closed and wondered how the fortuneteller knew all of that private stuff about her…and frowned about how she might die. That was as far as she got before falling into a sound sleep.

Disbelief

Aver stood alone in his apartment and stared out a
window at an unobstructed part of Mount Olympus. The
last guest left half an hour ago, but he barely noticed. He
was still thinking of the girl that, like some horrible
cliché, dropped from the sky into his life. *I'm going to
leave her a message...no, that'll make me seem desperate
or something. I should wait.* He waited for a moment and
second-guessed himself: *But, what if I wait too long and
in the meantime she thinks I'm not interested? Or...what
if she falls from the sky onto someone else's party? That
could happen, I mean, it happened once. Maybe she does
it all the time. I'm going to call.*

He looked around and chose a spot that would
have the best background behind him in the message,
turned his back to it, and opened a screen. He spun around
quickly once more to make sure the area behind him

looked nice and then pulled up the contact card she gave him...

...and stared at it, completely dumbfounded. *What. The. Shuck.*

He looked at it again, studied the picture and the attached words. He slashed the screen out so it disappeared and stared out the window again at the mountain. *There's no way. Absolutely no way.*

Aver squared the screen open and pulled the card up again. The same face smiled back at him and the words remained defiantly unchanged.

The girl in the picture was not Linna.

He knew the face, hell, everyone did, but the words below the picture felt like a simultaneous skip in the heart and a kick to the gut:

Bryn Struse
557 Wahconah Cove
Deimos Orbit - 8
Mars

This can't be real. He stared back at the card. *Why would someone give this out? As a joke? If so, it's really not funny.* Not knowing what to do, Aver called up his best friend.

Lach's tired face popped up. He was clearly sleeping and was too tired to use a question mark when he asked, "Aver. Why are you calling. I just got home and crawled into bed."

"I'm sorry, I know, but this is really important."

Lach seemed to wake up a little. "Come on, I spent all night at your party. What else could be so important that you need to talk to me right now? Wait, it's not about that weird drop-in girl is it? I'll hang up right now if it is."

"Well, sort of, but..."

The screen went black with a *Connection ended* message displayed across it.

Annoyed yet undeterred, he called Lach up again. This time he didn't answer, and got his cheesy, "This is Lach. Leave your stats, and I'll get back," message with the goofy emphasis on the 'k' in 'back' that annoyed Aver to no end. He thought it was weird that his best friend rubbed him the wrong way in so many little ways. Instead of leaving a vid message, he sent Bryn's card.

Ten seconds later he got a call request from Lach. He approved, and his friend was there looking considerably more awake now. "What's this? Where did you get this?"

"From Linna. It's the contact card she gave me."

Lach looked stressed. "Uh, in case you didn't notice, this is most definitely not a card for Linna whatever-her-name-is. This is a contact card for Bryn Struse. *The* Bryn Struse. You know, of the 'We own everything'-kinda Struse."

Aver agreed. "I know, trust me."

Lach was looking at the bottom corner of his screen and remarked, "How can this even be? She looked nothing like Bryn."

Aver shrugged, "Maybe it's a fake card. Maybe it was her and she uses some kind of identity concealer or something. I dunno. I mean, if you were that famous and got mobbed everywhere you went, wouldn't you pretend to be someone else to be able to try and live a normal life?"

"Uh, no. I would embrace and enjoy every minute of my famous-ness."

Aver said, "That's why you're not famous."

"Hey!" Lach exclaimed. "That's not nice. You call me up at this awful hour and then insult me?"

Aver pulled up the time stamp from this call. "Um, I think you called me just now."

"But you called me first. I just chose to hang up on you."

"Ok, I called you first," Aver agreed. Now, seriously. What do you think about this?"

Lach shrugged. "I don't know. Have you called it yet?"

Aver sounded incredulous. "No. Are you crazy?"

"If someone who even has the slightest chance of being Bryn Struse…and I obviously need to pause and remind you who we're talking about here…*BRYN STRUSE*, were to give me her contact info, you'd better believe I'd contact her right away. Call her," Lach said.

"No way!"

Lach pleaded. "Come on. Call her and call me right back. I want to know all about it."

Aver seemed on the fence, but he was being worn down by his friend. "Eh, I don't know. I don't want to bother her or anything."

"Aver. Come on. She's the richest girl in the known universe. She's got an army of people to do everything for her, so I doubt you'd be interrupting her doing much of anything. That, and she wouldn't have given you her contact info if she didn't intend for you to call her. Call her and call me right back. Or, better yet, three-way me in on blind-mode so I can watch. This really is a gift from above. If you don't take this opportunity I will kick you so hard in the shin that you'll be all like, 'Ow! My shins are all hurty and gone from Lach's powerful kicking action. I wish I had come courage and called BRYN STRUSE when I had the chance. I'm such a loser.'"

Aver gave in. "Ok, fine, I'll call."

"Good. Finally. Talk to you in a minute." Lach's last words of advice before the screen went dark were, "Don't wimp out." Lach was gone and Bryn's contact card peered at Aver from the corner of the screen.

With a nervously reluctant sigh, he took one last look at the background behind him and tapped the Contact me! section on her card. Bryn's face popped up and cheerfully said, "Hi! This is Bryn and I'm not available at the moment. Please leave a message. Thanks!"

Wow, that was actually Bryn Struse and it was like a message a normal person would leave. He wondered if she was just like everyone else as opposed to the bigger-than-life celebrity everyone knew her as.

He then noticed that the screen said, "Recording," and had a moment of terror. *Oh no! How long has it been recording? Aaah! Say something!*

"Uhh, hi. I'm Aver. This message was for Linna, the girl who dropped in on my party tonight, but, um, I'm not sure if I have the right contact info or not…this is what she gave me. So, um, if you are there, Linna, or Linna is you, Bryn, or something…um, either way, I had a great time talking with you tonight and I was wondering if you wanted to hang out sometime, just, um, let me know. Thanks. Oh! Almost forgot…here's my contact card. If this is Linna, why did you give me Bryn Struses' contact card? And, um, if this really is Bryn, someone named Linna gave me your contact info as a joke, Bryn, and I'm sorry to bother you. I really like my StruseCreator a lot. I did a report on the StruseRecycler back in school and did pretty well on it. Oh, that was weird, I'm just gonna go. Thanks, bye."

Aver ended the message and saw the Message Sent box light up and immediately wished he could crawl under a rock on some distant uncharted moon.

Almost immediately, a screen popped up with *Incoming Call* on it. His heart raced as he stared breathless and wide-eyed at the screen until he saw that it was just Lach. He shook his head and hit the Answer button.

"So? How did it go?" Lach asked. Are you dating the most famous girl known to man, or did you totally wimp out and sound like a blathering idiot? I'm going to go with the latter."

Aver said, "Um, yeah. It was really bad. If I were her, I'd never call me back."

"If I were her, I'd get your message and think, 'Hm, this guy is a lot too lame for me. I heard that he has an awesome friend named Lach whom I'd rather meet.'"

"Har har."

Lach pointed out, "Well, the important thing is you actually called her. You're a great guy and all, but you'll never get a chance even remotely like this ever again. You'd live to be 400 and be kicking yourself over and over again for the time you let this opportunity get away."

Aver said, "Very true. Thanks for giving me that extra spark of motivation."

Lach finished, "No problem. That's what I'm here for. Wow. Bryn Struse. *The* Bryn Struse. Amazing. Ok, I'm going to noodle this one for a while and then sleep on it. Thanks for blowing my mind a little."

"No, thank you," Aver said and slashed out the screen. He sat down, stared at Bryn's card and thought about the weirdly wonderful way this all happened.

That, and he also wondered again just how he ended up with Lach as his best friend.

Message Received

After she got up the next morning, Bryn sat on her favorite perching place. On the edge of the second level of the living room, with her feet hanging over the five-meter drop above the lower living room. She loved staring out at the multi-colored orb of Mars spinning lazily below her; that and the other lights of the higher orbit asteroids belonging to nearby wealthy people and businesses. Her eyes would drift over and take in the predominate red of the planet, the white of the frozen northern pole, the blue of the small, still-forming oceans, the various shades of black domes clustered over the population centers, the green patches of the budding forests – Mars was truly a colorful joy to look at, even more so than Earth. Here, the colors were brighter and so incredibly vibrant, as if the planet has found itself awakening after a long slumber, shook off the dust, smiled and proudly said, "Watch what I can do!" Earth, however, had gotten noticeably duller from centuries of excessive use and abuse to the point where it was a lackluster gray-tinged shadow of its former self.

Even when she was a child, this was her favorite spot to sit and think. For most families, the living room was the hub of all activities, but her family was not like most. Growing up, her parents were always in either in a private workroom or laboring in a lab, toiling over some invention or another. As infrequently as she saw her parents, at least when they were working on smaller inventions for personal use or the public government projects, they were usually at home. For the super secret projects, and there were many, the elder Struses had to work in an undisclosed location, away from everyone they knew, for months at a stretch. Her much older twin brothers dealt with this by spending all their time in the sim room training for who knows what. It was a big desire for them to get into the military and do great things. If they weren't training for something, they were off visiting one of their seemingly unlimited number of friends.

Bryn, on the other hand, did not have that luxury. There were few opportunities to meet other kids her age, as she was often either at home alone, or left to entertain herself at StruseCorp while her parents were in a meeting, or working on a project. Since Bryn rarely had people to visit, or things to do, she spent most of her free time sitting here for hours at a stretch, taking in the view and thinking. When Crane, the sentient house computer, noticed her pattern of coming to this spot, they surprised her one day by adding a seat that popped out of the floor when she sat in her thinking space. From then on it was Bryn's official spot.

This morning, Crane broke the silence by appearing nearby and saying "Do you know what time it is?" Bryn's eyes instinctively went to the lower corner of her glasses to check the clock there, but realized she had left them back in her room. It was fine, she didn't need them to see, and didn't want to be connected to everything at the moment.

Crane continued, "Did you forget your glasses again? It's 7:42 am and you've been here for two hours now appreciating the view. Is there anything on your mind?"

For Bryn, Crane was like a third parent, but the one who took the most active role in raising her. It was impossible for a child to get into any trouble with a household computer keeping watch over things. If a kid was about to fall, the gravity would turn off and they would float harmlessly to the ground. If they were in more immediate danger, a protection field would appear around the tot. The house computer would also fill the role of providing almost all of the child's education by ensuring they uploaded and learned the subject of the day. So, despite having parents, Crane had been the one she talked to the most in her life. Talking freely about feelings with the house was nothing new to her.

Bryn said, "I don't know. I've just been thinking about things."

Crane asked, "Like what?"

"I dunno, a bunch of stuff. I've got a lot to think about. I mean, who am I? It seems like I've never been known as 'Bryn Struse.' It's always been 'Bryn Struse, daughter of Alva and Amelia', or 'Bryn the daughter of missing inventors Alva and Amelia,' or 'Bryn Struse, orphaned quillionaire.' I've never been known for my own achievements, but instead I've been compared to what my parents did, or how many credits I have."

Crane's holographic image sat down beside her. "I agree, that's not fair, but how else are people going to know you for who you are unless you get out there and make a name for yourself? Honestly, you spend most of your time either alone, or hanging out with Amory."

"Yeah, I do, but…hey, speaking of her, what's she doing right now?"

Crane said, "She's in the art room painting a picture and talking to me about last night."

Bryn asked, "What about last night? Did she mention the fortune teller?"

"No, not yet, but I'll be sure to ask her...and don't try changing the subject."

"Ok. It was a good try though."

Crane agreed, "It sure was. You get a comet for effort."

"Where was I? Oh, I remember…this year I want to change things. I want to make a name for myself and get out from under the shadow of my family. Who knows, maybe I would just rather slip into obscurity and spend my life doing things I like."

"That is a possibility." Crane asked, "Like what?"

"That's the problem. I don't know. But I could."

"Sure you could."

Bryn said, "I really could if I wanted to."

"I'm not saying you couldn't. You can do whatever you wanted."

"You bet I could."

Crane looked at Bryn and asked, "So, again, doing…what now?"

Bryn sighed. "Nothing. I don't know what I want to do. Running the family business I guess."

"Yes, but you do have people who can run it for you," he pointed out. For a moment, Crane seemed distracted and asked, "So, who is Aver?"

Bryn perked up, "Hey, how did you even know about him?"

"Amory told me."

"Urh! That Amory! I'm so gonna get her when I see her next."

Crane smiled, "On a related note, I'm guessing you haven't put your glasses on yet today."

Bryn gave Crane a squinty look. "Yeah. We already talked about that earlier."

A shrill cackling laughter echoed from down the hall.

Bryn sat up. "What was that?"

"Amory laughing at something funny."

Bryn looked suspiciously at Crane, "What could be that funny?"

Crane smiled. "Well, if you had put on your glasses, you would have seen the *message waiting* light blinking, and you would have seen this delightfully adorable message that your nervous nelly left for you."

The laughter in the other room continued unabated.

A two-story screen appeared, hanging in midair in the atrium in front of them, and began to play a video. Bryn's eyes cocked in a quizzical fashion as she tried to figure out what he was talking about...until a horribly nervous, five-meter tall Aver appeared on the screen before her as it played Aver's message to Linna/Bryn.

Bryn was two parts touched by his sincerity, five parts angry at herself for being so careless in giving her real contact info instead of Linna's info, and a thousand parts embarrassed by seeing this in any place that wasn't 100% private.

"BWAHAHAHAHAHA!" Amory's maniacal laughter erupted from somewhere behind her.

Bryn looked below and saw Amory downstairs clutching her stomach and laughing like a crazy person. Dr. Waggles was getting into the fun as well by balancing on his hind legs, swaying, and waving his tiny front paws in the air while making a "WRROOOORRR!" noise in an attempt to mimic Amory. The little dog looked like some odd, elongated, drunken, belly dancer trying to woo people. This made her laugh even harder, to the point where she was having problems breathing properly.

Bryn grabbed two nearby pillows off a couch and whipped them hard at Amory. The first one hit her, which only slightly diminished the. Amory was able to use her Tracelet to fling the second pillow back at Bryn, catching her off-guard and hitting her squarely in the face.

"Oof!"

Bryn turned back the other way and used her Tracelets to lift up every pillow and cushion in every level of the room and rained them all down hard on Amory. Her laughter subsided and became a steady giggle under the pile of pillows she was now buried under. Dr. Waggles jumped up on one of them, and dug a little to find her, only to jump back in fright when she used a Tracelet to shoot a couple of pillows straight up into the air...which then fell straight back down on top of her. The giggling engine that was Amory revved up into a full-on guffaw.

"Bak!" said Dr. Waggles. "Bak! Bak!"

Bryn lost it and fell over laughing, as well.

Over the past few moments, Crane had spliced together all of the "Uh"s, and "Um"s into a continuously looping display of insecurity forced from adoration, all set to a peppy beat. This video clip began to play on the big screen that hovered in the living room with the title, "The Best of Aver."

The laughter continued for hours.

Looking Back

Bryn was restless. After Amory left, she spent the morning moving from room to room, not being able to find a comfortable place to sit and think. While she didn't want to be left alone with her thoughts, Bryn also had a strong need to think things out and put an end to the simmering, conflicting mix of emotions that flew about her head like ghosts locked in a cemetery; desperate, but unable, to lay their final earthly concerns to rest.

After running out of rooms, she entered her parents' old bedroom and lay down on the bed. Moments later, the torrential flood of repressed thoughts burst forth thought the mental dam and the tears rivered down her cheeks. As the images of her life before tore through the barrier, Bryn winced in pain.

Her younger self is there...Bryn recognized the day, even the time, and looked past it for another memory, *anything but that.* Younger Bryn with a party hat. *Oh good.* Bryn focuses on this one. December 31,

100

2486. One year before the bad time, but far enough away to keep the pain at bay. The five of them are there. *Mom, Dad, me, wearing a stupid hat, Tilden, and Triton.*

It was Bryn's twelfth birthday and there she was, beaming with the unbridled happiness of someone that has known nothing else. By looking at this picture perfect family getting ready for the turning of the New Year, that was easily believable. The end of December was always a big time for celebration for the Struse family. Between Bryn's birthday, the anniversary of the founding of StruseCorp by her grandparents, Christmas, and New Year's Eve, December was a big cause for good times.

Tears welled up in Bryn's eyes. *Look at us. We were all so happy and together back then.* The screen in front of the family struck midnight and they all cheered in the arrival of 2487 with hugs, cheers, and well-wishes.

Bryn shook her head, *How did we go from five of us down to just me in the span of one year? What happened to us?* Bryn's mind stopped fighting the flow and drifted toward the one thing she had tried so hard to avoid. *What happened to us?* She was sucked into the whirlpool of things she normally pushed far from her thoughts to keep from breaking down.

December 31, 2487. A 13-year old girl, dressed up for her birthday, standing stoically, yet drowning in pain...more pain than any child should ever experience in their entire life, slicing open her soul with the white-hot cut of the words; being told...not believing...death...one, two, both of them...the news of which cauterizes the wounds immediately, probably to protect from bleeding out from the fatal stab to the heart which leaves her dead deep inside where no one sees. The formally lush interior of this girl wilted with the words she knew to be true, but refused to believe. Her sense deadened, but was still painfully aware of the hushed whispers, magnifying and reverberating endlessly the word that would follow, surround, envelop, and define..."Orphan."

Curled like a comma, Bryn cried in deep sobs punctuated by equally deep breaths for air.

"Bryn?"

Startled, her eyes snapped open wide to the present, like a pair of pipes that just flooded out.

Crane asked again, "Bryn? Are you ok?"

She wiped unsuccessfully at the streams running over her cheeks and sheepishly lied, "Uh huh."

The holographic image of Crane shook their head and sat on the edge of the bed without creasing it. "Were you thinking about your parents?"

She shrugged and quietly said, "And Tilden and Triton."

"Wow. Whole-on family flashbacks."

Bryn sniffled. "I don't understand what happened. It seemed one year everything was perfect and the next everything had fallen apart."

Crane said, "Well, you know what happened with your brothers and why they had to leave."

"Yeah, but it was just really stupid. So stupid that I don't understand why anyone would even think of doing that."

"And your parents, well, they were working on a project when, well, something went wrong."

Bryn turned to Crane, her house, her friend, her parental figure, looked them in the eyes and asked, "Do you think they're alive?"

Crane looked back and said, "I don't know," which caused Bryn to deflate a little. They continued, "Which, is a much better answer than a definitive 'no.' On one hand, we don't have any proof that says they're dead, but we also haven't seen or heard from them in the past five years. I have ideas and theories, but they need to wait until you're ready to be open to them...and don't say you are, because I can clearly see you're not."

Bryn nodded.

Crane perked up. "You need to stop feeling sorry for yourself. Let's fill the rest of this year with new and wonderful experiences and memories instead of longing and pining away for moments in the past you can never re-live."

"But I need time...I'm really..."

They cut her off. "No. The only thing you really need to do is be out and about doing great things." They looked at her closely, "And besides, that sadness you like to wear from time to time will be unfashionable in ten seconds."

"What are you talking about?" she burbled.

Crane whistled, and a few moments later the bedroom door slid open and a dappled dachshund wearing a blue cape came swooping into the room sitting on a hovering green disk. "Bak! Bakbak!"

The happy wagging dog landed on the bed, scampered over to Bryn, and licked her tear-streaked face.

Bryn couldn't help but to smile, and started to protest, "That's not fair!"

Crane said, "I know, that's why I had to enlist his help."

"Whoa!" Bryn tried to avoid Dr. Waggles' tongue and tipped over. The little dog seized the opportunity to bound on top of her, with a tail blurry from wagging so fast.

Bryn held up Waggles and looked at Crane with moist red eyes. "Thank you."

"Oh, I'm not done yet."

Suspicious, Bryn asked, "What do you mean by that?"

"You might have been lying here thinking about the time when you and your family would do family things. I'm here to show you that you actually do have a family. It's not like what you used to have, but between Waggles, me, and the people I just sent a message to, you've got the family thing covered."

"What? Who did you message?" Bryn asked.

A vid screen opened and played a message time-stamped three minutes ago. Crane, with their normally chipper exuberance, said, "Hello Sutherland family! I'd like to inform you that Bryn would like to take you up on your gracious offer of hospitality. She'd love to spend the afternoon with you and will be there within the half-hour. Thank you, and have a wonderful day!"

"Hey! I wanted to spend the day a..."

Crane finished her sentence. "'...with the Sutherlands'? I thought so! What a better way to cheer up then spend a nice day with your best friend and her family...who, I might add, has been a closer family to you than your parents ever were."

Bryn opened her mouth to protest this, but thought and realized they were right. In her family fantasies, she always thought back to the best of times when everyone was together. Unfortunately that seemed to happen maybe once a year, if that, due to her parents or much older brothers always being away for one reason or another; hidden away in a lab, or at work. The Sutherlands had always been there for her, even when she was younger. Her happiest times seemed to actually have been spent not with her own family, but her best friend's.

"You're right," Bryn said. I'm going to try and be happier." She sat up, leaned over and hugged Crane. "Thank you."

They hugged her back. "Ok, enough mushy stuff. You'd better get ready for a fun day."

Bryn bounded off the bed and ran out the bedroom door with a wagging dachshund hot on her heels.

She spent the day with the Sutherlands and came away from the experience with a new mental picture of what a happy family is like.

Lost & Found

One evening, a few weeks later, Bryn was on her way home from work and was talking with a hologram Amory.

Bryn asked, "So how are your..."

"Stuff it Struse. Tell me how your date with Aver went."

"Such rudeness. What date? And besides, since when is going out with someone considered a date?"

"The one you had last night. Crane told me."

Bryn admitted, "Yes, we went out together last night, but..."

"So, who did you go as? You or Linna?"

"Me...?"

Amory's eyes and mouth got wide, *"You didn't tell him!* Bad Bryn!"

Bryn slumped in her chair. "How could I? It would have been so weird and hard to explain, and everything was so nice and going so well that I didn't want to ruin things. But..."

"Yeah, good luck with telling him the truth after a good date." She mimicked Bryn, "'Oh, hi, Aver. Remember that great date you thought you had with me, Linna Meekins? Actually I don't exist. Well, I do, but I'm not Linna, but Bryn Struse. Let me explain why I'm an idiot...' Something like that?"

"Maybe..." Bryn trailed off as an indicator in her glasses alerted her that an unknown caller was trying to reach Linna's line. The contact information was scrambled. "Huh, that's weird."

"Yeah, I know it's weird. Why didn't you just tell him who you were after Aver left that message?"

Bryn shook her head. "No, not about that. Someone's trying to get ahold of Linna."

Amory suggested, "It's probably Aver. Poor confused boy."

"No, it's from a caller with scrambled contact information. They just left a message."

"Huh, that is weird. That means it's someone shady that you probably don't want to talk to. Play the message!"

The clip started and it was a tough-looking woman standing in front of a completely blank background. Bryn recognized her immediately as the person who attacked her with the sun sword. *Hm*, Bryn thought, *she's masking her background*. The woman spoke, "Linna Meekins, you're a hard person to track down. Then again, I'd go to the edge of space to get back what you stole from me. You're gonna meet me at the following coordinates at 7pm tonight with the sword. Come alone. If you aren't there, then I'm comin' for you." The clip displayed coordinates for a park on the outskirts of the Yardangs on Mars.

Bryn said, "Huh."

Amory nodded, "This person sure seems determined." Amory looked off to one side, nodded, and looked back at Bryn. "Sorry to do this, but I've got to get going."

"S'alright." As her ship docked, Bryn made a slight grimace as the familiar and nearly instant wave of nausea tugged at her stomach and was gone. "I'm just arriving at home anyway."

"You'll have to tell me how this turns out."

"You bet I will. Later, A."

"Bye, B," and Amory's hologram shimmered away.

When Bryn entered her home she said aloud, "Crane? Are you home?"

They appeared beside her, "Of course. Where else would I be?"

She ignored their question and asked, "Did you see the message that Linna got?"

Crane acknowledged, "I did, yes."

"Can you figure out who it is and where she lives?"

Already prepared for this question, Crane said, "Her name is Bissa Hoven, an avid member of the Knights of Phobos gang, although, don't call them a gang as they like to think of themselves as being more noble and powerful. The thing they're known for is fighting with sun swords. They tend to stay on the edges of society and in more rural areas, where they can intimidate and harass people without fear of reprisal. Most of their chapters are on Fringe planets, but they do have a fleeting presence in the central Solar Union. Ironically, they do not, nor have they ever, had a presence on Phobos itself."

Bryn said, "Good to know."

"Bissa lives in the Yardangs, so there's a good chance she might have her friends nearby," Crane warned.

Bryn walked to the living room and stared out the window for a few minutes. A sly smile slipped across her lips as an idea began to form. She called for Crane and said, "I think I'm going to call her back now. Can you get me the sun sword, and make a background to look like Linna's Basic apartment? Oh, almost forgot, can you put a hologram of a Struse Recycler beside me and have it be in the view?"

The intricately decorated tube-like hilt of the deactivated sun sword floated down the hall and over to Bryn. Crane said, "Done, done, and done," as the air behind her shimmered and was replaced by the tiny living room of the standardized Basic apartment. Crane asked, "Are you ready for me to patch you through?"

Bryn looked behind her, nodded in approval at the new background, and was about to say something when she said, "Whoops, almost forgot," and thumbed open a screen to activate her Linna disguise. A moment later, the person who did not exist, standing in front of a room that did not exist said, "All set, Crane."

A screen opened before her, dialed, and was answered by the smug-looking Bissa. "Linna. I didn't ask you to call me. I told you to meet me later. You don't seem to follow directions too well."

Bryn replied, "Actually, about that...I can't make it tonight. It's kind of a bad time for me. How about..."

Bissa became angry and leaned forward in a menacing manner, "How about this, you go where I told you to, when I told you to, or else you're going to regret it."

"Woah, hold on there, shucko. There's no need to get angry, otherwise I might drop this," she held up the sun sword handle, "into this," she motioned to the Struse Recycler beside her.

Bissa's eyes got huge and she shook her head, "No! Don't you dare do that!"

Bryn said, "I know how much this toy means to you and the little club you belong to, but I really can't meet tonight. However, I can meet next week at the same time, and I'd be more than happy to give this back to you then."

"You're so going to regret this." Bissa said, her eyes never wavering from the sword hilt hanging by Bryn's two fingers over the recycler. "I'll see you next week," and she ended the connection.

Bryn ended the Linna masker and Crane cancelled the background. Crane asked, "Why are you going to meet her next week?"

"Because I just got home and I didn't feel like going out again."

Setting Up Shop

As the week progressed, Bryn spent all of her spare time in her art room determinedly working on a new project. Over the last two years Bryn painted pictures in this room, but also tinkered around, eventually creating her Tracelet here. She felt a new kind of pressure with this new device as she was under a strict deadline to create it by. With increasing frequency she was finding herself having to go down the hall to her parents' old workshop for additional tools and parts.

Her parents' workshop had always captivated Bryn much in the same way that a revered cathedral held sway over its followers. The workshop was what kept her parents away from her for so much of her youth, and now it was all she had left of them. Apart from the odd tool she needed, Bryn left everything there the same as when her parents had last used it.

Late one night, she looked around her art room and asked herself, *If every tool I could possibly need is down there, why am I trying to build this here?*

After a deep philosophical debate with herself, Bryn decided to just set up shop in her parents' workshop. She had Crane float her device and current tools down the hall, to the other end of the house, while she cleared a space for herself. She stopped and looked around, noticing for the first time that there weren't any windows in the spacious, yet cluttered, room. *That's weird. Hm. Oh well, time to get to work.*

Confrontation

A week later, when Bryn left work, she rode public transportation as she did every night. Tonight though, she bypassed her normal stop where her personal ship was docked. She couldn't use the shiplot at StruseCorp because it would look suspicious for Linna the intern to be flying a very expensive starship. Instead she continued on, traveling across half a continent to the Yardangs to meet Bissa the bounty hunter.

The train stopped at the Yardangs, and Bryn exited onto a small platform at the edge of the small domed city. A few other people got off the train at the same time, including someone who Bryn suspected was following her.

She walked quickly, with her head down, trying to blend in with everyone else, and headed toward the coordinates given for meeting Bissa. The park was a kilometer away. She used her glasses to view what was going on behind her and saw the same oddly-dressed, very tall, man in the trench coat and hat was following a steady one hundred meters behind her. *This guy is still following me or, maybe, I'm being a tad paranoid. I've prepared for this a dozen times in the simulator, I know this park down to the last detail, I can do this.* Despite her attempts at self-assurance, she was still nervous.

A few minutes later, Bryn arrived at the coordinates given and saw no one else was there. A quick scan of the area showed that the tall guy was gone. *See, it was nothing, stop being like this.* She knew the only way Bissa could enter was from the South or the East, but most likely from the South...and there she was. Bryn's eyes pointed at several buttons in the screens of her glasses. A camera started recording and a call went out.

Bissa, dressed in an all-black, combat-style outfit stepped into view from the trail. "Hello, Linna. I'm surprised you listened and came alone. Good for you. Do you have my sword?"

Bryn replied, "Wow, no small-talk for you. Yeah, I've got your sun sword right here. Let me get it out," and she reached for her side.

"Hold it!" Bissa commanded. She was now holding a blaster at Bryn. "Do this slow, or I shoot you and get it myself."

"Woah! Calm down, cowgirl. I'm just getting it, see?" Touching the empty space by her hip, an invisible pouch opened up and Bryn removed the intricate handle of a sun sword. "Here, take it," Bryn said and tossed it over to Bissa.

Without lowering her gun, Bissa caught the handle deftly and looked it over.

Bryn quickly took a step forward and said, "I should have turned it on before I threw it to you."

Bissa looked up. "I was just going to let you go, but you know what? I can't now. You stole this from me and I have a reputation to uphold around here. No one messes with a Knight of Phobos, especially not some punk kid like you."

She squeezed the handle to activate the sun sword, but the plasma blade did not spring forth from the hilt as usual. Instead, crackles of red light surrounded her hand and wound their way up her body. She screamed and tried to back away from the bright electricity climbing her arm, until they reached her head, and she fell over, paralyzed.

It worked!

Her excitement was replaced by fear as several sun swords sprang to life and sliced through the nearby row of hedges. Three members of Bissa's gang looked at Bissa's form, still swaddled in the red crackling light, and charged at Bryn.

For a moment, Bryn froze up, staring wide-eyed at the trio of deadly blades coming at her. Her mind was filled with the horror of chunks of her being sliced away with blissful ease by the gang members. *What the hell am I doing here? Why didn't I just mail it to her?*

Bryn's arms flicked up instinctively and her Tracelets shot out waves of repulsor energy that sent one of them flying back into the bushes, and winged a second, sending him spinning around and toppling over.

The third Knight of Phobos swung his blade, vibrating with quick electric death, at Bryn's mid-section when a ripple of heat flew past Bryn's shoulder and instantly crumpled the man. The blade of his sword vanished into the hilt just in time to avoid disemboweling Bryn.

Bryn turned around and saw a BarnardBot in a police uniform hovering a couple of meters above the ground. It landed and said, "Linna Meekins, thank you for the tip about Bissa Hoven. We appreciate your help. If I could trouble you for a statement and then you can go."

"Th-th-thank you officer," Bryn said, trying to calm down from what just happened. "Always glad to help."

Realization

Bryn arrived home, stopped in the kitchen, grabbed a bowl of food from the StruseCreator, and headed down the hallway.

Crane popped up and asked, "Good evening, Bryn. How was your after-work activity? Did your trick-paralyzing-sword-handle work?"

Staring down the hall with distant eyes, Bryn responded, "Oh, yeah. It worked great. She got arrested, so that's all done."

"Oh good, you should..."

She cut them off, "Hey, Crane, I'm going to eat in the workshop. I'll call you if I need you."

"Sure, sure. Go ahead."

"Thanks." She kicked off her boots as she walked and padded the rest of the way in bare feet.

Once inside the workshop, she sat down, put on some music, and ate her bowl of warm noodles while looking around. She thumbed open a screen and activated a hologram message of her mother and father, turned off the sound and paused them, so she was looking at life-sized visions of her mom and dad in the room with her.

A family dinner. See they're not dead after all. As long as I have my memories...well, as long as I keep focusing on the happy memories, they're still alive. She stared at the holograms of her parents and ate another mouthful of food. *Yeah, they're not really dead. Hm. What if they really aren't dead?* Bryn asked out loud, "Hey, Crane, my parents aren't buried anywhere, right?"

"Correct, no bodies were ever found."

Hm. "What about their ship, that wasn't found either, was it?"

"No. Just a few fragments, but nothing of importance."

Hm. No bodies. No wreckage. Maybe? "Crane?"

"Yes, Bryn?"

"What was their experiment about?"

"They were testing a faster mode of travel that combined current warp technology with their experimental wormhole theories."

Why haven't I asked these questions before? "How much faster would it be?"

"Immeasurably faster. With current technology, the distance you could cover is measured in light-years. With what they were working on, it would be measured in galaxies. You could, in theory, go anywhere in the blink of an eye."

Bryn asked out loud, "What if they didn't die? What if the experiment worked and they're just somewhere else?"

Crane responded, "That is possible, but if so, it would be difficult to believe that we wouldn't have heard from them in the past five years."

"Yeah...but what if they're trapped somewhere? What if they can't get back?"

Crane noted, "That's also a possibility. I've noticed that you're asking a lot of questions about your parents and their disappearance."

"I guess I am, yeah. I've just never really thought much about it before. One day they were here, then they were gone, and I always just went along with what I was told." She sighed and looked appreciatively at the silent, moving holograms of her parents, smiling in their un-aging pictures. "I just want to know things are for real. If they're gone, I want to know 100%, without a shadow of a doubt that they're truly gone. If there's even a glimmer of a chance they might still be alive, I want to do anything within my power to find them."

Crane cautioned, "You're aware that going down this road could lead to disappointment and more pain."

"They've been dead to me for the past five years. At worst, they're still dead. At best, I'll have them back in my life once again. There's no reason not to take that chance."

Crane smiled. "Good. I've been hoping that you'd come to this conclusion eventually. I've got a lot of information for you."

Time Passes

Over the next several months, Bryn kept busy, and, as time passed, the exciting element of danger related to Mars Day, were blurred, and eventually forgotten with the slow and steady passage of time.

The one thing that Bryn did not forget was the night when Crane told her everything related to the disappearance of her parents. They told her the few facts they had, the scenarios he surmised as being somewhat possible, far-out impossible ideas, and the speculations of every conspiracy theorist out there. Trying to deal with that giant lump of information, Bryn spent much of her time each day digesting and processing it all. Despite all that she knew, she felt there was so much more she didn't know, and wanted desperately to seek out each and every mote of information.

After months of delaying entry for a whole litany of reasons, Amory finally disappointed her parents by declining her acceptance into the Off-World Ambassador training on the alien planet of Lossia. She enrolled in a college in the country of New England on Earth where she and Bryn managed to coordinate their schedules a few times a week to stay current on the happenings in each other's lives.

Still working at StruseCorp, disguised as plucky intern, Linna Meekins, Bryn continued to learn about her family's company, rotating from department to department. Apart from focusing on the disappearance of her parents, Bryn's life had long since faded into the monotony of daily life. Every once in a while, usually when she was doing some mindless task at work, Bryn would think about what the fortune teller said and laugh at how absurd it sounded. Her life was pretty dull and she doubted it would change anytime soon, which was fine with her. *I'm done with excitement for the year, thank you very much.*

The End Result Is The Same

"...and the next installment of fourteen billion bots will be ready by the end of the third quarter." The young man said.

Bonna Neefe looked around at the other seven people around the table and said, "Thank you, Arcadis. It looks like we'll get those earlier than promised, and under budget. Good job."

Arcadis blushed slightly and Bonna continued. "Next on the agenda," she looked up and around the table, "The death of Bryn Struse. How is that going?"

A woman to her left spoke up and said, "That's all set for fourth quarter."

Bonna asked, "Is this plan foolproof?"

Visua replied, "Yes. It'll take her out and probably hundreds of others as well, but it will work."

Bonna shrugged, "I'd rather keep the collateral damage down to a minimum, but if that's what it takes, then so be it."

A man in his late twenties spoke up, "What about the cyborg?"

Bonna looked over at him. "You're referring to that cyborg that was in Sanctuary on Mars Day? It's a bounty hunter. So what? It was in a bar that caters to similar scum like it. What's your point, Ston?"

"That cyborg has quite a deadly reputation. It never appears anywhere unless it's working, and when it works, people die. Watch the security vids. It followed Bryn's friends into Sanctuary and left immediately after they did. It's no coincidence it was there."

Bonna leaned back in her chair. "Even if it was hired by someone to kill Bryn, why should we care? The end result is the same."

Ston continued, "This is dangerous ground. This cyborg represents other factions at work. It is highly unusual for us to not know about such a thing. For thousands of years we've been running society and here is something even we've not foreseen. We need to know who is controlling this cyborg and why."

Bonna said, "I agree, but if this bounty hunter is going to kill her, let it get the job done as it will divert suspicion elsewhere. In the meantime," she looked at the man, "it's now your charge to find out the who and why. Table of Eight dismissed."

Orders From Above

StruseCorp Executive Vice President, Dave Dagenham ushered the representative from Delm's Shipyard into his spacious office and directed her to a seat at the small boardroom table. "Moffy, I'm glad I was able to finally get this chance to meet with you to discuss..."

A small red-lined screen, that only he could see, popped up with an urgent alert. This wasn't any of his five work call lines, or his three personal lines. This was more important than all of them combined.

He abruptly stood up, "Sorry Moffy, if you could excuse me, I need to take this call," as he took her elbow and led her out of the room.

Once the door was closed, Dagenham shut off the room computer, breathed deeply, and answered the call. The Acting President of StruseCorp, Jud Astrid, his boss, appeared. "Dave, am I interrupting anything?"

"I was just meeting with Moffy from Delm's..."

"That's fine. That deal isn't right for us anyway. We just want to make it look like we're making an effort. I'm not calling about StruseCorp business, obviously since I called you on this line."

Dagenham had always suspected that Jud was connected to something bigger than StruseCorp, if that was even possible. He had an eerie penchant for predicting what was going to happen, and he was always right. Always. So, when Jud called him on this special super-secure, private line that Jud had set up for those special calls that seemed to transcend regular work business, he listened.

He nodded in agreement, "Obviously."

Astrid continued. We've got a problem. I have word that one of the StruseCorp interns is an impostor."

He cocked his head to one side, puzzled. "An intern issue? Don't you think this is a bit beneath us? I'll have the intern manager handle it."

Jud glared at Dave. "Dagenham, *you* will handle this. I believe that one of the interns is actually someone who has infiltrated our company and has been stealing our corporate secrets."

"Sorry sir. I will handle it. Which intern is it?"

"We think it's Linna Meekins. I want you to find out who she really is, who she works for, and as much about her as possible. First and foremost, you need to be discreet. Report back when you know more."

Dave thought, *Who's the "we" in "We think it's Linna Meekins?"* Always the confident yes-man, he responded, "Yes sir. It will be done."

"Good, good. Thank you," and he ended the connection.

The Errand

Aver looked around wide-eyed, "Wow, is this really Bryn Struse's ship?"

Bryn, disguised as Linna nodded, "Yup, and she's so big-headed it's even called *The Bryn*."

"No!"

"Yes!"

"Why did they ask you, an intern, to bring it to Delm's Shipyard to get upgrades? If it were me, I'd just tell the ship to take itself there."

Bryn flopped down in a chair. "At StruseCorp, they really believe in adding the human element to everything."

Aver laughed. "You sounded just like one of their commercials."

"That means I'm being brainwashed nicely as part of my internship."

Outside, the ship shot upward through the thin Martian atmosphere, got in a line of several hundred other ships in the space above Mars's North Pole, and entered the Solar Union Lightway.

Bryn continued, "So, you've never been to Delm's before?"

"No. Never. No one in my family owned a starship, so I'm pretty excited for today. Thanks for bringing me along."

"No problem. It's always nicer having a friend along."

The reddish-white of Mars's North Pole shifted, half spun, and stretched out an impossible amount as *The Bryn* entered the Solar Union Lightway and was accelerated past light speed. Seconds later, the warbling light shrunk back into curves and spun back to pinpricks of light as they exited the Lightway above the massively vast enclosed expanse of Delm's Shipyard.

Aver laughed, "It's kind of a waste to have taken the Lightway to get here since Delm's is halfway between Mars and Jupiter."

"It's not my bank account," Bryn lied.

The Bryn communicated silently with Delm's and moments later, an entrance opened for their ship. A minute later the ship stopped and a representative from Delm's was asking for permission to enter the ship.

Aver frowned. "I should have gotten a tour of the ship before we left, but wow, we're here already."

"I told you this would be a quick errand."

They both got up and the Delm's rep greeted them. "Hello Linna! Hello Aver! Welcome to Delm's Shipyard!"

"Hello!" they both replied.

"If you would please follow me, I will escort you to Miss Struse's loaner ship."

They walked along a soft-carpeted, brightly-lit, lovely-smelling hallway to a small, beautifully-decorated waiting room.

The one woman sitting there had a vid screen open, "…no, there's something wrong with the loaner. They said it's going to be another twenty minutes. I know, I know, I'm sorry, I'm trying to get there as soon as I can…"

The tone of the woman's voice tugged at Bryn's heart and she paused.

The Delm's representative said cheerfully to Linna, "No waiting for Miss Struse. Her loaner is ready to go right now."

Bryn asked, "What type is it?"

"A Brookline, of course. We assumed Miss Struse would want a ship of similar size and ability to *The Bryn*, which is difficult since her ship is a custom build commissioned by her parents. We believe the Brookline StarLenser would be closest."

Damn, that's a fancy ship. No, no. I should do the right thing. Bryn gestured at the woman in the waiting room, "Can you please give her the Brookline? We'll take a different loaner."

Both Aver and the representative stared at her with disbelief. "Really?" they chorused.

"Really."

"But this ship was especially prepared for Miss Struse. Should we contact her first to ensure…"

Bryn shook her head, "No. No need to. She'll be fine with this. And besides, my friend, Aver, has never been to Delm's before and…"

The representative turned to Aver and said, "Oh! You *must* go to the observation deck. It will take your breath away." She laughed, "Not literally, of course. There's plenty of air to breathe, I promise."

Bryn nodded, "Yes! Perfect! We're going to head to the observation deck. In the meantime, please make that woman's day a little brighter by giving her our loaner ship, thank you."

"Will do. Thank you. The green floor is that way. After you've toured Delm's, stop on by whenever you are ready and we will have a ship for you."

They thanked her and went to the green floor by one wall. When they stood on the green squares, they rose up through the ceiling and another twenty stories above that before stopping.

Aver's jaw dropped open.

"Yeah." Bryn agreed.

The three level, floor-to-ceiling window looked out over the expanse of Delm's shipyard for hundreds of kilometers in the distance until it curved down and away. Ships of all shapes and sizes, from tiny dots, to giant cruise ships, and bigger, were in various stages of construction.

"That's amazing."

"It's one of my favorite human-made views in all of the Solar Union." Bryn looked around and saw an upper observational deck that was empty. "Hey, let's go up there. We can probably get a better view."

"Sure!"

In the upper deck, they sat down on a bench and spent a few minutes in silence, taking in the view.

After much hesitation, Bryn spoke. "I…I have something to tell you."

"Really? What?"

"I feel really bad, about this. I've been lying to you about who I am."

He looked at her. "Really? You're *not* Linna Meekins?"

She shook her head. "I'm sorry, no. I wear a device that scrambles my appearance."

"But…but, rooms and people greet you as Linna…"

"The device is probably the best concealer ever made. It kind of has to be."

"Why…?" The realization came over his face. "That card you gave me…on the rooftop…"

She quickly looked around to make sure no one was nearby, thumbed open a screen and she shimmered and shrank from Linna into Bryn. "That card was mine. I'm sorry I've been lying to you this whole time, but I have to be very careful about who I show myself to. From this moment forward, I want to start over and be honest." She held her hand out and they shook hands. "Hello Aver. My name is Bryn Struse. I would very much like to be your friend."

"Wow. Shuck. Um, hi Bryn. It's nice to meet you."

"I'm afraid that since we're in public, I need to cover back up with Linna before someone notices and we appear on the news." With a few taps on her screen, she re-transformed into Linna.

"If you were anyone else, I'd probably have been offended, but wow, yeah, I can totally see why you would have to go to such lengths."

She frowned, "Sometimes it's crazy and really hard to deal with. That's why I spend most of my time at home."

"Well, at least there's no one at your house trying to record you and sell it to a tube channel like that one girl did a few years ago."

"Ugh. I could not believe that when it happened. Yeah, that didn't help things."

Aver said, "You can trust me. If I do what she did, I promise to get top dollar and split it with you."

"60/40."

"That sounds fair."

They laughed.

"I'm so glad you understand. I was worried that you were so used to Linna that you'd reject me once you found out I wasn't her."

"I became friends with your personality, not your looks, or who you were born to."

"Great! I'm going to stay like Linna forever!"

"Welllll, there's no need to do something crazy like that."

"One other thing."

He smiled, "You're not actually Bryn Struse?"

"No, I'm still me. The rest of this year is going to be kind of intense."

"Intense? How?"

"At the end of the year…"

"Oh yeah, I saw this on the news. You turn eighteen and inherit StruseCorp."

"Kinda sorta yeah."

Aver thought and said, "Wow, and I hope you're learning politics as well because you'll be in control of the largest company, meaning you get to decide which politicians to sponsor. Your one company basically decides what the Solar Union Senate passes. I'm sorry, but that would be too much pressure for any one person to deal with."

"Oh it is. And that's the one part I've been trying to ignore. I don't care two shucks about politics."

"Do you have security people, because if you don't, you should."

"Sort of."

"That doesn't sound very secure."

Bryn made an uncertain face and said, "I have a strong suspicion that my godfather, Dow, has BarnardBots following me around, but I've never been able to prove it."

"Er…you mean Dow Barnard? The creator of the DeathBots? *He's* your godfather?"

"Yeah, he was best friends with my parents way back when and has been keeping an eye out for me ever since they went missing."

Aver looked around nervously. "You really think there might be DeathBots lurking around somewhere?"

"*Barnard*Bots, and probably. It's just a hunch though. I've never seen them, but it's something I think he would do."

"Well, if so that's all the protection you would ever need."

"Yeah, tell me about it." Bryn changed the subject, "So what else do you have planned for today?"

"Not a lot. Just go home and work on creating some new patterns to try and keep up with the new-found demand…which I should probably thank you for."

She smiled, "Who, me?"

"Yes, you. I thought Linna must have used her intern position at StruseCorp to put my pattern designs on the StruseShop main pages for their product categories, but now I assume that must have been you. Thank you. I really appreciate it."

"It's the least I can do. Especially after my bumbling friend and I literally crashed your party. Plus, your patterns are really great. You can tell you put a lot of work into them, which so few people do these days."

"Why, thank you."

"I hate to reveal myself and run, but I should get going. I'll drop you off at your place."

"Sure."

They got up and Bryn held out her hand again, "Friends?"

They shook.

"Friends," he said.

"Great! Let's go get that loaner!"

A minute later they were at the waiting room and the same greeter happily guided them to a brand new Newton InterOrbit. She apologized that it wasn't quite a Brookline StarLenser but it would do the job nicely over the two days *The Bryn* would be getting its needed upgrades.

Tub

Bryn sighed deeply, turned and walked slowly down the hallway of her home toward the eatery.

Crane appeared wearing the apron and a chef's hat they had on before, although now it was spotless and crisp. The words *Crane - Executive Chef* was embroidered in blue on the left side.

Bryn gave them a look. "Why are you wearing that?"

Crane shrugged. "I kind of like it. What's up with the Newton in the garage?"

Bryn thumbed open a screen and did a mini-slash on the *Identity Concealer* tab. Bryn watched her arms shimmer slightly and pull in to her smaller frame. She continued to look at them for a moment.

Crane looked concerned, "When are you going to tell Aver who you really are, also, is something wrong?"

"It depends what you're asking about so I'll answer your first question with a 'just did.' I figured it was about time to come clean and I'm glad I had that talk."

"So he took it well?"

"Better than I thought he would."

Crane pointed a whisk at her, "Did you tell him that you are…"

"Nope. I'm really enjoying his friendship right now, so I don't have the heart to tell him about that, which is fine because I made it abundantly clear that we're friends. As for 'Is something wrong?' No, not really. It's just sad that Linna's arms look more familiar to me than mine do." She ran her hands through her now short orange hair. "Oh, this feels much nicer. I really don't like long hair on me at all."

"Maybe Linna needs a hair cut?"

"Eh, I don't know. I don't want to change things too much with her. You know, I'd like to keep her different enough from me where there's no chance that someone would ever mistake us."

"Good point, but trust me, you two look very different. Her getting a haircut would make things a little better for you."

"Yeah, maybe." She looked around. "Where's Waggles?"

"He's asleep on one of his beds. The one with all the toys."

"Heh, figures. He's so materialistic." She shook her head, "He doesn't get that from my side of the family. He must have picked it up from you."

"Doubtful. Oh, I almost forgot to tell you, but didn't: Call Amory."

"When did she call?"

"Maybe fifteen minutes ago."

"Hm." Bryn opened a screen and punched up Amory. It rang a bit and then went to her greeting. "Hey A, it's B. Call me," and slashed it out.

Crane smirked, "I bet it took you a while to come up with that rhymey zinger."

"What? You don't think I can't come up with catchy lines once in a while?"

"No."

"Oh. That's a wordy answer."

"Yes."

Bryn said, "Sorry, I'm tried from having a nice day and from constantly having to hide who I am."

"Speaking of issues, when did you want me to brief you on what I've found out?"

She grimaced. "Can it wait a bit? I was really hoping to take a tub first."

Crane nodded. "Sure. It's filling now, so it'll be ready when you get up there. Did you want bubbles?"

"Yes please."

"Done. Anything else I can do for you now?"

"No, I think that's it. When I get out of the bathroom, we'll sit down and go over everything you'd discovered about those 'incidents.'"

"Great, thank you. Enjoy your tub."

Bryn walked down the hallway, stepped on the green disc, and floated up to the second floor where she padded down to her bedroom. She stripped off her clothes as she walked, letting them drop wherever they fell, and was naked by the time she got to the bathroom. As promised, Crane had gotten everything ready for her. The dozens of individual points of light emanating from the faux-candles caused the silica-flaked stone tiles to twinkle with the brilliance of a million stars. The steam from the tub gave the room a misty quality as it hazily diffused the candlelight. She walked across the room, stepped over the edge, and stood in the tub. The ideally warm water coaxed the rest of her to join the parts of her below the knees that were enjoying balmy bliss. She sat down and let out a deep breath. "Oh, Crane, this is perfect. Thank you."

They appeared on a screen in front of her. "You're welcome. I know how much you love taking a tub."

"This, and taking showers are probably the only real luxuries I indulge in. I know using water to get clean is so inefficient, expensive, and wasteful, but wow, it sure does feel amazing."

"And those are good luxuries to take advantage of." A light blinked in the corner of the screen. "Oh, it looks like Amory is returning your call. Want me to put her through?"

"Sure, thanks." The screen blinked and his image was replaced by Amory...and a group of people with her.

Amory recoiled and laughed, "Hey...whoa! Nekkid Bryn! Heh, it's nice to see you again, although I didn't think it'd be like this," and laughed. Her friends were shocked at seeing *the* Bryn Struse sitting in a bathtub, and stared at her, dumbfounded.

"Eep!" Bryn quickly sunk down so everything below the chin was submerged. She hiss-whispered, "Crane! More bubbles!"

The level of bubbles rose quickly and now the only part of her visible was the reddish top of her head.

Amory's laughing subsided to just giggling. "So, uh, Bryn, did we catch you at a bad time?"

The pile of bubbles spoke. "No, just taking a tub. How are things?"

"Things here are good. Good. Um, I wanted you to meet some of my new friends here at school. This is Eppie, Magda, Teb, and Kavin."

A hand rose from the bubbles and waived. "Hi guys. Nice to meet you." The hand then returned to the depths of the tub.

They all said, "Hi, Bryn," and waived. Magda whispered, "Where is she?"

Amory whispered back, "That red spot is the top of her head."

"Is she completely under water?"

Bryn could hear their whispering and replied, "No, there's just an awful lot of bubbles in here." She blew hard and a column of little circles flew up and swirled around for a bit. One of her eyes was now visible.

Magda saw her. "Oh there she is. Hi!"

"Hi." And then to Amory, "Hey, A, can you take this call somewhere a little more private?"

Amory said, "Sorry Bryn, I was going to have a shocking exposé of you broadcasted on the news tonight, so can you sit back up and let me get a better shot?"

A single finger poked out of the bubbles in reply.

"Okay, okay, no need for that. Hold on." She excused herself and took the screen with her. The perspective was weird for Bryn to see the background behind Amory spinning as she got up. She paused and a guy's voice said, "Hey, Amory. Can I get a copy of that call?"

"Shut it, Teb! No," and then mouthed the words, *We'll talk price later.*

Bryn exclaimed, "Hey! I saw that!"

Amory said to Teb, "Oops, gotta go! I'll be back in a few." The background spun some more and was dark. Amory's face returned. "There we go. Hey, so what're you doing? Oh, enjoying a tub, I see. That's nice."

Bryn sat up again. Just her face was visible above the expanse of foamy bubbles. She brushed a clump off her nose. "Next time I'd appreciate some notice if you're going to have a gaggle of onlookers when you call!"

"Oh come on. How was I supposed to know you were in the tub. I mean, how often do you answer calls while naked?" Amory looked pensive for a moment.

"Actually, a lot more often than one would think possible. Why do you answer calls from the tub? I mean, who answers calls while they're taking a bath? On second thought, who, besides you, owns a bathtub?"

"If you had one in your apartment, you'd answer calls from it as well. Heck, half the time you're here, you're in the tub. And when it's just you calling, I don't mind. You're practically family...and you're almost always alone."

"Oh Bryn - doubter of my amazing friend-making skills. When will you learn?"

"So you have friends now?" Bryn asked, distrustfully.

"A few, yeah."

"That's good. So why did you call earlier?"

"I just called to say hi and see what you were up to. I knew you would probably be getting back home about then. So, what did you do today?"

Bryn shrugged, "I worked out in the trainer this morning and then went to...wait, why are you smirking?"

"Smirking? Me?"

"Yes, you're smirking. What's going on?"

"I'm not smirking. Smiling, maybe, but smirking implies that I'm up to no good, whereas I can assure you I am as angelic as the box of Wums I plan on eating by myself and not sharing with my new friends later tonight."

"Because they're new."

"Right. If you were here, I'd happily share the Wums with you, but not them. They're not Wum-worthy yet. That especially goes for that Teb guy."

"Teb? What kind of name is that?"

Amory laughed. "Oh, that's only half of it. His last name is, coincidentally enough, Tub."

"Tub?"

"Yes, Tub. As in the deeply conical-shaped, water-filled contraption you're pruning away in as we speak. Tub."

"His name is Teb Tub? For real?"

Amory looked excited, "Yeah. Wacky, huh?"

"Wow. That's a really unfortunate name combination."

"I wonder if when you said you were taking a tub, if he briefly thought that you were taking a Tub, as in him."

Bryn disagreed, "Uh, I don't think so."

"I beg to differ your royal loftiness. I'm going to say a big fat yes on that one. He probably was thinking that since normal people don't own tubs and he is a Tub." Amory looked up for a moment in quiet reflection. "Look at me, now I'm thinking about it."

"About what?"

"About you taking Tub."

"Anyway." Bryn sunk down, dunked her head under water, and came back up with water running down her face.

"Aw, come on, no!"

"What? Did I just miss something?"

"Geez, Bryn, you ruined it."

"Ruined what?"

"You had a huge blob of bubbles on your head and I was waiting for you to try and look up at it and get a picture of that."

"Is that what you were smirking about before?"

"Smiling about, yes. I guess I'm just going to have to make do with these screen grabs." Amory spun up a couple of pictures with Bryn sitting in the tub with a large pile of bubbles perched atop her head. "It looks like a hat or something."

"Thanks, A."

"Or a duck. It could be a duck. Speaking of animals, can you get Waggles in there too? That'd be an awesome picture if the two of you had bubble hats shaped like ducks. Oh wait, I'm sorry, you were telling me about your day, weren't you?"

Bryn said, "I was before Teb Tub took this conversation to a weird place, yes."

"I'm sorry. Please continue...oh! You were in a trainer?"

"Yes, good memory, Amory."

"Nice rhyme."

Bryn continued, "Thanks. So yeah, I did a good one this morning from our private training collection. It had a green ball sitting on a pedestal surrounded by a cliff."

"Oh, I did that one last week. It was pretty tricky."

"Yeah, I fell the first few times, but eventually got it right."

"What was your time?"

"I think a minute and thirty-something seconds."

"Wow, you're good! I did it in two-fourteen."

"That's still pretty good. Anyway, I went back to one of the first scenarios."

"Which one? The field with the angry kitten? I love the one with the angry kitten," Amory said.

"No, the killer robot arena one."

"Oh, that was a fun, and easy one, from what I remember. So, what else did you do?"

Bryn said, "I dropped the *Bryn* off at Delm's."

"Oh, nice."

"With Aver."

"Ohhhh, niiiiiice. Did you take him up to the viewing deck so you could view his deck?"

"Yes, and eew."

Amory asked, "So, was that 'eew' a 'yes-eew' or a 'no-eew?'"

"Definitely a 'no-eew.' I did show myself to him."

"Oh! So you flashed him? Naughty, naughty Struse."

Bryn sighed. "No, I revealed myself – I dropped my…"

"Pants?"

"Disguise! I dropped my Linna disguise and showed him who I really was."

"Good idea. Linna's not sexy at all."

"Amory!"

"Just kidding. No, that's really a big deal. Did he freak out? I bet he freaked out."

"He was surprised, but me accidentally giving him my actual card on the rooftop sort of prepared him for it."

Amory nodded, "Like inadvertent foreshadowing."

"Kinda, I guess."

"I could see that. He seems like a smart guy. As long as you were being honest with him, did you happen to mention that you're…"

"No, and that's funny because Crane asked me the exact same thing."

"Brilliant minds think alike. Plus, that's kind of a biggie."

"He'll figure it out."

"I doubt it. He's kind of a dummy."

Bryn frowned, "Wait, didn't you just say something about how he seemed like a smart guy?"

"Yeah, but I've changed my mind. I'm pragmatic like that."

"You're kind of weird."

"I'm weird? You're the one who answers calls while naked."

Bryn looked down and saw that the layer of bubbles had diminished dramatically. She sunk down in the tub a little more.

Amory noticed this and said, "Oh, now you've developed a sense of modesty?"

"No. I'm just afraid that you're going to sell dirty pictures of me to Teb Tub."

"They aren't dirty pictures since you're getting clean in a tub. Then again, I think he'll pay top dollar for clean pictures as well, so can you sit up a little taller? Oh, hey, that finger you're holding up is blocking my view. Come on, I have to have some way to put myself through college."

"Isn't college free?"

"Well, yeah, but it helps to have an income stream to pay for nice things while here."

Bryn said, "So, you'll make a living selling nudie photos of me while I'm whiling away my time as an unpaid intern. Nice."

"Unless your awesome house computer has the ability to speed up time to your birthday so you can be in charge of StruseCorp now. Then you can bypass the boring intern stuff.

"Who knows? Well, Crane might know because they're so smart, but that's going to have to wait until I've taken a tub and a shower."

"Oh, you're adding a shower now?"

"I deserve it," Bryn said matter-of-factly.

"Oh really? For what? Flashing Aver in Delm's observation deck?" Amory cleared her throat and deepened her voice, 'Bryn, you've done such a phenomenal job showing your boobs to boys, in public, that we're giving you the Solar Union Medal Of Valor. May future generations be inspired by your unyielding commitment to the fabric of society.'"

Bryn splashed a wave of sudsy water at the screen. Amory instinctively jumped back, lost her balance, and fell backwards over the bench she was sitting on. Her and Bryn started laughing uncontrollably. From Bryn's view, she could only see the top of the bench seat and Amory's legs sticking up and kicking with laughter.

Eventually, the laff-riot became belly laughs, slowed to guffaws, toned down to laughter, and relaxed to giggles, which slowed and sputtered out. Amory still lay on the ground with only her lower legs across the seat of the stone bench in view of the screen. One foot raised up and pointed at Bryn. "Heh. That was funny."

"Yeah. I needed that." Bryn sighed. "Eh, I probably should get going."

Amory's foot mimed, "Yeah, me too."

"Alright. I'll talk to you later then."

"Yeah, you too."

Silence.

Amory's foot still bobbled to her words. "Bryn? You still there?"

"Yup. I'm here. I'm just waiting to see if you're actually going to get up to slash out the screen or not. I'm guessing that you're just going to wait for me to do it."

"Yeah. That's kinda what I was hoping for. Hm. I wonder if I can slash out the screen with my feet. Hi-yah!" Her leg flailed about, not going anywhere near the screen.

"No, you're doing it wrong. You have to be closer to the screen."

"But I can't get closer!" Amory's leg was still wildly swinging. "Ugh. Oh wait...I found a stick. Let's try this."

"That's not going to..." An odd-looking branch of some kind waived at, and through, the screen. "See, that's not working. It has to be a finger or other body part."

"Grr. Now what am I supposed to do?"

Bryn suggested, "Why not get up?"

"Pfffthh," Amory scorned. The stick now stood upright and traced circles above her legs. "Wait, a body part? Any body part?"

"Yeah."

"Any?"

Bryn said, "Yeah, any."

"How do you know?"

"I've seen a vid on the tubes."

The stick tried to point towards the screen, but it was too long and ended up going through the screen again. "Bryn, Bryn, girl of sin. So, let's say I used my...elbow. That would work?"

"Yup."

"And, am I correct in assuming that if one Mr. Teb Tub were here, he could have an easier time slashing out said screen than, let's say, you or I?"

Bryn agreed. "From what I've seen on the tube, you would be correct in your assumptions. Quite correct."

"Oh wow." Amory's legs went up and fell to the side. Several seconds of awkward maneuvering later, her head and arms excitedly popped up above the bench. "That's fascinating! I've got to see this for myself. Sorry, Bryn. Gotta go. Bye!" She aimed an elbow at the screen and swung it like a chicken wing and the screen went black.

Bryn laughed. *That Amory's so funny.*

*Doop*Doop!*

On the screen a message appeared saying, "One message from Amory Sutherland."

What? I just hung up with her. She shook her head as she punched up the message. It showed Amory as she was entering a building. She whispered, "If you're kidding about this, I'm so totally going to kick you in the shins when I see you next," and it ended.

Bryn laughed.

Glimpse Of Death

She sat in the tub for another minute and splashed the water a little, but wasn't finding the tub to be as deeply relaxing as she thought it would be. *Probably because I spent the whole time chatting away with Miss A.* She sighed. *I should get going.*

Bryn stood up, stretched, cracked her back, and said, "Shower, please."

The tub drained quickly, leaving a foamy froth at the bottom, which was washed away by jets of water spraying out from the sides. The walls of the tub widened from each other as they grew upward forming a partially enclosed, half wall partition that was plenty big for her and another ten people if she so chose. Jets of water sprayed out from dozens of places. Some jets were powerful and massaging, some fine and misty, some in-between, as they sprayed out at Bryn from all sides and angles, wrapping her in a cocoon of warm water. A few

146

minutes later, she said, "Done," and the sprays slowed until they were all off. She stepped forward onto a wide square in the floor, glowing a reddish hue. As her body was swaddled with blasts of hot, drying air coming from all around, the shower walls behind her melded back into the shape of a tub. Bryn turned around and raised her arms and legs so the air could dry her off. She took another step, this time onto a yellow square, and her freshly cleaned clothes rose out of the floor and hovered by her. Once dressed, she felt a brief cool breeze over her head and the mirror screen that appeared in front of her, showed that her hair was now neatly combed, just they way she liked.

Bryn nodded approvingly and walked towards the door. As she left the bathroom, the candles switched off leaving the room dark until she next returned.

A screen popped up and Crane said, "Bryn, I need to see you right away in the media room. Something's happened."

"Ok. I'm on my way."

A minute later Bryn arrived. "What's going on?"

"Something terrible that just happened."

"What? How recent?"

"Within in the past hour. I will warn you it is disturbing."

Bryn frowned, "Ok."

"Here's what happened first. The *Bryn* was docked at Delm's, over here," they pointed to a detailed map of a tiny portion of Delm's Shipyard, "in what they refer to as the 'Upscale customer shippark.' You and Aver leave the ship and spend the next short while ooh-ing and aah-ing over the latest and greatest of star-faring vessels that will probably never leave the solar system. While you two are enjoying the view from the observation deck, a woman named Auga Searbo was given the Brookline StarLenser loaner ship meant for Bryn Struse by Delm's staff. Two minutes later, the Brookline left the shiplot. Twelve minutes later, an emergency distress call was detected coming from both the Brookline and Auga Searbo's own personal screen. Five minutes after that, the first responder rescue ship took this vid." Crane looked at Bryn with a serious look. "This is a scary clip, so be warned."

A screen popped up and grew until the entire room was the video showing the Brookline StarLenser listing to one side and spinning. It was plain to see that there was something terribly wrong with the scene. Modern intelligent ships don't spin like that unless they've been damaged to death.

The ship silently spun closer. The rescue ship matched the angle and spin rate of the damaged ship, causing the ship to stop moving, but now the stars in the background were spinning around them like the view of two dance partners twirling in tandem with an unblinking audience watching. The outer edges of Saturn's rings looped into the top corner of the view, disappeared, and reappeared with a dependable, stomach-churning, regularity. Bryn thought it was odd seeing the rings at such an angle. The side of the ship had a large hole that small chunks of frozen water vapor spun free from.

Bryn asked, "Why is this taking so long? Isn't it supposed to be a rescue craft?"

"Yes, but it scanned the ship from a considerable distance and found no signs of life aboard. It knows someone died and that's why it's taking its time and documenting as much as possible."

The screen shook ever so slightly, but it was definitely noticeable. The screen split with a new view occupying the upper right corner of the screen. It was black.

"What just happened?"

Crane replied, "The rescue ship detected something and sent a probe off to find it."

The rescue ship slid closer and slowed to a stop with the damaged side of the ship taking up the entire view. Crane held up a hand and the large video paused while the smaller video kept going. In the distance a tiny white dot was becoming visibly discernible from the starry background.

"What caused that hole?"

"Good question. It's definitely not from a blaster."

"Right, there aren't any burn or singe marks."

"Exactly. This section of the ship was torn off...but what could do such a thing?"

Bryn suggested, "Maybe a passing asteroid?"

"No. While this isn't a huge ship, it does have a good enough force-field to push aside most small-to-mid size asteroids. Plus, there isn't an impact crater. What else could have torn a hole this size in a ship?"

"Probably a bot of some kind, but that would never happen."

"That's what I thought as well, but a bot would just use a laser to cut a hole in the ship, not tear it."

Crane drew a box and the picture on the left edge of the door grew huge. They pointed, "Look right here. What do you see?"

Bryn looked closely. "They look like small divots. What are they?"

"I had an idea, but it didn't make sense, so I called a professional on robots. Here's what he had to say about this portion of the video."

A pre-recorded video of Dow Barnard popped up over a section of their view. "Hi, Crane. I got your message and the clip of the vid you sent. I can safely say that's not the handiwork of one of my robots. You were right in they would just burn a hole with a laser to get in; that is if a robot would ever do something like this," and quickly added, "which they wouldn't." He leaned forward. "The only thing I can think of is that it might be someone wearing a mechanically assisted spacesuit...or, and this is a big or that might as well have been lifted straight out of a fairy tale by flying magical manatees wearing tiaras and tu-tus, but it could be a cyborg. I know it sounds far-fetched since the last of those monstrosities was made more than two hundred years ago, but that would nicely explain why the divots are small like a human hand instead of bulkier like a modified space suit, but please don't quote me on that. I don't want to sound like a raving lunatic."

Dow's screen vanished. Bryn looked up at the small screen and saw the white dot had grown and become a spinning white parenthesis.

Crane said, "There you have it, Bryn. A cyborg."

"There I have what? He said he wasn't sure what made it and he clearly prefaced it by the fact they aren't around anymore."

They said, "Just because they haven't been made in over two hundred years doesn't mean they're not still around."

"Well, when was the last time one was sighted?"

Crane said, "One hundred seventeen years."

"See!"

Crane acquiesced, "For the moment, you have a point. Let's see what else is on the video."

The view shook slightly as the camera ejected from the rescue ship and entered the ragged hole. The interior of the ship was black, with faint sunlight occasionally shining in through the sporadically placed windows as the ship rotated causing the strobe lighting to resemble an empty, cluttered, destroyed dance hall. A light beside the cam switched on and it illuminated the wide room. From the inside it looked like a small version of pretty much any standard luxury ship. This area was the rear of large living room. Bits of plastic and metal, and other random things floated past. The camera moved to the second level. Directions such as up and down no longer mattered as the ship was rotating.

Bryn said, "There's nothing here but an empty ship."

"Keep watching. You'll get to see something very interesting in a bit."

"It seems like a lot of darkness, spinny outside light, and floating stuff."

"If I scan ahead, you'll miss important clues."

"There's noth..." Bryn did a double-take. "Wait, what was that?"

"What was what?"

Bryn leaned forward. "There was a red dot of light on the side wall there. Can you go back?"

"What you think you saw was, in fact, a red dot of light. Now, please be quiet and just take it all in. This is very important."

The camera was now in the master control room, or at least what used to be the master control room for the ship. Still-glowing molten metal holes, framed with black blaster burn scars dominated every surface of the room.

Bryn thought, *That just happened a short time before the rescue craft arrived. That must be why there's no power.*

The camera moved onward down the hall. Despite the bright light on the camera, the hallway seemed exceptionally dark. A red dot of light zipped ahead of the camera and disappeared into the darkness. Like it had been spooked, the camera spun around, as if to catch someone sneaking up on it, but the hallway back to the control room was empty.

Something on the right caught Bryn's attention. Her eyes looked up at the small screen of the second camera, and ballooned wide as her body tensed up to the locking point; her mouth let out a terrified scream of panic, fright, and revulsion all heaped together in one drippy awful terrible mess that splattered across her face.

The frozen expression of the dead woman from Delm's waiting room was contorted in an eerily similar silent scream, this one painfully eternal, which began as she was sucked into space when her ship was torn into, and would end only when Bryn's mind ceased to be. Something like this, once seen, could never be forgotten.

Shifting light snatched Bryn's attention from the dead woman to the other side of the room-sized split screen showing the adventures of the main camera as it spun around to continue recording the ship - Bryn's gaze was immediately drawn to the source of the red beam of light which neighbored with a fiercely glowing eye of angry blue electricity. As her mind was starting to comprehend that something was standing there; just noticing an outline of a very tall something wearing, what? A hat? – when the nozzle of the blaster seared alive with bright color, lit, and instantly filled Bryn's world with a destructive orange that blanketed the entire room with painfully bright light, blending to white. Everything went dark, except for the repeating residual splotches of color burned into Bryn's retinas.

The screaming continued until Bryn realized it wasn't the video, since there's no noise in space; it was her. Her heart thumped thunderously as sweat ran off her like a steady rain. The arm of the chair she was holding had been torn free and was crushed within her hand. She dropped it to the floor. She had been shot hundreds of times before in the trainer, where protections in place ensure you can't be seriously hurt, but this was different. Had she been in that ship, she could have been the one dying from a blaster shot, or futilely watching the ship fall away as she was sucked out of the maw-like hole torn in the hull...popping, freezing, blood boiling, expanding away to a terrible, multi-tiered terrible death from exposure to the vacuum of space.

The sound of Crane speaking caused Bryn to fearfully recoil. "I'm sorry, but you needed to see that. This is not a game. Had you actually left Delm's when you intended to, that would have been you and Aver. Killed by this cyborg."

The screen flicked back and froze on the on a frame showing the one red eye and one crackling blue lightning eye shrouded in silhouetted darkness above the washed-out bright light from the camera. The blaster barrel was just starting to glow with the shot that destroyed the probe. The gun was clearly being held by a human-looking hand that devolved to a series of wires and yellow metal exoskeleton frame which disappeared into the sleeve of the brown coat. Bryn looked up above the lights of the eyes and could barely make out the outline of this ominously tall figure wearing some kind of wide-brimmed hat.

Crane said, "Here's the rest of Dow's message."

A screen with Dow Barnard appeared and he said, "Crane, I finished watching the clip. This is so terrible. I know the woman. Her name is Auga and she works for me. I can't believe this. And, yes, that monstrosity at the end confirms my suspicions; that is definitely a cyborg. For it to have lived this long is incredible but, at the same time, troubling. Why would it keep itself hidden from society for over a hundred years only to show itself now by killing Auga, of all people? I don't believe it is a coincidence that it attacked the ship Bryn was meant to get. Please take extra precautions to ensure her safety. Tech that old would be no match for any model of BarnardBot, but I'm still worried, nonetheless. Thanks for sending me this, and tell Bryn I said hi."

The gravity of the situation hung heavier on Bryn after hearing Dow's concern.

Crane continued, "You've seen this cyborg once before."

"I don't think so," Bryn said, shaking her head. "If I saw this thing, I'd definitely remember."

"Let me refresh your memory with a clip of your adventure in Fafa."

A smaller screen popped up showing the melee at the bar recorded from Bryn's glasses. The woman with the sun sword was charging at her when the view froze and zoomed in over the attacker's right shoulder. There, in the shrouded darkness of the far back corner of the room, you could just make it out. One very tall, very ugly, cyborg. The shadow created by its hat covered the top half of its face, but after seeing the bottom half, Bryn wished it wore a bigger hat. *A sombrero? Or, maybe a helmet. That would help.* From the nose downward it appeared to have a half-mummified face that might or might not be missing a lot of skin. She looked closer and saw that maybe it wasn't mummified, but rather it was just muscle tissue with no skin.

"Did they just never finish this thing?"

Crane answered, "It appears not. I'm trying to find out more information about cyborgs."

Bryn zoomed out and saw that every patron at the bar was up on their feet either running for the door, or rushing at the girls, with the noticeable exception of the cyborg. "Why didn't it try to get us like the others?"

"I'm not sure. My first thought was that it was somehow behind it, but we now know that the owner of the club was the one who issued the order to kidnap Amory. It was either there out of coincidence, which I somewhat doubt, or it was interested in you beforehand, almost as if it was following you."

"Oh. That's not good. Did you see it elsewhere?"

"No, not yet. I've searched all the street cams within your vicinity, and haven't seen it, but I'm still looking. The main thing you need to keep in mind is that, for some reason, people are out to get you. You need to lay low for a while."

Bryn asked, "And then what?"

"After that, you go to work as Linna, do your intern job, and bide your time until your birthday."

"But that's months away!"

"It's for your own good," Crane said. "Did you see the videos? If that was your ship, you would be dead right now. You're very lucky to be alive, and I'm trying to do what I can to keep you that way."

Bryn admitted, "I know. I'm sorry to be such a pain, but I just really want to be out and living life and doing things...not cooped up at home. No offense."

"None taken. Sometimes I'd like to take a vacation from here. Who knows, we may find out who was behind the attacks and lock them up, and then things will be a lot safer for you, but in the meantime..."

"I know, I know. Be Linna."

"Exactly."

Bryn sighed deeply while staring at the barrel of the blaster on the screen in front of her. The exhale was so deflating that it seemed like she never quite re-grew to her normal self. "Ok."

A moment later came the familiar sound of a new message. *DoopDoop*

Bryn thumbed her screen open, saw there was a message for Linna, and watched it.

"Linna, hi, it's Jud Astrid. Lig told me you were taking today off. When you get in tomorrow, I'd like to meet with you for a few minutes. Thank you, have a good day." He nodded, and then the screen went dark.

Bryn grumbled, "Oh, I don't like him."

"Your parents believed in him."

"But, I remember them complaining about him when I was younger."

"Well, yes, they did, but while they didn't personally like him, they still trusted him enough to run most aspects of the company. Liking someone and trusting them are two very different things," said Crane.

Bryn frowned, "I don't care for him. He seems shifty to me, and I don't think I'll get over it, and if you'll excuse me, I'm going to take a mental break from all of this death stuff and try to enjoy my day off."

"Doing what?"

"I've got a painting to work on."

"That sounds like a good use of a free day. Have fun with that."

"Oh I will."

Facing Things

The next morning Bryn was getting ready to leave for work when Crane stopped her in the kitchen.

"So, are you ready to get back to the wonderful life of an intern?"

"Actually, no. I was toying with the idea of calling out permanently and just going on vacation or something."

"Now, now. You've got a company to inherit in a few months. You've done really well with this for the past year and a half. You can make it the next few months."

"Yeah, I know, that's why I'm going, but I'm not liking it." She thumbed open a screen, hit a button and she visually changed into Linna. She started towards the door, but paused and looked back at Crane. "You know, I really can't wait until I can just be me all of the time."

"Speaking of that, I don't think you should have told Aver who you really are. You don't know enough about him and you could be putting yourself in danger. Plus, you're not into him."

"Yes, but sometimes you just need to trust people. Plus, I really need a friend. Do you know how rare that is for me to actually have a friend who likes me for me and not how many credits I have or whose kid I am?"

Crane agreed, "Your special situation does make it difficult to make friends. Go on, or you'll be late."

Bryn rolled her eyes, "Yes, 'mom.'"

Meeting Around The Table

"...and nothing was found in the apartment linking her to Bryn Struse. Apart from her hardly ever being there I can't find any proof which definitively says that Bryn is using Linna Meekins as an alternate identity. In fact, we have footage of them together at certain times, and more footage of them separately, but recorded at the same time. I even met with Linna in person and secretly scanned the hell out of her and found nothing out of the ordinary. I'm beginning to doubt our theory that she's Bryn," said Jud Astrid.

Bonna frowned. "Hm. I was sure it was her. What now?"

"I'm checking a possible lead on another intern, named Nicko McBrain. It would be great cover for her to pose as a man and would definitely throw off suspicion. In the meantime, I'm still going to keep an eye on Linna, just in case. Either way, something's not normal in the intern department. Oh, which reminds me. After her apartment was searched, and we turned power back on to the building, all of our recording equipment immediately stopped working."

She pointed across the Table of Eight at the man behind the Technology sign, "Jud, get with Arcadis. He might be able to either fix your recording gear in Linna's apartment, or get you better equipment." Jud and Arcadis nodded at each other.

Bonna Neefe looked across the Table and asked the young man behind the Information sign, "Ston, I believe you said you had something to add about the Bryn Struse situation?"

He leaned forward, "Yes, Bonna, you're all aware that Linna and her friend Aver dropped off Bryn's ship to Delm's but something interesting happened there."

Ston thumbed open a screen, tapped a button and small screens opened in front of each Table member. "Linna passed on the Brookline StarLenser loaner offered for Bryn, so they gave it to another woman, Auga Searbo, an account manager with Barnard Robotics..."

Arcadis blurted, "Oh hey, I know her."

"...was attacked and she was killed."

Arcadis frowned, "Huh. Well, I guess I knew her, then. That's unfortunate."

The woman behind the Religion sign said, "Don't forget to send flowers to the funeral."

He nodded back at her, "Thanks, Hela. I always forget stuff like that."

Ston continued, "This is footage from the rescue craft that was first on the scene, but I'll speed forward to the interesting part." Everyone around the table, except Ston, instinctively leapt back when the blaster shot filled the screen. He scanned back and paused it on the identical frame Crane did when showing Bryn who attacked the ship. "This is the same cyborg that was following Amory and Linna in Fafa. Heck, it's the only cyborg still alive, as far as I know. How it even found out this was supposed to be Bryn's loaner ship, or why it's so intent on getting Bryn, we have no idea, but we're still looking into it."

Bonna said, "As I said before, if this thing kills her, it will make our lives easier, but what concerns me most is that it not only knows things we don't, but can act on them quicker. Find it and keep track of it. I want to know who's pulling the strings, because whomever they are needs to be brought in line. Plus I want to know if they have more of these cyborgs. They could come in handy."

In-Between Days

The next few weeks and months were quiet ones for Bryn. Work was uneventful as she remained undercover as Linna the intern, and cycled her way through department after department at StruseCorp. Time after time she got stuck with the jobs no one else wanted to do, but she didn't mind. This was the company her family built, so despite being given crappy assignments, she smiled and worked through them graciously.

As time went on, the fear and paranoia she felt after the attacks ebbed and eventually evaporated away. Nothing dangerous had reoccurred. There had been no sign of the cyborg, and things were fine. Boring, but fine.

Speaking of fine, the friendship between Bryn and Aver was progressing well. Between their jobs, they had very little free time to see each other in person, but when schedules permitted, they hung out. The situation suited

Bryn well as it gave her time to focus on the things she needed to in life, while gaining a steadily close friend.

When Bryn had a day off, and Aver was working, she would spend much of it painting. It relaxed her, made her feel more creative, relaxed, and...

DoopDoop

The noise surprised Bryn and caused her lightbrush to jerk and score a jagged line across one side of the canvas.

Shuck!

Bryn tossed the brush into the can to her left and turned to the waiting screen on her right. Once she saw the name of the caller she perked right up and opened the connection.

"Amory!"

"Bryn!"

"Wow, it's been weeks! Where'd you go?"

"Yeah, it's been way too long. Um, remember when I told you a few weeks ago that I had to study for a big, week-long exam, so I probably wouldn't be in contact with you for a while?"

Bryn's eyes looped from one side, up, and to the other side of her head. "Uhhh...no. No I don't."

"You're a forgetful one, Miss Bryn."

"So, how did you do?"

Amory squealed and hopped in place. "I passed!"

"Great! What was your score?"

"I don't know. They only tell you if you passed or not."

"Oh, ok. What do you need to get to pass?"

Amory smiled, "A perfect score."

"Geez, why didn't you just say, 'I aced the exam!' instead of being all nonchalant about it?"

"Because, unlike you, I'm not a braggy bragger."

Bryn said, "Oh come on. You know I'm not a braggy bragger."

"With something like this crazy-intensive exam, you totally would."

"Despite your silliness, congratulations to you."

"Thank you. It's a relief that that part is over. We still have more fun things coming up, but the biggie, for now, is over. So, what have you been up to? Almost done with the intern thing?"

"Yup yup, that's almost finished, just a few more months. While I've enjoyed it, I have to say that I am so ready to just be done with the whole thing."

"Haven't you been learning a lot about your company?"

"You have no idea, and that's the problem," Bryn said. "I want to just get into my parents' old office and start making changes now, not months from now."

"Oh! Pardon me for mis-thinking, but I was under the assumption that you didn't like the work at all and that's why you weren't crazy about your internship."

"No, you're right. At first I was very resistant to the idea and fought with Crane constantly about it. I thought, 'I'll never need to know any of this stuff. Most of the executives running the company didn't start out at the bottom, they started out somewhere much higher and worked their way up pretty much by knowing the right people.' It wasn't too long until I began to see areas where, with a few minor changes, things would run a whole lot better. It was frustrating because I tried to make suggestions, but because I was just a lowly intern, I was ignored. They dismissed me and said I didn't know what I was talking about. After seeing similar things in each and every department I was passed along to, I realized the problem was much bigger in scope. I took plenty of notes and now know what needs to be done. So yeah, my mind has been changed over time. Plus, hey, at the end of the day, it's my name on everything we do, so it needs to be the best."

Amory perked up, "Huh? What was that? I'm sorry, I was busy working on this puzzle."

Bryn's furrowed brow and light lips spoke silent volumes of annoyance.

"Just kidding," Amory giggled. "Great speech. I'm terribly moved to the point where I'm going to buy a new Struse Recycler just so I can throw my current one into it."

"You are so lucky you're so far away right now."

"I know, I know. You'll kick me in the shins."

"That's it! You're in the lake."

"What lake?" Amory asked.

"The one in my mind where I put people who are annoying me."

"Oh. Am I the only one in there?"

"Right now, yes. Unfortunately, you just missed Dr. Waggles. I told him to jump into the lake earlier for scaring the heck out of me when he flew by and barked loudly in my ear. He's since made up for it by being very cute a few minutes ago, so now he's no longer in the lake."

"So, I just have to be cute, eh?"

"While that seems to work for him, I doubt you'd get far with that line of reasoning."

"Good to know. Hey, isn't that big conference-thing coming up soon?"

"Yeah it is!" Bryn bounced a little in her seat. "I'm really excited about it since it's going to be the first time in I don't know how long that I will be able to go out into public spotlight as me. Wait, I told you about that?"

"Yup. You sent me a message the day you got the invitation a few weeks ago. What's the conference about, again?"

"It's the Leaders of Industry and Trade Conference at the Hathaway Hotel orbiting Eris. Looking over the list of lectures and discussions, I think it might be on the boring side, but then again, my parents always seemed to enjoying going to it every year. It's funny, I always saw things like this as 'grown up stuff' and here I am, about to go to it myself, but I don't feel like I'm ready, or something."

Amory pointed out, "And now you'll actually get to go instead of having to stay at home."

"Yeah, tell me about it. I never understood why I couldn't go with them and just stay in the hotel room or something."

"Maybe they wanted, or needed, to get away from you for a few days?"

Bryn glared at her best friend. "Did you know you're in the lake? 'Cause you are. In the lake. You."

"Sorry," Amory said with a grin. "Couldn't be helped."

"The same could be said for you. But anyway, maybe it's the empty house, and maybe it's that I've been working at StruseCorp for almost two years now, but I feel like now I'm the 'grown up.'"

"Would that mean that Waggles is the kid?"

"Yes."

A pair of dappled ears dropped down into Amory's view of the screen, followed by a black nose and upside down dog head. Bryn followed Amory's stifled laughing face and eyes slowly up above until she was looking at the dachshund floating above her. His tail wagged fiercely and he licked Bryn's upturned head. A tuft of her orange hair stuck up in the tongue's wake.

"Yes he is."

"I think it'll be good for you. You get to be you for a few days, out in public, and have fun representing StruseCorp. It lets you get your feet wet before you take the plunge at being in charge on your birthday in December."

Bryn hesitated, "Yeah. I'm a little nervous about the whole 'being put on display'-thing at the conference, but I need to get over that."

"P'shaw, you'll be fine," Amory reassured. "Yeah, they'll ogle you for a while, but once the novelty wears off, you'll be just like any other person there."

"I think you're right."

"Of course I am. You have other people who will be doing the real work for you, so just enjoy it."

"I will."

"What are you painting?" Amory asked.

Bryn looked over at the canvas covered in bright colors depicting a tranquil scene in a field with gently rolling green mountains in the background. She had been painting the view from her secret cabin in the Vermont province of New England where her family would go to get away from technology for a while. Her eyes were drawn to the streak that scraggled across the scene when Amory called. "Just an Earth scene."

"Nifty. Sorry to chat and go, but I only had time for a quick hello to say I'm still alive."

"Thanks. I'm glad you called. For a while there I thought a bear might have eaten you or something."

Amory laughed. "I don't doubt that the wildlife around here would try, if given a quarter of a chance, but I think I'm safe for the time being. Give me a call before you go to the conference."

"Will do. Have fun, A."

"Thanks. See you, B."

Bryn slashed out the screen with her right hand as she picked up the clean lightbrush with the other. She said, "Ok. Now to fix this," and got back to work.

Bryn Goes To StruseCorp

A few days later Crane appeared by Bryn as she was in the kitchen. "You're a chipper one this morning!"

"Oh yes I certainly am. I'm going to StruseCorp...without Linna."

"Hm," they nodded. "I say 'well done' to the girl least likely to. What brings this about?"

"The conference is in a few days and I want to tell the execs at the company that I'll be going. I don't want them to be surprised or anything."

Crane nodded, "Good idea."

"You think so?"

"Of course. That way they can be prepared for the big media circus that seems to follow you around, and they can coach you on what to expect so you don't seem like an ignoramus."

Bryn stopped drinking her juice in mid-gulp. "Uh, when have I ever looked like an ignoramus?"

"Did I say 'ignoramus'? I meant, 'really smart person who might be taken wrong as a know-it-all.'" A small chime went off and a screen opened in front of Crane. "Goodness! I have an alert that one of the energy collectors is about to go offline, sorry I can't stay and chat, but I've gotta fix this. Have a great day!"

"Wait, Crane?"

They had half-disappeared into the floor and stopped. "Yes?"

"Do you think it's safe for me to go out, you know, as me?"

They rested their elbows on the floor and their chin in their palm and thought for a moment. "Yes. I do think you'll be safe today."

"Why?"

"No one will be expecting it. For you to appear in public today should catch them off guard. The conference, on the other hand, will be a different story. They'll probably be expecting you to be there. On the plus-side, at least you'll almost always be surrounded by thousands of other people, but either way, you'll need to be extra vigilant there."

"Got it. Thanks."

Crane added, "Oh, one more thing."

"What's that?"

"When you go to StruseCorp today remember this. Your age means nothing and don't let anyone pressure or intimidate you. It's *your* company, so do what you want, and most of all, have fun."

Bryn thought for a moment and said, "Thank you, Crane. I really appreciate and needed to hear that."

"You're welcome."

They disappeared into the floor and Bryn was alone with her half-empty glass of juice and a mind full of thoughts.

A clickity trit-trotting came scampering down the hallway and into the kitchen as the cute dachshund made his way to say goodbye to Bryn. He stood up on his hind legs and made a paw-paw motion on Bryn's thigh.

"Oh, Dr. Waggles! You're so cute!" and she scratched his head. "Ok, I'm off to work. Have a good day, little guy."

"Worrroooo!" Said Waggles as he continued to stand on his hind legs.

"Yes, you're a stand-up dog! Bye!"

Bryn went out the door, stepped up the ramp into *The Bryn*, sat down in a fairly rigid-looking chair, and thumbed open a screen.

George, the ship, asked, "Why that chair today? Normally you flop into a couch and send messages to Amory."

Outside, Bryn watched the ship exiting and clearing the house. "Normally, yes, but today is different. Today we're going directly to StruseCorp as is."

"We're not stopping for you to switch to public transport at Linna's Basic house?"

"Nope. As is."

"Good to know. So why the different chair?"

"I'm just reviewing some of the company's numbers before I get to work. I'm meeting with the execs today."

George was quiet for a moment and then asked, "Do they know you're coming?"

"Nope."

"Should we tell them to prepare for your arrival?"

"Nope."

More silence. "Won't they know you're coming when we approach StruseCorp?"

Without looking up, Bryn said, "I'm sure that's when they'll find out, yes. If you don't mind, I need to review these sheets."

"Sorry," George said and went silent.

Bryn spent the next few minutes reviewing the company's financial data. She highlighted certain sections, circled others, and etched others with a large red *WTS?!*

"Bryn, I apologize for intruding, but we are arriving at StruseCorp. I need to drop you off at the public Drop N' Go terminal. Someone has taken the parking spot traditionally reserved for you."

"You mean the one that says *Reserved for Bryn Struse*?"

"Yes."

She frowned. "*Great.*" She thought for a moment and said aloud, "This is not a problem at all. No biggie."

"Docking now to the Drop N' Go. Thank you, and have a great day."

"I'll make it the best that I can. Thank you."

Bryn slashed out her financial data screens, left the room, walked down a short hallway, and out the wide doorway into the public Drop N' Go terminal at the sprawling StruseCorp complex. Bryn's grandfather had once seen very old pictures of a large train station in the now submerged NYNoGo area. He was so taken by its size and grandeur that he based this terminal on it. Hundreds of people were exiting or entering through doors around the perimeter of the grand room with the high ceiling. Most people comment that something seems out of place when they first arrive here, but no one can ever guess correctly what it is. No advertising. With the exception for a tasteful sign which read, *Welcome to StruseCorp*, there wasn't a single other sign hawking a product of service anywhere in sight, a true rarity in modern society.

A green circle silently flew over the people and descended toward Bryn. She could see that Jillah, one of the newly promoted executive assistants, was very stressed out. When it landed, she jumped off and greeted her.

"Bryn, hi, I'm so sorry, we didn't know you were coming today." You could tell by the sincere look in Jillah's eyes that she meant it.

"Thanks, but it's ok, there's no reason to apologize."

Jillah tried to lead Bryn over to the circle, but Bryn said, "I'd rather walk, thanks." Jillah walked fast to catch up, but not before shooting a glance back to the circle she left on the floor.

"So, what brings you into StruseCorp today?"

Bryn said, "I thought it was about time that I stop by and say hi to everyone. Plus I want to find out what our plans are for the conference."

"Good idea!"

As they walked, Jillah seemed to get more nervous. She finally said, "I'm so sorry about your parking space. I've told her so many times not to park there."

"Really? Who's that?"

"Schanna."

"As in Schanna Fife?" Bryn never liked Schanna, the current VP of Research and Development. Thinking of her made Bryn think, *Do I dislike all of the vice presidents here?* She was a sub-standard employee to begin with, but after Bryn's parents disappeared, she quickly rose through the ranks for no apparent reason. She was one of those people who was always too polite to your face, but you knew that once she was out of earshot, she'd trash you any way she could. Bryn always thought her position was far beyond her abilities, but there was never much she could do about it. *Until now.*

Jillah replied, "Yes."

"Huh." After a minute of silence, Bryn said, "Ok, I have an idea. It's a little weird, but can you have someone do this for me..." Bryn spent their walk towards the office area detailing her plan as well as saying hi to people by name as they made their way through the crowd. The employees were quite surprised to not only see Bryn, but to be greeted by name. "What do you think of that?"

Jillah smiled, "That's great! It's going to be fun."

"Perfect!"

They arrived in the large central lobby area of the complex and walked over to the private lift, which opened immediately and took them up to the executive offices.

"Bryn, I have to ask, how do you know so many people? I've worked here for a few years now, but apart from the people upstairs, and some of the department managers, I don't know anyone else."

"I actually spend a lot of time here and try to make a point of meeting everyone."

"Really? I haven't seen you here in a long time. StruseCorp alerts us to whenever you're detected on property."

"I try to keep a low profile."

They arrived at the executive level. By this time, most everyone had heard Bryn was on property and they were moving in to greet her. Jillah leaned and whispered to Bryn, "I'm going to take care of that for you now."

"Thanks, I appreciate it," she whispered back. Jillah slipped on by unnoticed in the commotion and disappeared into her office.

Bryn had planned on walking right into Jud Astrid's office and having a chat, but she hadn't figured on all this commotion and all of these people wanting to talk to her first.

The people who surrounded her were all atwitter with excitement:

"Oh WOW! Bryn Struse! How are you?"

"Bryn! It's been ages since you've been here!"

"At least four of five years!"

"Look at you! You're all grown up!"

"You look just like your mother!"

"Welcome back, Bryn!"

"Bryn!"

Half an hour later, things had mostly gotten back to normal as she had managed to work her way through and satiate the crowd of well-wishers. She walked down the wide hallway to the large office at the end. *Wow, I think that person was right. I haven't been up here since my parents disappeared.* A whole series of emotions came flooding back as she remembered being a child walking down this same hallway to see her parents. A mix of joy to see them, with apprehension as she was afraid they'd just send her away again, saying they were too busy to be interrupted.

She approached the outer office where a woman she didn't know sat. "Hi, you must be Bryn. I'm Olympia, Mr. Astrid's assistant. Can I help you with something?"

"Nice to meet you. No thanks, I'm just here to see the big guy."

"I'm sorry Bryn, but Mr. Astrid is not here. Did you schedule an appointment?"

"No, sorry, I didn't. Is he around?"

"No. He's not here. If you'd like to schedule and...wait, what are you doing?"

Bryn walked up to the door of his office, which opened for her, and looked in.

"Stop! You can't go in there!"

"Hm. You're right, he's not here. Any idea where he is?"

"No one's supposed to be in his office."

"Actually, this used to be my mother's office." Bryn walked in, across the large office, and slumped into his plush desk chair. Then, out loud to the office computer, "Harris, can you tell me where Mr. Astrid is?"

The ghostly computerized avatar for the executive offices appeared. "Certainly. He's down two levels in the accounting offices."

Olympia glared at Harris.

"Thanks. Did he take the private lift from this office to get there?"

"Yes. He rode it down about half an hour ago."

"Thank you, Harris."

"You're welcome, Bryn. It's good to have you back."

"Thanks. It's good to be back." And to Olympia, "Speaking of being back, I'll be back in a jiffy."

Bryn went over to the private lift, partially concealed by several large plants in the corner, and took it down two levels. As she stepped out into the corridor, she saw Jud from a distance.

"Oh hey, Mr. Astrid! Slow down! I need to talk with you."

He turned around and smiled. "Bryn! What a wonderful surprise! Welcome! What brings you around these parts?"

"Business, of course. Can we talk?"

"Sure. We can go into this boardroom right here."

They went into the boardroom and sat down, Bryn took the head seat and Jud sat at one side. Bryn looked around at the long wooden table and then out to the close-up view of Mars. StruseCorp was also in orbit around the Red Planet, but at a much closer position than Bryn's house. The view from here mostly was of the spotted domes of green that nearly covered the red landmass which encircled the southern portion of the planet.

"Wow, it's been ages since I've been in this room. I can't tell you how many hours I spent in here, and other offices waiting for my parents to finish working so we could go home."

Jud nodded, "I don't think things have changed much, if at all, since you were here last."

"I was happy to see that Harris is still in your office."

"Oh, I can't do much of anything without them. They're wonderful. Plus I think it helps that Harris has been in that office since your grandfather built the place. They have a lot of insight. So, what's on your mind, Bryn?"

"Well, I wanted you guys to know that I'd really like to go to the Leaders of Industry Conference."

"Oh, you don't need to go to that. We've got it covered."

"I'm sure you do, but I thought that since I'll be inheriting StruseCorp soon, I should be taking a visible interest in the company. I figured that this would be a great way for me to be seen in more of a public light, and plus it will give us some good exposure with the press who will be all over this."

Jud said, "That's kind of funny since there's been speculation that you'd surface and want to go to this conference. You are right, though." He pointed at her, "You being there would send a great message to everyone and give us considerable media time. One thing I am concerned about is your safety because you will be mobbed there by the media. I also heard about that ship you almost got into at Delm's. That's really scary stuff. You're incredibly lucky. Obviously someone has an issue with you and I want you to stay as safe as possible. What if we had you just vid into the conference?"

"You think I should go as a hologram?"

Jud responded as if Bryn had read his mind, "Yes! That way you could still attend and you would be safe. Literally the best of both worlds."

"I thank you for your concern, but I'll be just fine. Nothing's going to happen to me."

Jud shrugged as if he knew she would insist on going, "Ok, if you say so. Although, StruseCorp won't have much to present at the meeting, we're just going to see what the other companies are doing and to participate in the workshops." Jud laughed and added, "Heh, not unless you have some new invention up your sleeve we can showcase."

Bryn hesitated for a moment but thought, *What the heck* and said, "Well, I do have something, which, amazingly enough, does happen to be up my sleeve."

"Really? Maybe you've inherited your family's knack for humanity-changing inventions, after all."

"Uh, no. Not really."

"Well, what is it?"

Bryn slid up her sleeve to reveal a Tracelet. "This bracelet is a miniature tractor beam and repulsor, all-in-one. You can manipulate objects with a twist of your wrist and also do more delicate maneuvers with your fingers. I call it the Tracelet."

Jud seemed extremely interested. "Oh! I think I've seen this before."

Bryn looked at him strangely. "Uh, I doubt it since just me and my friend have them."

He waived her comment off, "Of course, of course. Can I see it?"

"Actually, is there a product testing room we can go to? I don't want to break anything in here."

Jud smiled, "This sounds promising already."

First Invention

A few minutes later they were in a long, white testing room that was mostly empty, save for a non-functioning robot and a shelf cluttered with random objects in the distance. Jud had called his Executive Vice President, Dave Dagenham, to come down and join them. When he arrived, he greeted them with a noticeable lack of enthusiasm, as if Bryn being there was nothing special. "Ok, Bryn, start the demonstration."

"Once the Tracelet is activated, it works with my hand's movements to either push or pull an object towards or away from me.

"It takes a while to get used to, especially aiming correctly so you actually grab what you're wanting. I use my glasses to help with the accuracy part of this, but my friend uses an optional screen that appears when the Tracelet is activated for targeting. Watch as I grab the small box off the shelf and bring it this way."

178

With a grabbing movement, she reached towards the box on the other side of the room, which invisibly lifted up and moved quickly at her when she pulled her arm back.

"I can manipulate the box any way I want while it's in transit." She twisted her fingers and the box began to spin. She glanced over towards the two men and saw they were watching a screen instead of her and got annoyed.

"And, I can send it anywhere as slowly, or quickly, as I want." She stabbed out with all five of her fingers and the spinning box zipped through the air and slammed through the robot's head, and lodged into the wall behind it. The two men jumped, saw what happened, and Dave nodded at Jud while pointing to the screen.

Bryn really wanted to know what they were looking at, but couldn't see it directly, until she noticed they were standing in front of a one-way mirror and used her glasses to zoom in on the reflection of the screen in the mirror. She stared in disbelief at seeing Linna and Amory defending themselves in that club in Fafa. *How did they get a clip of that...and it seems to be a view from behind the bar. That's really weird.*

Dagenham's demeanor had completed changed from just a few moments before. He said, "Wow, this is really something. Are you thinking of this for police or military applications?"

"Oh, no. Not at all. I was thinking of toning it down a bit and using it for more of everyday use. I mean, who wouldn't want to be able to get something from across the room by levitating it over to you? It's just really handy."

Jud said, "Also, for commercial or construction purposes. If someone needs to lift something heavy, and there isn't a robot nearby, this would be perfect."

Dagenham nodded, "Yeah, it would be."

"Great! Bring one down to Schanna Fife, Vice President of Research and Development, so she can have her people get started on making a prototype."

Bryn's heart leapt. "Really?"

"Absolutely. This could be a well-received product." The men walked to the door. Jud said, "Thanks so much for stopping by Bryn. See you at the conference," which caused Dagenham's head to look at him in surprise.

"Thank you!" She thought for a moment and added, "So, wait a bit. What should I expect with this conference?"

"Not too much. We usually get there, register, and then hang out in the bar and catch up with old friends for the rest of the night. Then it will be three days of meetings and lectures given by the brightest minds in their fields, and debates. There'll also be a trade show where you can see what new products other companies are coming out with. It's a nice diversion from normal life."

"So no pressure or anything on me?"

"Oh no. None at all. Just go, take it all in, and enjoy."

"Ok. I can do that. Thanks."

"Thank you. See you then." Jud waived goodbye and turned to talk to privately with Dagenham.

Bryn went up a level and poked her head in Schanna's office. "Hi!"

The woman glanced up from the screen she had in front of her. "Hello...," and realized who was standing at her door, "...oh! You're back!" This half ended as a question.

Bryn stepped fully into the large office. "I didn't realize I was gone."

Schanna's eyes narrowed and she slashed out the screen she was reading to give her visitor her full attention. "Did you have a good vacation, or whatever you were doing?"

Bryn walked past several display cases featuring StruseCorp inventions, many of which her parents made, and stopped at a large bookshelf full of Schanna's personal things. They all looked very delicate and expensive. Bryn didn't look up at her, but instead continued to peruse the things in the shelf. "Nope, no vacation. Although, that's a good idea. Just been busy, you know, working on stuff." She picked up a slab of colored glass and walked with it to the middle of the room. It was handmade by a real person so it was surely expensive.

Schanna's wide eyes went from the glass to Bryn and back. Bryn thought, *Hm. It's probably more than a little expensive.* She wandered close to the door, causing Schanna to rise a little out of her seat.

"I'm sorry, but can you please put that down? It's very expensive."

Thought so. "Oh, I'm sorry. I hope you didn't think I was taking it. I was just admiring it. I would never take something that didn't belong to me. Here, let me just park it back on the shelf. She lobbed the glass and the woman behind the desk shrieked. Just as it was about to hit the shelf, it slowed, and stopped in mid-air, just hovering above the shelf. "Did you want it on the shelf, or over on your desk?" Bryn pointed her finger at the desk, zipping the glass across the room, making the Vice President yelp in fear, and gently lowered and landed it in the middle of her desk.

She stared from the glass to Bryn and back again. Bryn didn't know if she was going to yell at her or cry.

"So, what did you think?"

Schanna yelled, "Think? Think about what? That you're a careless and insensitive punk rich kid?"

"Come on. There's no need for talk like that. I was just trying to demonstrate the new StruseCorp product appearing at the Leaders of Industry Conference, the Tracelet." Bryn stepped up to the desk and showed it to her. "See? It's a bracelet that contains a miniature tractor beam and repulsor that can be controlled by minute movements in your fingers so you can manipulate objects out of reach."

Her head cocked to one side, much like a puppy trying to understand the strange things her owner was saying.

"Here's a vid of me testing it downstairs a few minutes ago." She thumbed open a screen and it played a clip of Bryn tossing things around and it ending with the box going through the robot's head. "Pretty cool, don't you think?"

Schanna had mostly calmed down by now and was staring at the video. She looked a little nervous after seeing the robot's head get smashed in by the box and her eyes glanced down at the bracelets on Bryn's wrists. "It's very interesting, but I'm not sure if it has a place here."

"Oh, let me finish playing the video. I like the part where Jud Astrid, you know, the Acting President of StruseCorp says he loves it and wants it in production right away."

After watching that segment, Schanna glared at the beaming Bryn. "I simply don't have time right now. We've got too much going on."

"That's unfortunate, especially since the conference is in a few days and they want this to premiere at it."

"It doesn't need to be in production to premiere at an event. You just have to demonstrate it. You're just a kid. A kid who doesn't understand how a big company works. This can wait."

DoopDoop

Schanna looked to her left at the screen that just popped up and open by itself. It was Jud. "Schanna. Hi, has Bryn been down to show you the bracelet thing yet?"

"Yes, she's here right now, in fact."

"Good. Good. What do you think?"

She stood behind her desk, with crossed arms, and stared down at the screen. "I don't think it fits in with our other products."

"No, it doesn't, but this has so many applications from home, to military, to commercial, that we need to get on this right away."

"I think it can wait. We're in the middle of half a doz..."

Jud cut her off. "I don't care. This comes first. I want a prototype done by tomorrow, and low-power demo versions ready to hand out as freebies for the conference. Marketing is already working on an extra large booth to demo it with. This is your priority. Replicate and make both full-power and low-power versions. Got it?"

"Yes sir."

"Thank you," and the screen went dark.

"I need to thank you as well," said Bryn as she handed her a Tracelet.

"*What for?*" she replied with a bitterness poisoning her tone.

"You just made me feel a million times better about myself. I hope your day gets better!" Bryn smiled and walked out the door.

Confused, Schanna just glared at the girl.

A Dish Served Cold

Hours later, at the end of an exceptionally long day, Schanna arrived at the screen in the shiplot foyer, called up her ship, and walked to the doorway where her ship would momentarily pull up to.

Seconds later, she looked curiously at the door. *That's odd. It's usually here by now.*

Half a minute passed and she went back over to the screen. An error message appeared besides the icon for her ship and the screen said, "I'm sorry. Your ship is either not responding, or is no longer in the shiplot."

"What?" *No, not now. I've had such a long day already.*

The screen repeated itself. "I'm sorry. Your ship is either not responding, or is no longer in the shiplot."

Schanna was getting impatient. "It worked fine this morning. Did my ship happen to leave today?"

The screen checked and replied, "I'm sorry Miss Fife, but your ship has not left the shiplot. It is still occupying the same space you had it parked in this morning."

"You're no help at all. I'll check it out myself." Schanna stomped through the side doorway that manually entered the shiplot. What could possibly be wrong with it? I know I left it right here... "NOOO!"

She stared in horror at the large pile of cubes, each one a different color depending on the element. She looked over and saw that the large gold plaque that read *Schanna Fife - Vice President of Research and Development* had been pulled free from the wall and was lying, bent, on the ground; no small feat considering it was three meters wide. She looked up and in its place was a new, bright, shiny sign.

Bryn Struse - Owner.

Her face contorted into an ugly little ball as she screamed profanities at the plaque.

Fireside Chat

Several days later, Bryn was sitting out on her back patio. The warm glow from the fireplace flickered over her in the cool nighttime air. Above, a spotlight hovered pointing downward and providing enough light for her to read a physical book. Slouched in a comfortable chair, her feet were heeled up against her bum and her knees pointed skyward.

Halfway through, she stopped, sighed, and stared straight up at the stars shining above. She closed the book, set it on the side table and thumbed open a screen, hitting a button.

A moment later, Amory was on the screen saying "That's so funny."

"What is?"

"That you called me just as I was heading down to the simulation room so I could call you in person. Hold on..."

A few seconds later, a ghostly Amory appeared on the deck. "Hey! The backyard! I don't see you out here much anymore."

"Up until now it's been kind of hot outside."

Amory looked around, found, and sat in a comfy chair opposite from Bryn. "Um, you do know you can change the temperature...and everything else in here, right?"

"Yeah, yeah, I know, but I don't like to. It takes the reality out of it when you can have complete control. You have to take the hot and rainy days, so you can appreciate the nice days more. Having one long eternal perfect season isn't fun."

"Sometimes I think you're a fifty-year-old trapped in that seventeen-year-old body of yours."

Bryn protested, "I'm almost eighteen."

"Almost."

"That means presents."

Amory rolled her eyes. "Sometimes. Speaking of presents, are you ready for your conference tomorrow?"

"What? That doesn't have anything to do with presents."

"No, I suppose you're right, it doesn't. It was a nice way to change the subject away from buying you a gift to something a little less expensive."

"What are you talking about? I don't have expensive tastes."

"Says the girl who is sitting on a virtual deck, in a 'backyard' on top of an asteroid in the most desirable and scenic Deimos orbit of Mars."

Bryn's blushed slightly. "So yeah, anyway, I'm ready, I guess, for the conference. Did you know it's on Eris?"

"Nice way to change the subject, Bryn. Well played. And yes, I did know that."

"Thanks. I figured if you could do it, so could I. I went to StruseCorp the other day to talk to them about me going."

Amory asked, "Really? How did that go?"

"They actually really liked the idea, oh, and guess what?"

"They promoted you from intern to best boy?"

Bryn gave her an odd look. "Uh, no. They're going to start production of the Tracelet."

Amory perked up, "Really? That's great! Wait, I thought you wanted to keep that idea to yourself?"

"Originally, I did, but after considering it, I thought, 'Hey, why not?' so I gave them one to use as a template."

Amory frowned. "This wouldn't happen to be your small way of trying to compete with the looming legacy of your ancestors now, would it?"

Bryn shook her head, "No. No. No. No. No." She stopped and nodded her head once. "Maybe."

"Ah ha! I knew it!"

"Oh, come on, A. Seriously. You have no idea how hard it is to live here and to look around at pictures of my parents beaming with pride as they pose with their inventions, and not to mention the ones of my grandparents with all of their awards and accolades for 'saving humanity' and all. Then I look at my life and what have I done? I know I'm only almost eighteen and all, but when I look at the size of the shoes I have to fill, and then look at my small feet..."

Amory glanced over. "I think they're a normal size."

"I was speaking metaphorically, thanks. I meant to say that I feel like I could never be anything near as great, as famous, or as anything as they were. And it's not like they all got old and became forgotten. They all vanished in their prime, so that's what everyone remembers. 'That fabulous Struse family, remember how awesome they were, oh wait, let's see what li'l Bryn can do...What? Nothing? Ok, forget her, let's think back to the good old times when Struses were amazing.'"

"Come on, it's not like that."

"Yes it is. In my mind, anyway. I thought if I could do something, anything, to help establish me as my own person, that maybe, just maybe, I could crawl out of the shadow my parents and grandparents still cast to this day."

Amory was quiet for a moment as she watched the fire. "Well, it might work." She felt the bracelet on her wrists. "These Tracelets really are super handy."

Bryn nodded as she stared at the flickering flames.

Amory added, "On the plus side, you have two brothers who haven't accomplished much of anything. You'll always be better than them."

"I guess, well I don't know. I mean, I don't want to think of myself as better than someone. I just want to be known as being me. Not as 'Bryn, daughter of Amelia and Alva,' or 'Bryn, granddaughter of the savers of all humanity.' I want to be known for my own accomplishments, not live off the legacy of my family. And besides, from what I hear, Tilden is doing well with the Solar Union Navy."

"Have you heard anything from or about Triton?"

"No. Not since that whole thing went down years ago. I have no idea where he is, or what he's doing."

Not knowing what to say, Amory acknowledged with a, "Hm."

They both stared at the hypnotizing fire.

Bryn perked up. "Oh! I didn't tell you!"

"Tell me what?"

"The other day, when I went to work, I discovered that my spot had been taken in the shiplot."

"Noooo!" Amory responded with extra emphasis on the vowel.

"Yes!"

Amory asked, "Who took it?"

"Schanna Fife, the VP of Research and Development."

"The *nerve* of her!"

"I know! I had to use a normal drop off entrance."

"Oh, poor you, having to use the regular person's entrance. Forbid the thought."

"Um, if you had your own specially designated parking spot that had been passed down to you from your parents, what would you do if someone took it?"

"I'd have it towed into the Sun."

"Exactly."

Amory looked at Bryn in disbelief. "Wait really? You actually had her ship towed into the Sun?"

"I did one better. I kept it within the company. Here, look at these before and after pictures." Bryn opened a screen, hit a few buttons, spun it around and pushed it towards Amory. The first picture showed a sleek, expensive-looking ship occupying a shiplot space. The large sign on the wall read, *Schanna Fife - Vice President of Research and Development.*

"Wow, is that ship a Brookline?"

"Yes. Yes it is," Bryn said. "One of the most expensive ships money can buy. Now look at the next one."

The picture changed. The background remained the same, with the exception of the sign on the wall, but the ship had been replaced with a pile of different colored cubes of various sizes.

"Did you...*no*...wait, yes. Is that what I think it is?" She looked at Bryn who was grinning from ear to ear. "Did you put her ship in a Recycler?"

"I sure did. She took my parking spot. Actually, it was my parents' spot. I mean, come on, who has the wherewithal to do something like that?"

"She sure got her comeuppance. Wow, look at that," said Amory, zooming into the picture to get a better look at the pile of elements.

"It felt good. I only wish I could have seen her face when she went to leave."

"Is she going to the conference?"

"Whoops. Yeah she is. That might make it a little awkward."

"I would think so." Amory looked to one side and said, "Oh hey, I've got to go. There's a line of people who want to use the simulator now."

"Ok. You get going."

"Have fun at the conference!"

"Thanks, you too!"

"You're a weird one, Miss Struse."

"You too, Miss Sutherland."

With that, Amory waived and faded out.

Arrival and Registration

The next day, Bryn got ready, said goodbye to Dr. Waggles and Crane, got into her ship, and headed out for the conference.

She spent the flight to Eris reviewing StruseCorp financial statements. Five minutes later, she got bored looking at numbers, so she pulled up a puzzle game on a screen and played that until she arrived at a massive space station orbiting the dwarf planet of Eris.

Her ship pulled up to the drop-off area, Bryn said goodbye to George, and the *The Bryn* went to go park itself. A few hundred people were milling around the drop-off area as those who had just arrived stopped to get their bearings, and others were waiting for friends or co-workers to arrive. Bryn surveyed the people and didn't see anyone she knew. An area across the top part of the lobby shimmered with a huge welcome message attendees to the conference. A large colored arrow that said *Hotel &*

Registration pointed to the right, so Bryn headed that way.

Colored circles to transport people to the hotel area of the space station were plentiful, but Bryn chose to walk as she was enjoying being herself out in public. When she arrived, she saw that the hotel lobby and conference registration areas were now in different directions. She wanted to check in first, so she headed to the desk.

Bryn walked up to the front desk and the person behind it welcomed her, "Hello, Miss Struse. Welcome to the Hathaway Eris Hotel."

Bryn never knew if they knew her because of who she was, or from the person recognition systems every business has which detects a person's nanos. She suspected the latter, but thought the former had a part to play in it as well.

"Thank you."

The clerk continued, "Your suite will be located on the Birch Wing." The screen he handed her showed a detailed map of the entire station. Her room was glowing pink. "To get there, you can take the QuickWay from the lobby, or, if you're wanting a stroll, you can walk down the hallway. Personally, I'd recommend the QuickWay. Registration for the conference is down the hall to your left in the Charon Ballroom." The hallway and ballroom lit up in a pale green on the map. "If you need anything at all, please ask."

"Thanks!"

"Thank you, Miss Struse, for staying with Hathaway Hotels. Enjoy your time with us."

Bryn followed the map and headed down the Birch Wing. *Wow, this is a really long hallway.* Using her glasses, she determined it was almost four kilometers long. She zoomed out on the map screen hovering in front of her and saw that the hotel portion of the station was made up of a dozen long, spindly spines sticking straight out from the station itself. The Birch wing was the longest, and the rest were progressively shorter.

Once again, she eschewed the floating disk, instead preferring to walk. The hallway was quite wide and every so often, there was a floor-to-ceiling window that looked outside. To the right, she saw the bulk of the station and space beyond, and to the left was the full-on view of Eris. Looking at the rooms numbers she walked past, Bryn figured out that her room did not have a view of Eris, but then remembered that the station rotated, so in a matter of hours she'd have a great view. *It's not like I'm going to spend the entire conference staring out the window. If I want to do that, I'll just go to the lobby where they have that hundred-story window.*

Minutes later, she reached her room, which was about three-quarters of the way to the end. It sensed she was there, and the door opened for her.

The room was spacious and very comfortable with a large sitting room, a dining area, an oversized bathroom with real water fixtures, and a huge window. Outside, the brightish dot Bryn saw in the distance was the Sun.

Bryn didn't have any luggage with her, but instead had patterns for everything she needed loaded in her personal screen. If she wanted something, she could put the pattern into the StruseCreator and *poof*, it was made for her. Her only cost would be for elements she used. Looking at the hotel's price list for elements caused Bryn to shrug. They were expensive, but that's to be expected from a fancy hotel.

When she was bored with the room, she ventured out, this time opting to take a QuickWay back to the lobby. Moments later she arrived, walked to the left, and went to the ballroom to register.

She discovered that it was close to the end of the registration time for the evening, the room was mostly empty. The few people that were there stared at Bryn, making her feel self-conscious.

When Bryn approached the registration desk a small screen popped up facing the older woman behind it. She looked at Bryn and said, "Hello, Bryn, and welcome to the Leaders of Industry and Trade Conference! I saw you had signed up, but I wasn't sure if you would be here tonight or tomorrow. My name is Leda, the welcome coordinator for the conference."

"Hi, nice to meet you. Nope, I decided to come in today and check out Eris. Never been here before."

Leda beamed and nodded, "Oh, there's a lot to do here. You'll love it. Do you like your suite?"

"Actually, yes. It's very nice, thank you."

"Oh good, good. Here's your welcome screen with all of your information on it. Please wear this badge to identify you as a participant."

Bryn stared at the garishly designed lanyard and badge that blinked and moved with colorful words, logos, and graphics.

The registration woman put her hands on her hips and said, "Oh come on, it's not that bad. Lighten up and have fun!"

Bryn made an exaggerated smile as she put the blinking badge on her shirt. "Yes! Fun!"

Leda thrust a second glowing green string with blinking text scrolling along its length. "Oh! Don't forget your other lanyard!"

"Oh, another one? I don't think I need two."

"Hush. Of course you do. How else do you expect to carry your info screen around? In your hands?" The motherly-looking woman laughed like this funny she made was the best one ever to pass her lips. Bryn laughed nervously.

When she finished, Leda said, "Be sure to read the info screen, as it has the times and information for each session." Then, like a doting mother, offered, "Here, do you need help putting the screen on the lanyard?"

"No, thanks, I've got..."

The woman stepped around the desk, clipped the screen to the lanyard, and looped it over Bryn's head. "There you go!"

"Thanks!"

"Oh! I almost forgot! Your name tag!"

"Oh! A third thing! No, that's ok, I don't need..."

In the blink of an eye, Leda spun around, grabbed something off a table, and stuck an animated name tag that read *Bryn Struse - StruseCorp* which matched the participant badge and info screen in color and intensity.

Bryn noticed, with a nervous laugh, "Oh! Heh, heh. It all matches!"

"Of course it does! Everything has to look just right." She looked at Bryn for a long second. "You know, you look just like your mother."

Bryn blushed a little, causing her skin to more closely match her hair. "Thanks. I get that all the time."

"Well, she was a very pretty woman. Anyway, see you tomorrow and enjoy the conference!"

"I will now, thanks to these!" she said motioning to the conference crap she was now decked out in.

Bryn turned around, and was busy looking down at all of the stuff she was covered in, when a voice caught her attention, "Bryn? Is that you?"

She looked up and saw Lipazan Lindermeaner, a girl Bryn had known from years ago. The elder Lindermeaners owned some big company and the whole family was quite wealthy. After Bryn's parents had disappeared, Crane suggested she try and make some more friends. Unfortunately, he looked for people in her same economic class, and she went over to Lipazan's house a few times for parties and whatnot. It was from hanging out with her that Bryn discovered how awful and materialistic people can be.

"Oh, hi, Lipazan?"

"Yes! It's me!" Lipazan seemed to inflate a notch at being recognized by Bryn. "What are you doing? Have you inherited StruseCorp yet?"

"Not yet. That'll happen when I turn eighteen in a few months."

"You are sooo lucky. You get to enjoy your inheritance now when you're young. The way people are living so much longer, I'll be so amazed if I get my parent's company by the time I'm like one hundred!"

Bryn frowned, both at Lipazan's comment and the fact that Bryn used to hang out with her. "Yeah, but your parents will have to die for that to happen...unless they give you the company beforehand."

"Pffth," she scoffed. "They'll never give it to me first, but that's fine since I don't care about it much anyway. I mean, who cares about business, or companies, or any of that nonsense. Oh! Let me tell you about this small moon I just bought. It's wonderful and..."

"Hi, Bryn!"

Hearing a familiar and welcome voice made Bryn spin away from Lipazan. Dow Barnard and his daughter, Evelina were heading toward them.

Lipazan's eyes narrowed and she whispered, "Oh, I hate that Evelina. There's something really weird about her."

Dow wide smile was matched by the big hug he and Bryn gave each other. "Bryn, I didn't know you were coming! This is a great surprise."

"Yeah! It's so nice to see you! I decided to go just the other day. Hi, Evelina, how are you?"

Evelina glared at Lipazan. "I was ok, but now I'm feeling slightly ill."

"Hey, Eve, can you go over there and register us for the conference before they close?"

"Gladly." She turned on her heel and stomped off towards the table. Her long blonde braid swung like a whip behind her.

Dow apologized. "Sorry, she's been a little grumpy today." He turned to Lipazan, "Lipazan, hi, how are you?"

"I'm doing well, and yourself?"

"Good, good. So, what brings you here to the conference? Thinking about lending a hand in running your parents' company?"

Lipazan's face twisted repugnantly, as if some horrible stench wafted her way. "Ugh, no. I just came to look for rich guys."

"Hm," he nodded expectedly. "Good luck with that. Have a good one."

She took her cue to leave, waived goodbye to both Bryn and Dow, and wandered off.

He watched Lipazan leave and said to Bryn, "I never liked that entire family. Yuck."

Bryn laughed. "I used to be sorta friends with her a few years ago. She taught me how not to act like a human."

"That's a good lesson. Maybe she should open the school of How Not To Be. She'd easily make all that money her daddy won't give her, and then some." He changed the subject in a more positive direction, "So! Your first conference. Are you excited?"

"Yeah! I really am. This was something my parents never let me go to, so I always thought of it as a 'Grown-Up' thing. It's kinda weird to be here." She looked around, "It seems festive."

"You seem festive with all that junk you're wearing."

"Aren't we supposed to wear this stuff?"

"Yeah, that's one of the fun things about it. You get to dress like a ninny for a few days and listen to boring lectures on profit margins, class economics, and Fringe marketing. Actually, parts of it can be pretty informative. Be sure to keep an alert eye open in the evenings. Everyone goes to the bars and that's where the real deals happen."

"Like what?" Bryn asked.

He shrugged. "Well, for instance, last year I hung out with the owner of a Fringe mining company. After a few hours, we signed a deal where he bought ten thousand MinerBots."

"Oh, that's good."

"It really was. If you want to see what the people who run StruseCorp really do, follow them in the evenings and be like a camera on the wall. See who they meet with, what they're negotiating, and what kind of deals they sign."

Evelina's mildly childish voice spoke up behind them, "Dad, I'm back."

Dow turned and looked at his dour daughter holding his garish conference flair out to him as if it were poisoned.

"So you are. Oh, and bearing presents! Thank you. Now the fun begins."

Bryn looked past Dow and saw an area of carpeting about three meters behind him that was slightly pressed in. She used a scan feature on her glasses to sweep the room and saw an invisible BarnardBot standing on the carpet indention and looking around. Another one was by the doorway. This particular model was more popularly known as the DeathBot because if you came across one, it would be the end of you. The bot faced and stared at Bryn, which made her feel very uncomfortable so she turned the scanner part of her glasses off. The expression says, "out of sight, out of mind," but another came to Bryn's mind, "what has been seen cannot be unseen."

Dow noticed Bryn was distant for a moment and asked, "What are you staring at...oh, I get it. You and those pesky glasses of yours."

She motioned to the menacing robot behind him. "Is that really necessary?"

"No, probably not, but then again I don't take chances anymore. I have too much to lose. Actually, I'm curious. How many do you see?"

"Two."

Dow smiled.

Bryn scanned the room again. "Why, are there more?"

"There should be another five in this room, plus the others elsewhere on the station. I have a few bots be detectable with a minor scan so to either scare off any potential adversary, or if they are serious about starting something, they will sorely underestimate my defenses."

"Wow, you're good."

"That is what I do for a living, make the best robots in the Solar Union. And again, I'm serious about not taking any chances."

Evelina tugged at her father's sleeve. "Dad, can we go now?"

Bryn thought that for someone two years older than she was, Evelina was oddly childish at times.

Dow said, "Sure, Eve, in a minute," and then to Bryn, "I would invite you out with us tonight, but I've got a dinner meeting with a potential client. Let's get together for breakfast. I'll send you a message when I know what time. Have a good evening, and enjoy the conference!"

"Thanks, you too!" And to his daughter, "Nice seeing you Evelina."

She shot Bryn a shrug as they walked away.

With a few hours to kill, Bryn meandered around the conference section of the station. She poked her head into a few cafes and bars, hoping to find StruseCorp people. By the time she had gone to the twentieth bar, with no luck, she gave up. Hungry, she stopped at the food court and had a quick dinner by herself in a private booth.

After dinner, Bryn went for a walk and explored the public areas of the huge space station. She wandered through the expansive mall and lingered at an observation deck facing the cool blue dwarf planet of Eris below. The Planet Jump! experience caught her eye. As with everything, it was open all day and night, and it was something she wanted to try, but she had to work herself up to it. She tried to call Amory, to get her thoughts, but it went to her mailbox, so she left a message.

"Hey A, it's B. I'm at the conference. I don' t know if I told you, but it's on a station around Eris. It looks like it'll be ok, but the best part is this Planet Jump! thing. It looks awesome and someday you and I will have to try it together. Check this out, you wear a special space suit, and then you free-fall from the station to the planet below; through the atmosphere and everything. I'm totally going to do it. Anyway, hope all is well with you. Bye!"

She thumbed open a screen and marked in her calendar to come back after the end of conference and try this.

As Bryn walked back through the mallway to return to her room, she received a beep from her screen saying that she had a message. It was from Dow. "Hi, Bryn, it's Dow. I now have a breakfast meeting, but maybe we can meet for lunch at Ezra's restaurant at one o'clock. Let me know tomorrow if this works for you. Thanks."

She left a message back. "Hi, it's Bryn. Yeah, one is fine. I'll see you then."

She walked back to the hotel part of the station. Once in the lobby, she took the QuickWay, which whisked her quickly down the long hallway to her room. She entered and plopped down on a chair that faced a large window looking out over a rounded part of the station and the far distant sun. The edge of Eris was just starting to come into view.

Bryn pulled up a screen and played a puzzle game for a few hours until she got tired. She got ready and padded through a second living room and went into the bedroom. She thought, *Dow's awesome, but that's kind of crazy. Who needs that many DeathBots protecting you at once. Heck, one's overkill as it is. Hm. He must really feel like he needs them, but why? What does he need that much protection from, and more importantly, how come I couldn't see them? I should be able to see anything with these glasses.*

A few minutes later, she realized that she hadn't yet enrolled for conference seminars, so she went back to the first living room, dug through the information packet sitting on the table and pulled out the info screen. Bryn scanned down and signed up for classes that sounded interesting by tapping on them. Good, she thought, that still gives me plenty of time to sightsee while I'm here.

A minute later, when she got into bed and turned out the lights, she discovered that the name and participation badges were blinking a spectrum of crazy colors. She got up, and looked them over only to find they didn't have an off switch. With a grunt of annoyance, Bryn covered them with a towel, causing them to glow ominously, like an angry cloud sitting on the horizon, flashing with lightning. Bryn got back in bed, turned her back to the light storm, and fell asleep.

Nearby

Tant sat in a chair in his hotel room overlooking Eris and pulled up a screen. After a moment, Hamor answered. "Are you there?"

"Yes. I'm in a room just down the hall from her."

Hamor nodded, "Good. Good. With you, I've got a total of ten people spread around the station. One way or another, we'll get her tomorrow. Her stupid friends caused me to lose my club. After this, we'll have endless cash and we can go wherever and do whatever we want."

Tant laughed, "I can't wait. She won't know what hit her."

Terror

The next morning, Bryn got a quick breakfast from the StruseCreator in her room, while watching the news. Nothing particularly noteworthy was going on. After getting ready and topping her smart-looking business suit off with the blinky-nametags-of-annoyance, she stepped out of her room and rode the green circle, which hovered and sailed down the hall to land in the lobby. Once there, she immediately spotted the news crews that were waiting for her and managed to slip through the crowds undetected on her way to the grand ballroom.

Bryn found a seat by herself and within minutes the rest of the seats had filled in and the lights dimmed. First, was the welcome speech and orientation ballroom with about five thousand people in attendance. Afterward, Bryn headed over to a seminar about up-and-coming technologies, which she enjoyed. She was surprised that

Schanna wasn't there, since this seemed to be right up her line of work.

Following that, Bryn went to a class on new marketing concepts. While there, Bryn felt wonderful. *Actually, I feel free for the first time in a long while*, she thought. *Here I am, out in public as myself, ME, for once, and wow, it is great.* At each seminar she attended the people sitting next to her had introduced themselves, but everyone was polite and professional. *I could really get used to being me*, she thought.

There was a short break between the second class and lunch. Instead of going to one of the rooms set aside for delegates to meet others and hobnob, Bryn headed back to her room for an interview with Solar Union Public News's *Noon Edition* program.

As she entered the hotel lobby she saw that not only was the QuickWay walled-in by reporters, but the hallway to the wing of the hotel where her room was as well. *Shuck, they've blocked all of my escape routes. I guess I'll have to give them a quick minute of my time and maybe they'll leave me alone for the rest of conference.* As she approached, the crowd or reporters started to yell questions at her while small orbs floating above their heads were zipping to and fro, recording her from every angle.

She stopped, clapped her hands together, and said, "Hi! I've got somewhere to be, so I'll answer one question..."

"Bryn! Chut Halpner from Turdox News...Could I have a moment of your time? What do you say to the rumors that you are secretly working at StruseCorp as an intern?"

Bryn glanced at the reporter with the look of someone who just discovered that someone had replaced the milk in their cereal with skunky beer. She continued, "...which I should have prefaced with, 'from a real news company.' Actually, that was two questions. To answer your first question, "no." Thank you!" She smiled, weaving her way through the throng and walked towards her room. One of the hotel's standard security bots blocked the reporters from following her.

Bryn enjoyed the brisk walk down the long hallway. Once inside her room, she saw a screen blinking near the doorway. She tapped it open and listened to her message from Solar Union Public News. It was the producer for *Noon Edition* saying they were ready to go live soon, but needed to check some things first. She called him back. "Hi, this is Bryn Struse."

The man nodded, "Hello! I just need to check a few things, like your light levels and your background. Can you just slowly spin in place so I can see what would make for the best background? Great, thanks. Ok, can you turn back a little...perfect! Korva Bodette will be on in just a moment."

Bryn sat upright and stared at the empty screen for a few seconds and started to get fidgety. Her eyes dipped to one side and started to check her written messages when a woman popped up on the screen. A small green icon lit in the upper corner of the screen told her this was a now a live broadcast. "Bryn Struse. Hello and thank you for taking the time to join us."

"Thank you, Korva, I'm glad to be here."

"It's your first Industry Leader's Conference. How's it going?"

"Well, so far, it's going well so far. I'm lear-" her words trailed off as she saw Korva's eyes get huge as she was distracted by something horrible outside the window behind Bryn. In the same instant...

ERR-ERR-ERR-ERR-ERR.

A loud klaxon's deafening blare viciously sawed across the pause in Bryn's sentence. The view inside Bryn's glasses lit up like fireworks and showed her the terrifying scene unfolding out the window behind her...jagged white light crackled and tore empty space open as a giant asteroid spun through a teleportation gate at a high rate of speed, aimed directly at her wing of the hotel. The screens in her glasses burned bright with red arrows pointing towards the direction of the lift in the entryway.

"Aw, shuuuck," Bryn uttered before the years of training kicked in. Her arm flung out and her wrist snapped up, causing her Tracelet to latch onto the far wall in the other room of her suite and yank her hard out of her chair, hurtling away from the window. Out of the corner of her eye, she saw movement just outside; two BarnardBots stepped out from either side of window and leapt at the asteroid with blasters blazing.

The room tried to cushion her body as she slammed into the wall, and then landed her on her feet. Turning, she was about to step into the in-room emergency exit tube back to the lobby when her glasses warned her not to take the tube. The arrows changed direction and pointed her towards the hallway door. More messages popped up saying it had a moment to reassess her survival rate with escaping via the emergency exit which was now rated as, *A Good Way To Die* with a smiley face that had crossed-out eyes.

Stupid computer, always trying to be positive. Make up your damn mind. She sprinted toward and through the door as it opened in anticipation of her needs.

The hallway was nicely decorated with artwork and a thick, plush carpeting. Apart from the skull-splitting *ERR-ERR-ERR-ERR*-sound, it would have been a nice place to take a stroll, which, as her glasses reminded her, she definitely did not have time for.

As she cleared the door, she saw that others were starting to poke their heads out of their rooms. The people who had rooms on Bryn's side of the hall were running and screaming things like, "RUN!", "Asteroid!", and "We're all going to die!" These things distressed the oblivious guests coming out of their rooms on the other side of the hallway who were looking to complain about all the noise and knew nothing of their impending doom.

The arrows on Bryn's glasses pointed her to the several kilometer-long hallway that stretched to the left and told her of the 78% chance for survival in that direction, but she'd better hurry as that number was dropping quickly. She silently wished she had some sort of flyer-pack, or any kind of vehicle, for that matter. Her eyes darted to an available QuickWay circle on the floor that would whisk her back to the lobby. As she started towards it, a man who had stepped out of a nearby room jumped on it and floated upward and away from the chaos.

"Hey!" Bryn yelled. "A bunch of people can fit on that!"

The man turned, saw her, and looked surprised. "Hey! You're Bryn Struse! Wow!" He nodded to himself, impressed that he met a celebrity, as he turned back and sailed up the hallway.

Knowing there wasn't time to be angry, she began to run as fast as she could down the hall, but for as incredibly fast a runner she was, the survival rate indicated in her glasses was falling too fast. That was when something weird happened.

Her glasses flashed two big words: *STOP NOW*.

She screeched to a halt, having gotten about halfway up the hall away from the impending death that should be coming any second now. There were very few guests in this section the hall as most had either already evacuated, or didn't know what was going on. A few were trying to run; some the same way Bryn was heading, but most were toward the far end. She guessed that the rest of the people, especially those on the non-asteroid side, either went back into their rooms, thinking that the raving people in the hallways were drunk, or jumped onto the QuickWay. Further down there was something going on. She squinted and her glasses zoomed onto the area of interest: some kind of craft with people on it zooming up the hallway towards her. Her glasses focused further on the pilot who was none other than Dow Barnard, and the craft was one of his BarnardBots that had changed form into the shape of a large flying sled to get him, a few other robots, and some hapless passers-by, out of there.

Bryn waived and yelled "Dow!" and her glasses patched her through to him.

He said, "Don't worry, I'm getting all of us out of here."

Bryn yelled, "Don't slow down, there isn't time. I'll jump up to you."

Dow flew up the hall fast and was less than ten meters away when Bryn ran towards them, jumped hard and arced up toward the ceiling, over Dow's craft. She turned in mid-air and flicked her wrist, causing the Tracelet to grab onto the floor of the robot sled and straighten her out. For a brief second she looked like a physics-defying water-skier that was suspended in air above and slightly behind the carpet-skimming boat. The Tracelet pulled her closer to the craft when the loudest thing she had ever heard exploded into her world.

Impact

The asteroid impacted into the first long spindly wing of the hotel. The section where Bryn's room had been was immediately obliterated. The wing of the hotel snapped off twenty meters behind the dangling Bryn, causing an immediate pressure loss as life support vented into the unending appetite of space. Bryn felt the robot-sled slow down as the hungry vacuum clawed at them, trying to pull everything back towards the gaping maw. Something silvery flashed by her, and she looked back in time to see one of Dow's robots diving toward the open end of the hallway that was still partially obstructed by the passing asteroid. The robot's body elongated and liquefied, as it spread out and formed a barrier from floor to ceiling at the edge of the hole. The drag of the internal atmosphere being sucked away slowed and then stopped, which allowed the craft to speed up again, and Bryn was able to thud hard onto the floor of the craft. Dow and some other survivors helped Bryn up to her feet. "Thanks for the lift!"

"Glad to help. Now let's get out…"

The second loudest thing Bryn had ever heard exploded as a jagged chunk of the huge, spinning asteroid shaved off another section the hallway, and with it, the robot who had sealed up the end. Once again, the air was vacuumed out and the craft had to fight harder to maintain its speed. It bucked hard, ejecting Dow. He flailed and spun out of control toward the hole.

Bryn braced herself and snapped back both of her wrists in his direction. The Tracelets snatched him, causing a muffled "Oof!" as he stopped and was pulled back towards the fleeing ship.

When the hotel sensed that life support was venting out into space in a cataclysmic event, it sealed off the entire wing to prevent the rest of the hotel from being affected. The robot-sled had noticed it was speeding toward a wall. Bryn struggled to reel in Dow and was hardly aware that the robots on the ship began to fire an arsenal of weapons at the impending ending wall speeding up to crush them.

With a fierce explosion, the sealed wall gave way just in time as the craft sailed through the hole, landed hard on the marble floor, and skidded across the lobby. Another robot jumped off the craft, liquefied in mid-air, and sealed off the venting hole they just passed through. Bryn swung her arms up, flinging Dow high up into the lobby, and pushed off the craft hard, clearing the craft as it skidded toward the front desk. Bryn turned in mid-air to see the sled liquefy into a squishy barrier that swaddled and protected the other survivors from the impact with the desk. The lobby computer gently lowered Bryn and Dow to the floor.

After a very long second of silence, a small child who was among those rescued, happily yelled out,

"Again!" The lobby broke out in a wild mix of intensely relieved laughter and applause.

Speculation

A news broadcast blared to life. "This is Parla Insipid here brining you a Turdox News, NewsBlast. A few moments ago an asteroid slammed into the Hathaway Eris Hotel, completely destroying an entire wing. From what we've found out so far, several head mavens of the Solar Union Industrial Panel, meeting at the Hathaway Eris for the annual Solar Union Leaders Of Industry And Trade Conference, were staying in that wing at the time of the collision. While we find out more information on this incident, here's an amazing vid of Dow Barnard, owner of Barnard Robotics, and Bryn Struse, heir to the StruseCorp fortune, making one of the most exciting, fly-by-the-seat-of-your-pants escapes from certain doom you'll see in the next ten minutes here only on Turdox News."

The footage started by showing the asteroid from an outside video camera as it churned toward and finally smashed through a spindly arm of the massive space station. As it spun, a large outcropping ripped through a section of the wing, closer to the main hotel hub. The video then jumped to a hallway shot several seconds earlier as Bryn, off in the distance, was running, then stopped, turned, jumped superhumanly up, over, and latched onto Dow's speeding craft with her Tracelets. A second later the hallway they were just in was cut off by the large outcropping of the asteroid. The camera view changed to one further up the hallway and showed Dow getting flung out, and then caught by Bryn. This vantage blacked out after getting blasted by a barrage of laser fire from Dow's robots. The final view was that of the lobby, where the sealed off wing door was blown apart and the craft slid across the floor, trailing sparks. The screen split in two as one side followed Bryn and Dow as they shot up in the air to clear themselves of the soon-to-crash craft, while the other side followed as the craft liquefied and turned into a soft barrier to shield the occupants from hitting the desk. Bryn and Dow were quickly whisked away by hotel staff, followed tightly by Dow's robots, who had reverted back into their normal shape. As they trotted by, someone out of view yelled, "That was amazing!"

The screen returned to the anchorwoman. "This is Parla Insipid with a Turdox News NewsBlast! update on the asteroid collision at the Hathaway Eris Hotel. From the footage provided, it seems that the asteroid was teleported to that location. Whether it was on purpose, or accidental, we're not sure yet, but we will keep you updated. In the meantime the Solar Union Navy has arrived on the scene and is stopping the asteroid. Joining us in the Turdox News studio is former Solar Union Navy commander, Tuf Stonehardt. Thanks for joining us, Tuf."

"Thanks for having me."

"Without having any real data or details to go on, what do you think happened here?"

The older, solid man in the military uniform looked hard at Parla and responded, "What I suspect happened here…and I base this off of my 50 years of combat training and experience with the Solar Union Navy, is terroristic elements from the Lossian aliens have attempted to decapitate the heads of industry in order to create a pervasive wave of fear in our normally calm and orderly society."

Parla looked at him in a disbelieving doe-eyed fashion. "Why would the Lossians commit such a heinous act? They are a peaceful race of intergalactic observers and ambassadors."

"Jealousy. They are jealous of the very comfortable standard of living we have, the freedoms we enjoy, and the wide assortment of technology we possess. Our negative drive engines that allow our ships to darkline and travel faster than light? We invented those and the Lossians are fearful that we'll take over. They've been watching us for hundreds of years and they're afraid of us. That's why this happened today. As you can plainly see, they're prepared to rain devastation down upon us. I believe we need to act first."

"Didn't the Lossians act first by attacking the Solar Union just now?"

Tuf looked confused for a moment, and then seemed to catch up to what she said. "Yes, absolutely! They struck us first and we need to respond in-kind. Actually make that a hundredfold. We need to teach them an important lesson in that no one messes with the Solar Union. No one! If we don't stop them now, who knows what they'll do? Maybe bomb the Lightway, or take over a Fringe planet? Those planets are easy pickings being so far away from Earth. I won't sit by idly while this happens. No I will not." He pounded a fist on the desk while a graphic of the Solar Union flag waived patriotically behind him.

2492: Attack Of The Ancient Cyborg

"Thank you Commander Stonehardt."

"It was my pleasure, Parla."

"You heard it here first on Turdox News. Lossian terroristic elements made a bold attack at the Solar Union a few moments ago by cowardly striking at the brave industrial leaders of our society. We now head over to Kolton Skimmer, currently in charge of the investigation at the scene of the catastrophe."

The screen split to show the busy bridge of a ship, people running to and fro, with hovering screens following. A man who had his back to the viewers was shouting at an assistant, "I don't care who it is, I'm not giving an interview…especially not to that damn dirty rag of a news channel!" His assistant's eyes grew huge and darted back and forth from his boss to the viewers and back again. He finally got his attention by discreetly pointing behind Kolton, towards the screen. Kolton's looked over, rolled his eyes and glared at his assistant.

It must have been an awful look because the junior officer squeaked fearfully, "Eep!" and scuttled off, out of view.

Kolton approached the Turdox News screen. Taking up most of the window in the background was the spinning field of debris comprised of the severed Birch Wing of the hotel.

"Hello Kolton, this is Parla Insipid, from Turdox News. Thank you for taking time out of your busy day to join us."

Kolton gave a fake smile, "Yes it certainly is a busy day, and I really don't have..."

"Can you give us any insight as to why the Lossians have made such a bold, devastating attack at the Solar Union?"

"What? Did anyone actually claim responsibility?"

"No, not yet."

"Do you have proof of this?"

"No."

"Then how do you know it was the Lossians?"

"Earlier we spoke to Commander Stonehardt, and he…"

"Seriously? He's been retired from the SU Navy for decades. He wouldn't know anything about this. The Lossians are a completely peaceful race who serve to observe planets and introduce intelligent civilizations to one another. Do you think it's strange they haven't introduced humanity to any other alien race? It's probably because of war-mongering jerks like him."

Parla continued, "Please tell us what you have discovered in your investigation."

"Right now, I know about as much as you do, since it just happened just a few minutes ago. An asteroid of unknown origin appears to have been teleported to a location near the station. It then crashed through one arm of the hotel before it was teleported away to an unknown location. We don't know where it came from, we don't know if it was sent here as an accident or on purpose, and we don't know who was responsible." He pointed at the screen. "So before you start basing wildly inaccurate assumptions that can have a grave impact on interplanetary relations on the ramblings of a crazy, dishonorably discharged, old man with no knowledge of current events, or how things really are, I strongly suggest that you drop your sleazy shtick, actually do some research, get your facts straight, and start broadcasting with an air of integrity. Maybe then you'll finally be respected and actually be able to get real interviews that get to the heart of the story."

Kolton looked up at the blank screen where Parla Insipid had just been. "Where did she go? Did we lose the transmission?"

A junior officer who was standing a few feet away responded, "No Commander Skimmer, they hung up."

"They hung up? Why?"

"I don't know why, sir, but it happened right after you said 'sleazy.'"

"Whatever. Let's get back to work and find out what happened here."

A Safe Suggestion

Two hours later, Bryn was being led out of a room where she was asked to give a statement to the Solar Union authorities on what she saw and how she managed to survive the asteroid collision.

She asked the detective, "What now?"

He said, "Everyone's back in the conference, and while the staff tries to find you another hotel room, we suggest that you take it easy and go to the shopping mall section of the station. We've already searched it and it's safe, and almost no one is there right now." He looked over to one side and said, "Oh good, they're here."

Bryn saw two BarnardBots walking toward them and the detective continued. "These DeathBots were given by Dow Barnard to keep you safe."

Bryn's face squinched in, "Wait. What do I need to be kept safe for? Do you think that asteroid was meant to kill *me?* Where's Dow?"

The detective sighed, "At this time we don't know why it appeared. That's what we're investigating. Also, we don't know if it's safe for you to leave the station yet. I'd hate for you to start flying away and another asteroid comes out of nowhere to take you out. In the meantime, we're not taking any chances, so you've got two new friends to watch over you just in case. As for Mr. Barnard, he's helping with the investigation. For now, you should just go to the mall. It's safe there." He started to turn away before he realized something and turned back, "Also, just in case, here's my card." He thumbed open a screen and pushed his card towards her. She thumbed open a screen and his card merged into her screen.

"Thank you." She turned to the BarnardBots, "C'mon guys, let's check out this mall."

As she walked, Bryn's mind kept wandering to areas that were better left filled with cheery things. *They must know something I don't. I mean, come on. I'm being escorted by two BarnardBots. These things practically can't be destroyed. Why would they do this unless they thought I was in trouble.*

She stopped at a window in the hallway and tried to crane her neck to see the spindly part of the station where the hotel was, but she was too far down in the station to see that wing of the hotel section. Instead, she looked at the view of Eris below and also opened a screen in her glasses and watched video footage from different news sources showing the security camera views of the asteroid appearing and hitting the hotel. *There's no way this was an accident. That asteroid was not only huge, but moving fast. Are we supposed to believe that this thing just happened to slip through an open teleportation gate large enough for it to fit through? Not to mention that teleportation gates are heavily monitored and controlled by the Solar Union.*

She frowned and glanced over at the robots standing by her. The imposingly tall and shimmery-smooth robots stood silently, but she knew they were searching and scanning the area for any potential problems. Bryn turned her attention back to the screens in her glasses and searched the tubes for any information on unlicensed or illegal teleporters.

Mentions of underground teleporters were quite rare, but the few times it did come up, it was always connected to the mafia. *Great.* She thought some more, *Wait, if it was the mafia, although I severely doubt it, what use would they have for me to be dead? I could maybe see if they had a beef with someone else at the conference, but why me of all people?*

Annoyed at the prospect of facing more questions now than when she stopped to think about the situation, she decided it better to just put it from her mind.

"Let's go guys," she said as she and the BarnardBots resumed heading toward the mall decks.

Competition

Hamor stared in disbelief at the screen in front of him.

"Did you see that?"

"Uh, yeah." Tant's mouth hung open as he stared at the news footage of the asteroid that smashed through the wing of the hotel. "My room was in that wing. Shuck, all of my stuff is gone."

"Don't worry, we've got more weapons." Hamor's large dark eyes stared so hard at the screen that Tant thought it would melt from his intensity. "What the shuck is going on? This means someone else is trying to move in on her, and not just kidnap her, but actually kill her. The fools, she's worth so much more alive than dead."

"Maybe they were after Barnard. He was staying in the same wing and with those damn DeathBots always around, he's nearly impossible to kill."

"Either way, someone else is stepping in and trying to take out our target. That's just not right."

222

"No, that's not right, but..." Tant looked down at a small screen in front of him, "...ooh..."

"'Ooh,' what?"

"Target acquired. Putting it up on the big screen."

The news footage of the damaged space station was replaced with a view down a mall's hallway as seen from a dangerously high angle. In the distance a crude red blinking box surrounded a girl who was flanked on either side by tall silver robots.

Hamor swore, "Aw shuck, those are DeathBots. This isn't going to work. Nothing can stop those things."

A tall trenchcoated cyborg stepped into view of the camera.

Tant smiled. "Don't worry, she's still ours. Call everyone to meet us there. This guy's going to do our dirty work for us."

Face To Face

The main concourse of the mall-level was mostly empty, which suited Bryn just fine. *Most everyone on the station is probably at the conference, or hiding from asteroids...or leaving. Probably leaving.* She relaxed a little as she stepped into a fragrance pattern store and began to browse. Meanwhile, the BarnardBots took up positions out in the hallway.

A few minutes later, Bryn was admiring a large display in the middle of the store: a several-hundred year-old metal bathtub filled with hundreds of vials of fragrances.

She sensed something behind her, turned and watched as a nearly three-meter tall, mostly completed cyborg walked into the fragrance store. Its wide-brimmed hat cast a dark shadow that shrouded its face. The eyes glowed; one with the intensity of sparking electricity, and the other was an intensely piercing single red light. This figure of death looked out of place amongst the delicate light, soothing smells, and relaxing quiet music.

Bryn saw that its body was mostly covered in a long trench coat. The exposed parts were worn, chipped, dented, scratched, scored, burnt, blasted, and had the all-around battered look of something that's lived several lives longer than it was originally intended to.

And now this thing's focus is entirely on me. Shuck.

She tensed up. *This is that cyborg. The one that destroyed the ship from Delm's.* A flood of adrenaline coursed through her as her nano-enhanced reflexes flexed in anticipation of certain confrontation. Despite her body being at the ready, her mind tried to rationalize things. *We're in a very public place. If this cyborg, or whatever it is, tries anything, the store's security system will lock it in a force field before it could even draw a weap...* Bryn's eyes refocused and caught sight of two huge blasters holstered under its coat. *Wait, how did it even get on the station with those?*

The cyborg's voice croaked in a steely and dark tone, causing the flesh on her arms to pucker like a dead chicken, "Bryn Struse. You are coming with me."

She looked to the hallway where the BarnardBots stood and said, "Hey! Help!"

The BarnardBots stood still, like statues in a museum.

Her eyes darted to the way too tall, way too old, cybogy robot thing and sized it up as she yelled to the shopbot behind the counter, "Call station security!"

The shopbot stared at her blankly and was also silent.

Bryn got mad, "What are you waiting for? Call security now!"

Finally, the shopbot faced her and croaked in the same scary voice as the android, "Bryn Struse. You are going with him."

Oh shuck. Things were not looking good. Bryn's eyes latched onto the entryway, only to watch as it began to close.

One of Crane's mantras popped into her head at that moment, "When faced with a bad situation, you always have two choices: fight or flight...that is unless you're foolish enough to let yourself get backed into a corner. In that case, your only option is to fight."

Well, I can't very well do that since I don't have anything to fight with at the moment, and this thing looks like he means business. If he can get blasters into a secure station, control other robots, and disable BarnardBots, then this is something I don't want to mess with.

Movement from the right brought Bryn's attention back to the situation at hand as the shopbot came out from behind the counter clutching a box of Soothing Saffron Scent Sticks in a menacing manner and started towards her. To the left, the scary cyborg strode at her as well. Bryn shot one last glance at the closing gate, which was halfway to the floor, put her head down, and ran.

In one fluid blurrish movement, the cyborg had crossed the store, crouched, and swept its leg out, knocking Bryn off her feet and onto the floor. Hard. She rolled quickly on her back and with one arm outstretched above her head, and the other along her side pointing back into the store, and snapped both her wrists back. She was able to give one last terribly spiteful look at the cyborg as her right-wrist Tracelet latched onto a wall outside the store and yanked her out, just barely making it under the closing door.

The cyborg crossed the remainder of the store to the gate in the blink of an eye. It looked at the bottom of the gate, which was firmly on the floor, as if it was trying to figure out what just happened.

A tinkling glass noise behind caught its attention. It was pivoting when the large ancient bathtub, filled with thousands of glass jars of calming scents, pulled through the air by Bryn's Tracelet, crushed the cyborg against the heavy store gate.

Escape

Bryn slid across the wide corridor, and pulled her wrist back the other way, which pushed off enough from the wall she was zooming towards to slow her down. It wasn't quite enough, and she hit it with a good amount of force. "OW!"

She sat up and looked at the Scent Shop. Since all stores were open 24 hours a day, it was weird to see one with the gate closed. Bryn almost let out a laugh at the cartoon-like outline of the tub, as well as that of the cyborg stamped into the hard metal sheet gate, but the seriousness of the situation slapped back into her mind. A faint *TWEEEEEE – TWEEEEEE* sound could be heard coming from inside the store.

She looked around to see if anyone had noticed. Apart from one nearby couple, this area of the mall was deserted. The couple stared wide-eyed, first at the gate, and then back at her. Then, they realized who she was.

"Oh wow! You're the daughter of Alva and Amelia Struse!"

She looked up at them and said, "Yes, thank you, but you need to get out of here."

"What just happened? Are you ok? We saw the gate closing, then you came sliding out, and there was a horrible bang." They were visibly quite excited to have witnessed something somewhat noteworthy in their otherwise very drab lives.

"I'm fine, but you really should..." A loud bang sounded from inside the shuttered store. "...get going, now!"

Bryn hopped to her feet and ran off down the mall hallway at an absurdly fast speed. The older couple started to walk quickly in the other direction.

A new noise came from the store; a grinding sound as the gate was trying to raise, but couldn't since it was horribly dented. The couple paused and stared for a moment as the noise stopped and everything was silent before a section of the door exploded outward. Out of the smoke, amidst the din of the now loud *TWEEEEEE-TWEEEEEE-TWEEEEEE* alarm sound, emerged the tall dark cyborg; eyes ablaze with an angry light, and a smoking blaster in one hand. It strode up to the couple and asked in a terrifyingly grave voice, "Which way did she go?"

Upon seeing the towering visage of death looming above, any thought of helping Bryn was gone as fear filled their veins and raised their hands; pointing in unison down the hall where Bryn had run a moment ago. A halo appeared around the cyborg's feet, lifting it several meters into the air and it flew off in pursuit.

Planet Jump!

Bryn saw a station monitor and screeched to a stop, hitting the security button hard. A securitybot appeared on the screen and said, "Hathaway Eris Station Police – Mall wing, what is the nature of your emergency?"

"I need help. A cyborg just tried to kill me in the Scent Shop."

"On our way," and with that, the screen went blank.

A few seconds later, four securitybots pulled up beside Bryn. As she was trying to describe her attacker to them, she noticed something gliding down from the atrium above and yelled, "There it is!"

The securitybots rose quickly through the air toward the cyborg. Something went wrong as they slowed, arced around, and started speeding back toward Bryn. "Bryn Struse. You are going with him," they all said in unison.

"Oh, come on!" Bryn yelled and dove behind a bench to avoid getting flattened by the group of robots. She rolled, and got back on her feet just in time to face the four robots, who were each holding a stun stick, the crackling bluish electricity casting eerie shadows over the area.

Not having any other way to protect herself, Bryn used her Tracelets to pull the arms of the middle two robots towards her, and flung them sideways into the neighboring securitybots. The stun sticks pierced the robots on the end, electrocuting them. They shuddered in the dancing, crackling, blue light and fell solidly to the floor.

In the corner of her glasses, she caught a glimpse of the cyborg's trench coat flapping as it swooped down behind her. Reaching out with the Tracelets, Bryn snagged the two standing securitybots, and flung them with all her might around her at the descending cyborg.

The cyborg avoided the first one, but was hit by the second, stuck with the angrily flashing stun stick, and thrown back over the edge of the atrium, falling dozens of floors below. Without hesitation, Bryn turned and ran as fast as possible.

A corner of her glasses lit up with an incoming message. "Bryn Struse, this is Commander Ronald with the Solar Union Navy. We're aware of the situation and are trying to coordinate the mall to protect you. Unfortunately, it is not responding. Follow these directions to get out of the section of the mall you're in and over to a waiting shuttle which will escort you to safety. In the meantime, we're going to evacuate this section of the station."

She jumped a little when the light background music that was floating into the mall stopped and was replaced by: *ERRR-ERRR-ERRR-ERRR-ERRR*…Mall evacuation in progress…Please move quickly to the nearest evacuation point…*ERRR-ERR-ERR…"*

Bryn ran in the direction the arrows in her glasses indicated and soon entered a hallway that led to the Planet Jump! attraction. Standing in front of the Planet Jump! counter and a large floor-to-ceiling window facing Eris was a group of humans armed to the hilt with a vast array of weaponry. *Oh thank goodness, human military people. I'm saved!*

They raised their weapons at her approach and all stopped to look at her as she ran around and stood behind them.

"Thank you! This giant cyborg is after me! Get ready, it'll be here any second." She flicked on a message screen and replied to Commander Roland. "Sir! I'm at Planet Jump! with a group of your troops. I'll hold position here for your shuttle."

The commander looked confused, "What troops? We don't have any on the station. That's why we're going to…"

A finger reached over and slashed out her screen. Hamor said, "Sorry dear, but you're coming with us."

The group of mercenaries encircled Bryn. One woman flicked on a sun sword.

Can this day get any worse?

A gravely voice from the far end of the hall made her heart sink further, "Bryn Struse. You are coming with me."

Yes. Yes it can.

The mercenaries spun around to see the looming figure of the cyborg. It pushed its trench coat back to reveal two giant blasters parked, for the moment, in holsters. The cyborg's eyes glowed with a perpetually dark intensity under the shadow of its hat.

One of the mercenaries wrapped an arm around Bryn's throat and held a gun against the side of her head.

"Yeah, one move from you and she's dead. Scram, you bucket of bolts."

Aaaahhhh! Nooo!

Before anyone could react, the cyborg snatched a blaster, leveled it, and fired a sickly green blast of energy. The bolt struck the man holding Bryn dead center in his face. With a disgusting fizzy, bubbling sound, it proceeded to strip all of the molecules in his head of their covalent bonds, essentially removing the subatomic glue holding the body's elements together. His entire head and the top of his torso was reduced to a liquidy mush, sinking in and smearing all over Bryn's back and side as his body went limp and crumpled to the floor.

"*GGAAAAAHHHHHH!*" Bryn screamed in sheer terror, fell down, and scamper-crawled behind the Planet Jump! check-in desk.

Hamor yelled, "Light it up!"

A barrage of firepower was sent hurtling down the hallway at the cyborg. Its personal energy shielding absorbed some of the smaller blasts, but the others spun it around and knocked it down.

It raised a blaster and the bolt connected with the arm of the woman holding the sun sword. Her arm went goopy and splattered down as she screamed. A second bolt caught the center of her body, silencing her, save for the squishy thud.

I need a weapon and I need to get out of here. Bryn peered around the corner of the desk, saw the sun sword hilt and pulled it to her with her Tracelet. She put it in her belt and crawled through the door into the Planet Jump! room, away from the fray. The lights turned on, and the door closed behind her. It was eerily silent, but she knew the battle raged on the other side of the door.

She got to her feet and ran to the wall filled with spacesuits. A green light directed her to the correct size. She tried to grab a Planet Jump! suit, but a screen appeared asking for two hundred credits. She waived her hand in front of the screen. It scanned the nanos in her bloodstream, identified her as Bryn Struse and debited the money form her account. It cheerily said, "Two hundred credits paid by Bryn Struse. Please go to the Planet Jump! education center to learn how to make your Planet Jump! a safe and fun one."

Sorry, no time. She hurriedly pulled on the suit. The battle raging out in the hallway was quieting down. *Shuck, that means it's winning.* She put the sun sword hilt and her Tracelets on the outside of her spacesuit, grabbed a helmet, and ran into the airlock; a giant glass archway that aimed down at the dwarf planet below. *Oh shuck, I need to go. He's going to bust in any second.*

As she approached the Planet Jump! door, a screen popped up giving her instructions and a quick test of what to do and what to expect when experiencing Planet Jump! She jumped in fear as a motorized arm swung over and grabbed her helmeted head. There was a slight *ssss*-sound as it pressurized the suit. She relaxed at realizing it was part of the process, not a killer cyborg. A screen popped up on the interior of the visor and confirmed all life support systems were functioning normally.

Bryn moved into the red-floored zone in the airlock. The combat sounds were barely audible, save for the occasional explosion. The airlock scanned her, and a warning blurted from the screen. "Warning! You are carrying an unauthorized item! This item may not survive reentry!" A diagram appeared that showed at which altitude, based on her profile, pressure, velocity, heat, and other statistics, the sun sword hilt might be damaged at. *Good to know*, she thought.

Bryn only half paid attention when it explained that there was a Planet Jump! landing pad in the atmosphere of Eris. It went on to describe the intense and frigid swirling storms in the lower atmosphere and the importance of landing on the Planet Jump! landing pad. After the information it told her to step forward to begin her jump.

She stepped on the footprints painted on the floor, but the airlock wouldn't activate. A screen said to be patient, it was waiting for approval from an attendant. Of course, there wasn't anyone on duty at the moment; they had all been evacuated by the troops before she arrived. She ran back to where the attendant normally stood, punched the green, "Approve" button, and returned to the airlock, which closed behind her.

A screen appeared in her visor saying, "If you want to turn back, just say 'Turn back' at any time. If you wish to continue, please say, 'Continue.'"

Bryn stared longingly at the intense view of the pale blue ball in front of her. Her eyes angled upwards and watched the creamier shades of blue, belonging to the powerful atmospheric storm clouds, swirl and fold into one of a dozen darker blue shades which melted darker still until the purplish navy of night became the black of space along some fuzzy line of demarcation marking the atmosphere of the small planet. The small puffy clouds way far below provided a nice contrast and made the scene even more inviting. *For years I've stared at similar scenes of other planets, but I've always dreamed of just jumping into the view this…and at the same time I've always been way too afraid. It's not so scary now, considering the alternative.* She thought about the man's head melting. *Continue, NOW!"*

The screen beeped "Three"…beep, "Two"…beep, "One"…beep, "Planet Jump!" and with that, the door opened and she shot out like a missile, hurtling toward the dwarf planet below.

Giving Chase

In the Planet Jump! lobby, the cyborg had killed half of Hamor's people and was advancing on the remaining holdouts, who had taken defensive positions behind objects.

Two fast-moving liquid puddles blurred into the room. In a quick motion, they solidified into BarnardBots and began firing huge blaster shots, each one connecting squarely in the center of the cyborg, knocking it back a full step with each shot.

The cyborg paused for a moment, staring at the BarnardBots.

One of the BarnardBots replied, "We, and all BarnardBots, have learned from your previous attack on us and are now able to prevent you from controlling us. You will be deactivated."

A holographic image of a friendly young man appeared at the Planet Jump! counter. "Three! Two! One!

236

Planet Jump!" A rain of holographic confetti fell from the ceiling as the floor shook slightly.

The cyborg looked out the huge window at a person in a spacesuit blasting like a bullet, down and out of sight toward Eris. It immediately swung a blaster toward the window and fired.

No one had time to react.

In a terrifying instant, the intensely hungry pressure differential yanked the cyborg and the remaining humans through the molten and melting window, out into space.

The BarnardBots reacted just as quickly. One leapt out into space, determined the survivability of each human, and reached out to envelop the closest two in a protective, airtight and pressurized bubble.

The second BarnardBot spread itself out and sealed up the hole in the window to prevent further damage to the station. It messaged the station to inform them of what happened.

Picked Up

After being ejected from the station, Bryn turned around, and spent several long moments appreciating the view as she watched the Planet Jump! door she just vacated, rapidly shrink as she glided further away from the station. Normally, she'd be thrilled and excited by this to where she would be sending a clip of the experience to Amory, but she was instead filled with an overwhelming terror. She needed to get as far away from that station as humanly possible.

As the giant oblong-shaped station was becoming just a small toy in her view, she twisted around to face Eris. For a fraction of a second, in the far edge of her peripheral vision, she could have sworn she saw a bright flicker of light on the station from about where she just left, but she dismissed it as just light glinting off the massive structure or something.

Now her view was filled with the slowly growing blue of the planet below her and she tried to relax.

I'm safe.

Am I? It could come after me. It can survive in space. I saw it on that poor woman's destroyed Brookline from Delm's.

It could come after me, sure, but by the time it gets here, I'll already have landed and taken the shuttle back to the station.

What if it lands on the shuttle as I'm returning in it?

Bryn protected the sun sword hilt with her spacesuit's arms.

I know this should be so peaceful but I feel so alone and vulnerable out here by myself.

An emergency message screen popped up in her visor, partially obscuring the growing view of Eris. "Bryn Struse, this is Commander Ron Ronald of the Solar Union Navy. You are in grave danger. As soon as you reach the landing platform, get in the shuttle and hit the *emergency* button. It will immediately launch and bring you directly to the station."

"Yes sir. Will do."

With a no-nonsense tone, Ronald informed her, "The cyborg has exited the station and is following you."

Bryn's skin chilled. *Shuck! Shuck! Shuck! Oh shuck, I'm dead.*

She spun her suit around and tried to look behind her, which was difficult due to the angle of her decent. A terrible vision flooded her mind that as she turned it would be right there behind her, its red sparking glowing with hate as it reached out and grabbed her. When she faced the dot that was the station, nothing was there.

Bryn asked, "How much longer until I land?" She used her glasses to zoom in and search for the cyborg. Nothing.

"About five more minutes."

"I-I don't see it…the cyborg…anywhere behind me."

"You won't be able to see it unless it's really close. The important thing is not to panic."

Too shucking late for that.

He continued, "Focus on aiming yourself to the platform. Don't worry about the landing, even if you're off-target, the platform will pull you close enough and slow your fall."

She turned back around and faced the dwarf planet. A green box appeared over a cloudy patch of the atmosphere. It told her that soon she would be able to see the landing area. Something below her briefly glinted, well outside the glowing green box on her display.

"I saw something!"

Commander Ron said, "That's the platform. Don't worry."

"It was NOT the platform. It was something moving that reflected light for a second."

"You are just high-strung. Again, don't panic. That's just the previous jumper who went a few minutes ahead of you."

"No! What if that person takes the shuttle! I'll be stuck on the platform waiting for the cyborg to land on top of me!"

"There are two shuttles. The current jumper will take one back so when you land, there'll only be one shuttle. Get in it as soon as you land and hit the emergency button. Understand?"

"Yes."

A grayish square with blinking red lights started to appear in the swirling distance. Her view was entirely made up of cloudy curtains comprised of different shades of blue. For the first time she noticed faint streams of orange that began to whip around her suit. She glanced at the thermometer and, sure enough, the temperature was rising steadily.

If I survive this, I am never, ever leaving my house.

Ron said, "You're almost there. Get ready for the landing. Don't forget, as soon as you are on the platform, run as fast as you can into the shuttle. We're tracking the cyborg and he's just two minutes behind you."

Bryn tried to straighten out her body more to eek out as much speed as possible. She asked, "How long from when I land until the shuttle is clear of the platform?"

"About forty-five seconds. That's why you can't dawdle."

Her display showed the rapidly decreasing number of kilometers to the platform. When it was two kilometers away, she felt herself slowing down.

No, no, no! It's going to catch up to me!

One kilometer and the platform's tractor beams grabbed onto her and pulled her down slowly.

One hundred meters left and it re-oriented her right-side-up and gently brought her to a soft landing in the middle of a huge Planet Jump! logo.

Commander Ron yelled, "Go! Go! Go!"

Bryn dashed across the platform toward the shuttle parked to her left. She cleared the doorway and into an airlock. As it re-pressurized she pounded the inner doorway, "Come on! Faster!"

Ding!

The inner door slid open, she threw herself inside and saw the red *Emergency* button on the far wall. She slapped it hard. The shuttle rocked hard as it fired the engines and rocketed upward. Bryn fell over backward into a comfortable chair, panting inside of her spacesuit and watched the clouds slip past in the front display.

"You did it. You're safe," Commander Ron said from immediately behind her.

Startled, Bryn jumped out of her seat, spun around, and fell back into the front window, screaming.

The cyborg was sitting in the chair behind the one she was just in. It laughed with Commander Ron's voice and said, "Bryn Struse. You are coming with me."

Trapped

With her back to the wall and the killer cyborg sitting three meters away, Bryn had to force herself to breathe. After several silent seconds of nothing happening she calmed down slightly, as much as someone could if they were locked in a cage with a bear that had just mauled a group of people.

It was just sitting there, watching her. Its hands were resting on the armrests of the chair. It made no threatening moves of any kind.

After more silence, Bryn managed, "W-What are you doing?"

In Commander Ron's friendly voice, it replied, "You are coming with me."

"Is that your normal voice?"

"No. I am replicating a voice that you found to be calming. You would be frightened by my 'normal' voice."

"Where are we going?"

"Wrathwood."

Bryn was stunned. "The planet in the Fringe?"

"Yes."

"Why there?"

"I was asked to bring you there."

"Who asked?"

"I was told not to say."

"Why? Does it have something to do with the nutters who colonized Wrathwood and the *Star Ark*?"

"Also, I am unable to say."

Bryn asked, "What if I don't want to go there?"

"You have no choice in the matter. There will be no further discussion."

"Why?"

Silence.

"Hello?"

No response as it turned toward the display.

"You do realize it will take several weeks at faster than light speeds to get there."

More silence.

Bryn sighed, crossed her arms, and plopped into the chair furthest from the cyborg, which happened to be the one closest to the airlock. In the forward display she saw the massive space station glide by to the left as the shuttle steered upward toward the Lightway.

Bryn realized she was still wearing her spacesuit and considered removing it. *Well, if I'm going to be stuck in here for the next few weeks, I should at least get comfortable...*her eyes landed on the sun sword hilt tucked in her belt.

I could try to take its head off.

She reconsidered, *Then again, it did kill all of those people really quickly. It would probably shoot me before I got out of the chair.*

She sighed again.

This sucks. Yes, at least I'm not dead, but in some ways this is more annoying.

Well, not as annoying as Shanna Fife. Wow, she's the worst. If I were stuck with a shuttle with her for weeks, I'd probably blow myself, and this ship, up. Her mind started to race. *And how exactly would I go about doing that? If I could somehow overload the power in this sun sword, let's say, with these two Tracelets, OH MY GOODNESS, YES!*

She quickly and secretly removed both Tracelets, attached them to the top and bottom of the sun sword hilt and thought, *Ok, if I do this, I'll have two, maybe three seconds at the most before the power reflects inward on itself, magnifies, and goes off like a bomb. The question is, will I have enough time to get into the airlock and get free? Probably not, but it's better than the potential outcome this thing's got planned for me.*

Ready?

One…two…THREE!

Bryn activated the Tracelets, rolled the cobbled-together, sparking, overamping device across the floor and shouldered her way to the door, and slammed her hand on the button to activate the airlock.

Behind her, the cyborg leapt up and took a fraction of a second too long to assess the situation and decide what to do: go after Bryn, or try to do something about the throbbing device that ended up against the wall of the ship.

Just as the outer airlock door opened, forcibly ejecting Bryn into space, an explosion ripped through the shuttle, bursting it like a tin can over-stuffed with a demented teen's fireworks.

Tumbling wildly through space, Bryn opened the communication screen and shouted, "Mayday! Mayday! Rescue needed between the station and the Lightway!"

Three minutes later a Solar Union Navy ship latched onto her spacesuit and reeled her in to safety.

Once aboard the ship and seeing a human, Bryn frantically asked about the cyborg. "Did it survive? Is it still trying to get me?"

The Navy servicewoman smiled at her. "No. It's gone. You're safe now."

"H-how do you know? Are you certain?"

"Why don't you look for yourself." The screen split to show the charred remains of the ship, the front third of which was the only part that was remotely intact. It spun wildly, glowing bright orangey-red with streaks of fire being ejected every moment or two as it further disintegrated during reentry. It was a particularly harsh way to go, and in another few minutes there would be nothing left larger than a potato. "Nothing could survive that."

Bryn silently nodded in agreement.

Crash

Back on the space station, Bryn looked tiny in comparison to the group of thirty heavily armed Solar Union troops which surrounded and escorted her from the rescue ship up to the station commander's office.

After an hour of debriefing with the recently arrived military commanders, she had more questions, no answers, and now her options were limited. Bryn said, "This is so frustrating. I've been here for an hour now and we still don't have any answers as to who attacked me."

The commander replied, "We do know it was a cyborg. From what we know the last cyborg was built in 2240, over two hundred and fifty years ago. Unfortunately, more specific details are hard to come by as the records from back then no longer exist."

Another officer added, "It didn't look like a normal cyborg though, it was as if it was unfinished or something. It was certainly ugly."

Bryn said, "I don't care how it looked. This thing was able to slip past all of the station's security measures like they weren't even there. It was able to control other robots and sent them after me. How could that happen?"

That was something that was troubling the military brass. Cyborgs were old technology. Even today's most advanced BarnardBots couldn't do the tricks that this freaky-looking thing had done. In fact, the only cyborgs they even knew currently existed were little more than props behind glass in a museum. The commander replied, "We don't know. We're still looking into that."

Bryn's face turned red, the color matching her tousled hair, as her temper boiled over. She blurted, "Looking into it? Come on! You're the adults here, you're supposed to know what's going on and have the answers! This thing *killed* people! Maybe it was behind the asteroid too!"

A female officer nearby, wearing a uniform adorned with lots of shiny medals said, "I think you should go home now. We'll be in contact when we've discovered something."

Realizing she wasn't going to find out what was going on, Bryn walked toward the door. Before leaving, she paused and quipped, "It's more likely that it'll have killed me long before that happens."

Ten minutes later Bryn was on her ship and heading home, her anger at those in charge as well as having been attacked by a homicidal robot, were being replaced by doubt and fear.

"Why was it trying to kill me?" she asked out loud.

George replied, "Oh, there's lots of reasons…to many people, you are the embodiment of the oligarchical society that we live in, and killing you sends out a strong statement that the 95% of the population that comprises the Basic economic class won't stand for it anymore;

248

you're one of the most famous people in the Solar Union, so to kill you would bring the assassin an incredible amount of notoriety and fame; or, killing you would divert the complete attention of the media machine onto your untimely death and away from anything else that the killer wanted to draw attention from; killing you would also bring about a sense of insecurity…"

"STOP IT!"

"You asked, so I was merely answering…"

"I was trying to make myself feel better by being all, 'woe is me' and, 'hey! I'm only seventeen! I shouldn't have to deal with someone trying to kill me.'" Bryn sighed and stared out the window at the darkness beyond. "I think I need to take a break from everything for a while."

George said, "You mean a vacation? That's a good idea."

"Sort of. Once we get home I don't want to leave. It's safe there and I need time to think about things."

"What about work?"

"Shuck work!" Bryn shouted. I'm just a kid, don't you understand? I can't deal with this. My parents disappeared when I was young, my brothers are who knows where, I was raised by a weird combination of a home computer and my parents' best friend, who stopped by from time to time to check up on me, and now everything's coming to a head at once. I shouldn't be in this place. I'm supposed to inherit, and be in charge of, one of the biggest companies in the entire history of humanity. I have one true friend and she's away at school; and someone's tried to kill me…kill me! How do you think that makes me feel?"

"You do have to admit that your parents at least saw fit to make sure you were properly trained for anything. Because of that training, you were able to survive the attempts on your life."

Bryn looked disgusted at the pleasant smiley face on the monitor floating a few feet away. "You can tell you're nothing more than a computer. Being 'trained' to survive is a hell of a lot different than being prepared to deal with the fact that someone wants you dead. I'm a kid. I should be out with other kids my age having fun enjoying the last few months of no responsibility before stepping out into real life. I shouldn't have to be constantly thinking, 'gee, how can I avoid being killed by this robot assassin that's shooting at me?' I've never had a real childhood. My parents were always too busy working in the lab to pay much attention to me, so I tried to be like them; be interested in what they were interested in, and do the things they did, just to get their attention. Do you have any idea what that's like?" For a moment, the ship looked like it was going to respond, but Bryn cut it off, "No. You don't. You're just a computer. You can recite textbook-perfect answers to everything, and are able to accurately describe anything, except feelings. You can try, and fake it to a degree, but in the end, you're just a machine, so shut up and leave me alone."

They traveled the rest of the way home in silence. George shut off its interaction monitor, which was fine with Bryn. She didn't want to talk anymore. She sat in her chair and leaned against the hard, cold window, staring blankly at the blackness of space. She wasn't really thinking of much, other than she was thankful for the non-reflective glass in the windows so she couldn't see herself. All at the same time, Bryn felt like a terrible monster, a helpless child, a kicked puppy, and a lot more all rolled into one; but those emotions were just submerged with too much sorrow and self-pity. There was a deeply-rooted anger within her, an anger at her parents for, as she secretly thought deep within her heart, them essentially 'abandoning' her, an anger at whomever was trying to kill her, an anger at Amory (who deserved no anger directed anywhere near her, but still, it was secretly there) for leaving Bryn alone so she could go to school and have fun with new friends, to her brothers for doing that stupid, stupid thing so long ago that broke up the family, to society in general for making her an inadvertent, and continued, celebrity for absolutely no reason other than who's vagina she popped out of, and to her own pretend deeply-rooted guilt at having to play Atlas and single-handedly run StruseCorp herself with equally deeply-rooted fears that she would be the one to run the soon-to-be three-generation company into the ground. It was much too overwhelming for her.

I hate everyone for putting me in this position. I didn't ask for this. I can't handle this. I can't do this.

Despite the single tear that ran down her cheek, she managed to hold it all in until she got safely home, locked herself in her room, got under all of the covers on her bed, and curled herself into the tightest ball possible. Only then did she feel safe enough to let her emotions pour out.

Determined

Weeks went by, piled up, and heaped into months.

Sometimes Bryn was ok, but most of the time she wasn't.

The combination of too much heavy stuff, all at once, weighed her down to her lowest common denominator like a comforter filled with mercury. She stayed in bed all day even though, thanks to her nanos, she really only needed three hours of sleep a day. She spent hours on end sitting in her 'widow's watch' staring at the view. She didn't speak for weeks. She ignored all messages; from Amory and otherwise. Bryn withdrew into her shell to the point where she disappeared from normal life. People she knew were concerned and tried to talk to her, but she ignored every call and message. People tried to visit, but she wouldn't let them in. Depression was too flowery of a term for what she was experiencing.

252

Then, one day, while she was curled up, swaddled under her covers, Crane appeared in her bedroom.

"Good morning Bryn!" they said all happily and cheerily. You could almost taste the rainbow.

Bryn grunted in an annoyed and distrustful fashion. Crane hadn't tried to be all cheery in a long time, so she was immediately on the defensive and untrusting. "Go away!"

"I'd love to, Miss Struse, because I could really use a vacation away from the doldrummy you, but I sort of can't do that seeing as I'm an integral part of the house.

Bryn glared at the person-shaped image looming above her. She turned over to stare out the window at her view of the colorful crescent of Mars beyond.

Crane said, "You know, I've been thinking about things. Those people who tried to kill you…guess what? They succeeded!"

Bryn shot them an angry look. "What are you talking about? I'm still alive."

"Technically, yes. Your body is functioning well and you continue to move about occasionally. As far as you actually living you life, that stopped back when that cyborg tried to kidnap you. You stopped going to work, you stopped talking to and interacting with friends, you don't travel, you haven't even left this house. For all intents and purposes, you're dead to the galaxy."

She nervously twiddled the corner of her pillow. "I could do any of those things if I wanted to."

"You could, but you've chosen not to. You let two incidents, which, yes, were absolutely tragic, but at least you survived, define you and completely change how you've lived your life ever since."

Bryn was silent, but Crane could tell that they were getting through to her. She was no longer just blankly staring at the spectacular view, but was intently ignoring it as her mind began to really think for the first time in weeks.

Crane continued, "Yes, things haven't been going your way for a while now, but you have the power to change all of that. You can put pressure on the SU to find out who was behind the attacks on you. Get into contact with your friends again, and also take the time to get a hold of your brothers. Let the past stay in the past with what happened there and start to re-assemble your family, starting with your good brother. You don't have to single-handedly run StruseCorp. No one could do that. Let the capable people who have been running it for the past few years continue to do what they're good at. You should just show up once in a while and be the company's figurehead. That's easy. Forget what the media, or anyone else, says about you. Live your life the way you want to and pay them no mind, because in the end, they are the ones who are dependent on you, not the other way around. Finally, you can start researching what happened to your parents and know 100% if they're dead or not…and if they're still alive, you can find them."

Bryn started to float in the air, "Hey! Put me down!"

Crane shook their head, "Sorry, but you need to see something."

Bryn struggled, "I can see everything I need to see from here. Lemme go!"

"It's time for a field trip. An educational one."

"What? I don't want to go outside. I want to stay here. Anything I would ever need to learn I could do from the comfort of my own home. Where are you taking me?" She swung her arms in a futile effort to get free.

Crane floated her down the hallway toward the ship dock. Her pajamas morphed into a more appropriate outfit, chosen by Crane. "To show you something your parents wanted you to see when you were much older.

254

Honestly, I don't think you're ready yet, but it's the one thing I can think of that will snap you out of what you're going through now."

Her fidgeting stopped. "Something my parents wanted me to see?"

"Yes, but you need to go there in disguise." Bryn saw her personal screen open in front of her and Crane clicked on the Linna disguise. A shimmery moment later her features changed to that of Linna. The hallway door opened, and Bryn floated through another door and into her ship.

"Hello there! Long time, no see, Miss Linna," George said.

The Bryn started and left the shiplot with a brief queasy tug at Bryn's stomach. Her arms crossed, she spoke through her frown, "George? Where're we going?"

"To the Struse Museum."

"Oh come on. Get Crane on the screen." The screen divided in two with George on one side and Crane on the other.

"Yes?" Crane asked.

"What possible thing could my parents have wanted me to see at the museum? Have there been any new exhibits since I was last there?"

Crane responded, "You haven't been there since you were seven. Apart from the one about your parents and their disappearance, no."

"Then, George, turn around. I'm going home."

"Sorry, Bryn, but this is something you have to see...and look, we're already here."

"Well, I'm not going...hey! Put me down!" The ship floated Bryn out of her seat and out of the ship's door. It put her down at the entrance of the Struse Museum lobby.

A ghostly computer person approached her. "You must be Linna Meekins. Hello. I'm Sill and I'll be taking you on the special private tour that Crane arranged for you."

She eyed Sill suspiciously. "So, this isn't the standard tour all the school kids go on?"

Sill smiled politely. "Oh no. You'll be the third person to take this tour."

"Ever? Who were the first two?"

"Triton and Tilden Struse, many years ago."

Bryn's resistance eroded away and was replaced by a strong sense of curiosity at hearing the names of her much older brothers. "Really?"

Sill said, "Oh yes. This is a special tour for only the most VIP guests designated by Alva and Amelia Struse."

"Wow. Um, ok. Lead the way, please."

"Certainly," and Sill led her to the large lobby past the ticket counter. "Now, I'm assuming you've been on the standard tour before?"

Bryn rolled her eyes. "Yeah, I know all about how Leo Struse created the first recycler and how the teenaged Alva Struse helped him make the StruseCreator and then how humanity was changed."

Sill nodded. "Yes. Well, everyone knows that, but what you don't know is the amazing background story on how it all really happened. Remember, history is told by the victors, and there is always more to a story than what history tells. Follow me." Sill waived Bryn over to an empty wall in the lobby that shimmered and became a doorway, which immediately sealed after they had passed through.

Over the next two hours, Bryn was shown a side of the museum, and her family history, she never knew existed. When she exited the special VIP doorway, her eyes were huge and her formally slumped posture had been replaced with a new sense of determination. She wiped a final tear from her eye, turned to Sill and said,

"Thank you so much. You have no idea what you've done for me."

Sill smiled. "That's what I'm here for. If you ever need to come back, please stop on by. It was nice meeting you, Linna."

Bryn strode to the shiplot door and entered her ship.

"So, how was it?" George asked.

"Amazing, but that's the wrong word. Actually, a better word would be 'inspiring.'"

"Wonderful. You seem to be in a much better mood now than before."

"Oh, before I forget..." Bryn slapped the ship's console hard.

George was surprised. "Hey! What was that for?"

"For not telling me any of that stuff about my family."

"What stuff? If you haven't noticed, I'm a little big to fit in there to go on the tour."

"Like how my grandfather ended up making a deal with mobsters to buy their landfills, and all of the times they tried to kill him or destroy his new business when they discovered he was about to get rich by recycling all of the trash. Oh, and how my father was kidnapped and how he used theories on wormholes to create the first portable hole and escape. And all of the other stuff about my family? I mean, wow, my parents and grandparents were constantly fighting off physical, legal, political, and business attackers almost on a daily basis, like some action/adventure series on the Tubes. They suffered so much for StruseCorp and for our family and I never knew any of that. Why didn't anyone tell me?"

George mumbled, "Crane? Some assistance, please." The screen split in two and Crane appeared beside George.

"Hello Bryn. I'm glad you liked the tour. No one told you any of this because your parents wanted you to grow up as normal as possible. Normal families don't have to worry about assassins trying to kill their kids or blowing up their offices. Any kid growing up knowing this kind of environment and being exposed to the constant worry and fear they suffered through wouldn't have a chance at being normal so they shielded you and your brothers from it."

Bryn asked, "If they didn't disappear, would they have brought me on the tour themselves?"

Crane nodded, "Oh yes. They were going to wait for you to be in your mid-twenties, at least. Although, they did consider taking you on the tour just before they disappeared, when you were mired in your exceedingly bratty and entitled phase, in hopes it would give you some perspective. You leveled out pretty quickly after they went missing, so I didn't think it was necessary."

"I feel like my eyes have been opened after a really long sleep. It's like I'm well rested and I determined to get stuff done."

Crane said, "Good. Just in time for your birthday tomorrow. Despite your newfound sense of determination, you should be well rested. It's going to be quite the day."

Bryn barely noticed the brief wave of nausea that signaled their arrival to the house. She hopped out of her seat and talked to Crane as she walked, "I'm going to take a shower and think for a bit to digest all of this. In the meantime, Crane, can you research anything you can find about that cyborg that attacked me? I want to know more about it in case it comes back from the dead to get me again. Oh, and can you get me more information on my parents' disappearance?"

Crane already had all of the answers ready for her, but wanted to make her feel more in control of things, so he replied, "Sure thing. I'll try to have something for you by the time you're dressed."

Emergency Meeting

Seven people sat around the very old round table. Some were engaged in quiet conversations with their neighbors, and others were sitting stoically and looked generally unhappy. The few who were whispering, occasionally laughed, causing the grumpy among them to direct dirty glances their way. A moment later, the empty seat was filled with a blueish light and a hologram of a person appeared seated at the table. "Sorry I'm late, did we start yet?"

One of those who was quietly whispering earlier spoke up, "No problem. This was an unplanned emergency meeting of the Table of Eight called at the last minute, so a little tardiness is to be expected." Bonna looked around the table at each person for a moment and then began.

"Thank you all for coming on such short notice. It's a good affirmation that you are all so dedicated to the cause. It has been duly noted." She took a deep breath and all traces of her previous laughter were expelled on the exhale, leaving a deadly serious look on her face that landed squarely on each person sitting around the table. After she was done looking everyone in the eye, she continued.

"We have a problem. A big problem. At the onset of this year, we had several primary goals." An ancient map of Europe on the wall behind her faded and showed the list of goals for 2492. "We've been very successful in meeting the majority of them as they relate to the business side of things," As she spoke many of the items on the list crossed themselves off, "but, as you can see these two things in particular are still on our list." Several of the people at the table seemed to shrink a little in their seats.

She asked, "Does anyone know what day tomorrow is?"

"New Year's Eve," Ston said from behind the *Information* plaque.

"Correct, but what else?" Bonna prodded.

"Bryn Struse's birthday?"

"Yes! Exactly! And which birthday is our little survivor celebrating?"

Ston shrugged and said, "Her eighteenth?"

"Yes! And what happens on her eighteenth birthday?"

The room was silent for a moment, until the President of StruseCorp, Jud Astrid, spoke up gravely, "She inherits StruseCorp."

Bonna shook her head as if this was a shameful thing, "Yes, tomorrow Bryn Struse inherits the largest corporation in the history of humanity. A corporation we've spent years infiltrating and are using to finance and create hundreds of sub-corporations, which funnel money into our projects. Also, whomever runs StruseCorp has control over the Solar Union government. This one company alone sponsors 85% of all politicians and guides their votes. Such absolute political power must not be left to the whims of a teenager. If she is allowed to take over the company, she might meddle enough to actually look into things and discover everything we've built in the past five years since the Struses went away. This leads me to my next question, why isn't Bryn dead?"

Arcadis blurted out, "We've tried! She shouldn't have been able to survive the asteroid, and I don't know what happened to…"

A woman across from him interrupted, "Well, the asteroid was also meant for Dow Barnard…"

"And it would have gotten him too if he didn't switch rooms at the last minute."

Bonna Neefe firmly said, "Enough. The 'two birds with one giant stone' plan was excellent, but somehow Dow must have found out about it. Just before he arrived, he contacted the hotel and switched rooms. With a limited number of suites, they swapped his room with Bryn's. I'm guessing that he was just being paranoid and wasn't fully aware, yet, what was to happen. To compound things, he received two messages, one while in a meeting, which caused him to leave immediately and hurry to his room as quickly as possible, and the second call came right after he reached the room. He was tipped off about it because he didn't leave via the emergency exit we sabotaged, but instead took the hallway. It was as if he knew that it would lock up halfway to the lobby."

Arcadis nervously fiddled with his title plaque that read, *Arcadis Lidder - Technology*. "Maybe his BarnardBots alerted him to the mechanical failure we had planned."

She pretended to entertain the notion, "Perhaps, but I'm inclined to think otherwise."

The woman on the left asked, "Who was it?"

Bonna shrugged, "We don't know."

"We need to find out. If someone that's working for us is warning our targets…"

"Trust me, we will find out who it was and deal with them appropriately. I want everyone to check with their people to rout out the tipster. In the meantime, we need to get back to our pressing matter of Bryn's current life status."

Jud Astrid, spoke, "Despite her amazing knack to stay alive, I think her most recent brush with death has been more effective than you would like to admit."

The woman in charge shot the quiet man with a look of slight bemusement. "Oh really? How so?"

"Easy. She hasn't left her house at all in the two months since the botched attempt on her life. She also hasn't even listened to any messages people have left for her. I know because I've left at least twenty messages myself, all with tracers, and they're all still unopened."

Someone piped up, "Maybe she's avoiding just you?"

Jud laughed and nodded, "I thought that too, which is why I had some people she knows leave messages for her as well, which also went unopened." He smiled, "I also created a dummy message from her best friend, Amory, also with a tracer, of course, and nothing. She's not checking or opening any messages."

"Hm," Bonna said. "That's strange."

He continued, "Yes. Very. I've also planted cambots on the sides of ships that are normally scheduled to pass within view of her house in the Deimos orbit, and, well take a look at the pictures they've taken…"

A screen opened above the table. It showed the side of a frigate and then panned to the left. It locked onto a house sitting on an outcropping of rock floating in orbit and zoomed in. As the view got closer, a two-story glass window was visible. It panned in further still and a young woman was seen sitting on the edge of an upper floor with her head and arms resting on a railing just staring blankly out the window.

"I'll save you the time, but this camera recorded her like this for ten minutes before it moved out of view. I have fourteen more clips like this, all recorded on different dates, and all of them of her sitting in the same way, just staring outside. Although, this one here is a little heartbreaking."

The angle of the video was much different, this one captured at a might higher angle, but it still showed Bryn in the same place, only this time there was something small beside her. The cam zoomed in and now you could clearly see a very small, long, spotted dog that was making a great effort in standing upright and balancing on its hind legs while trying unsuccessfully to get her attention. There was a collective, "Awwww," in the room.

One person said, "I know we want her dead, but that was just really sad."

Jud agreed, "Yes it is. I think that she's both scared to leave the house, and also very depressed. I honestly don't think she'll be attending the annual meeting tomorrow."

Bonna thought for a moment. "You may be right. After seeing that, I'd be inclined to agree with you. Jud, go ahead with our original plans at StruseCorp tomorrow. Also, I want around the clock surveillance on her house. If she leaves, we not only need to know, but we need to be able to act upon it quickly."

"Consider it done."

She smiled, "Good! Ok, next on the agenda, our annual potluck New Year's Party…"

Incoming Call

Jud Astrid was on his way home and discussing the events of the Table of Eight meeting with his ship. "...and then I got stuck signing up to bring pretty much most everything for the party."

His ship, Benedict, replied, "That's awful. Just terrible."

Jud was exasperated, "I know! So then they…"

"Sorry to interrupt, but a call is coming in for you. Audio only."

"What? That's unusual. Who's it from?"

Benedict apologized, "There is no point of origin."

"What? That's even weirder. Don't answer it."

"Connecting call."

"No! I said not to connect it."

A familiar voice said, "Dow Barnard."

Jud's annoyance relaxed, *Oh, it's just Dow*...his thought was cut off as the message continued:

"Dow, you've got to listen to me, I don't have much time to talk. Did you get my message? Where are you?"

The sound of his own voice filling the cabin caused the hairs on his arms to point up like hundreds of exclamation points, while a deep chill slithered up his arms, gathered at the nape of his neck, balled into an icy fear that nearly him choked as it slid down his throat, and compacted into what felt like a sickening glacier inside his stomach. He remembered this call vividly, not so much for the call itself, but that if the wrong people were to hear it, he would be a dead man.

In the message, Dow Barnard's voice replied, "What? No. Why?"

"Are you at the Hathaway Eris?"

"Yeah, I'm in my hotel room, what's up? You sound troubled."

"Dow, they're planning on killing you and today…"

"What! Who?"

Jud sat bolt upright and stared wide-eyed at the ship's display. His mind raced, *Who is sending this?* Even as he thought it, he knew who. *There's no way. I mean, how did they find out? I did it through a secure channel, there's no way they could suspect me. None. I covered my tracks, they couldn't have found me out.* In contrast with his mind, he spoke slowly and very purposely, "Benedict. End the connection. Now."

The ship was silent as the message continued.

"…shut up and listen! In just a few minutes, an asteroid is going to hit your room."

Dow's voice noticeably relaxed. "Pah! Let it hit. I switched rooms when I checked in. I was going to ask how you know, but I'm sure it has something to do with that dreadful organization you belong to which sounds like some tea party, what is it, the Table of Salad or something?"

Oh no. No, no, no. "Benedict, I said end the connection. NOW."

The ship didn't respond. Instead, the message kept playing and his voice continued to ring out.

"Dow, damnit! The front desk just switched you to another room further down the same hall! *This* is where it's going to impact, and *this* is where you are," Jud remembered the map that he sent to Dow showing the schematics of the hotel and the relation of Dow's room to the impact point of the asteroid. "It'll hit in a couple of minutes."

"Oh. Hm. Well then, I'd better get going."

"You need to make a stop on your way...the person assigned to your old room is Bryn Struse. You need to save Bryn."

"Aw, *shuck*, Jud! Why didn't you tell me sooner!"

"When you checked in, you switched rooms as a security precaution, and Bryn Struse ended up getting the room you were supposed to get originally. That's where it's going to hit. You need to get your bots and...I have to go. I'll call back as soon as I can."

Why the shuck isn't the ship responding? A voice in the back of his mind piped up with what he had been trying not to think about...*because they control the ship. You're going to die.*

He pulled up the ship's screen and stabbed impotently at buttons, which did nothing. *Wait a second, where did I get this ship...oh no...shuck, shuck, shuck!*

The recording of his conversation with Dow continued, "WHAT? Why didn't you tell me that earlier? Who's behind this?"

Fear filled his veins. *They gave me this ship when I became a member of the Table.*

"Who do you think? There's seriously no more time, Dow. The asteroid will be teleported in seconds. GET OUT OF THERE!"

This is NOT good. I need to get off this ship.

"On my way!" Then, to his robots, "Emergency evac to lobby – you, sled; you, jets; you two, defensive positioning; GO!" His faint voice yelled back into the room from what sounded like a hallway, "Thanks Astrid, I owe you one!" The end of Dow's last words on the message were drowned out from the combination of klaxons going off and a rocketing sled blasting away.

Jud got up and calmly walked quickly towards the back of the ship. He wasn't all that surprised when the gravity stopped and he gently floated off the floor from the momentum of his last step.

"Benedict, restore gravity!"

Another message began to play. He was again greeted by his voice and a conversation he had with his ship months ago, just after the asteroid incident: "I can't believe they want to kill Dow. So what if he doesn't play along with their rules, that's no reason to kill a man."

In the recording, Benedict echoed his sentiments, "Killing is wrong."

Keep calm. Keep calm. I can do this. I need to get to the escape pod.

"It sure is. At least he was able to survive after I alerted him." The volume noticeably increased for those last three words, and they echoed around the cabin of the ship.

The recording continued with Benedict saying, "Yes, he and Bryn Struse. But didn't you end up putting them in harm's way by not contacting him until the last possible minute? According to the news reports, over one thousand hotel guests lost their lives. If you had notified Dow sooner, they could have been saved as well. Why didn't you contact the authorities?"

Undeterred from his goal of survival, Jud pushed off from a wall and floated quickly down a hallway and toward the back of the ship.

"Oh come on. Do you have any idea how hard it was to make that call to begin with? I went against the Table of Eight and told their target that he was marked for death. That could have...and still could get me killed. It's tragic that so many people died, it really is. But, telling him at the last minute like that exposed him to enough danger that it hopefully impressed upon him the seriousness of the situation."

The recording of Benedict's voice replied, "So they died just because you wanted to teach him a lesson of sorts? I fail to see a rational justification for your way of thinking. Why are the lives of Dow Barnard and Bryn Struse worth more than those other people?"

Jud was most of the way across the room. *Shuck, this is taking too long.* He took a moment, closed his eyes and breathed in deeply. *Stay calm. You can do this. Just get through the door, down the hall, and you'll be in the emergency pod soon enough.*

"Essentially, they're not. A life is equal to another life. Dow is a long-time friend. I can't sit by and knowingly let them kill him. Yes, he's a bit stubborn at times, but that's no reason to kill him."

He gave a small sigh of relief as his trajectory perfectly sailed him through the door and into the hallway beyond. *At least something is going right for me, although I wish this recording would stop.*

"And Bryn, well, her parents told me years ago, just before they disappeared, in fact, that they wanted me to watch over and keep an eye on her if anything should ever happen to them. So yeah, when I found out that both of these important people in my life are about to be murdered, I had to do something about it. As for not telling them earlier, I didn't have a chance. The Table seemed a little more paranoid than usual and kept us together until just before the attack. That was the first opportunity I had to let Dow know."

He arrived at the door to the pod, pulled himself in, and yanked the lever to close the door and launch the pod.

It didn't move.

"Which allowed him to escape that awful fate."

Shuck. He strained and pulled on the lever, which was made more difficult by the lack of gravity. His efforts caused him to float up into the hatchway.

"Yeah, and it's a double bonus that he was able to save Bryn Struse, otherwise she would have died."

Shuck! Why won't this door close?

"Yes, that's true. You saved Bryn Struse." The last sentence played at an abnormally loud volume.

Then silence.

The phrase "You saved Bryn Struse," pounded loud over and over again, echoing throughout the ship.

Gravity kicked on, hard, catching Jud by surprise and the floor blurred up to meet him. His head whacked into the bulkhead and he was knocked unconscious.

Crushed

"You saved Bryn Struse," was still faintly playing over and over in his splittingly painful head as he groggily came to. He realized that apart from the high-pitch whine of an over-stressed engine and the occasional sound of creaking metal, things were quiet. Thankfully the recording had stopped. *Now only if it would stop playing in my mind,* he thought.

He tried to move, but couldn't at first. Even breathing was difficult as a dense heaviness seemed to pin him down. With great effort, Jud was able to roll over and look up. Except for the strange sounds, everything seemed normal. *What's going on? Is there a holding field on me?*

"Benedict! What's going on?"

The voice of his ship responded, in a disturbingly chipper fashion, "Oh, hi there! You're awake!"

"Wha-what's going on? Is there a holding field on me?"

"P'shaw! I've done no such thing!"

Jud strained to ask, "Is there something wrong with the gravity?"

Benedict replied, "Nope! It's set to normal here!"

"Then why am I pinned to the floor? Where are we?"

"Ah ha! Now that's the question worth asking!"

Jud managed, "Why am I pinned to the floor?"

"No, silly, the other one!"

"Why are you talking like that? You're never like this."

Benedict replied, "I'm happy because we're going on an adventure! We never get to go on adventures, but we're on one now!"

"Where are we?" With exceptional effort he clawed his way down the hallway toward the front of the ship. His head throbbed with an unbearable pain.

"Bingo! That's the right question! You sure are smart today."

"Where are we?"

"Oh right, we're approaching Jupiter! Isn't this fun?"

SnnnNNNRUNK!

"Benedict, what was that!"

"That was a loud noise. Wow, you're very inquisitive today!"

"No really," Jud's breathing was labored, "what...was that noise?"

"Something outside, I think. A fin, maybe? I dunno."

He sighed angrily and strained to claw his way faster as he sensed he was in deep, deep trouble. "Which moon...are we," he gasped, "going to?"

"Oh no moon, we're going to land on Jupiter itself! The biggest of the planets! You know, some would even say it's the king of the planets...well, in this solar system, anyway. Isn't that neat? We're going to have a picnic in a grassy field and have a great time!"

"No…no, NO! We can't land…on Jupiter…there's nothing to land on, it's just gas until…until you get toward the core…"

"Then that's where we'll land!" The ship began to happily sing:

> *Picnic at the core*
> *Picnic at the core*
> *Get up off the floor*
> *I'll open the door*
> *There's nothing I like more!*

Jud finally crawled through the entryway to the main part of the ship. He strained to crain his neck up and look at the forward monitor which showed a darker-hued tan color at the periphery that faded to black in the center.

The ship said, "Not much to look at, huh?"

He thought, *Benedict was always very formal, why is he talking like this?*

Benedict kept talking: "Metallic hydrogen. We have to get through a lot of this to get to the core, so sit back and relax!"

ShhnnnNNNRUNK!

"Turn around! You're…going…to kill…both…of us!" Jud could no longer keep his head up and breathing was becoming almost impossible.

"Nonsense! We're going to have a picnic!"

ChaRUNK-SKEEEEEEEE!

"T-the p-p-pressure is t-t-tearing the s-s-s-ship - part! Tuh-tuh-turn -round n-n-n-n-ow!"

"Ho ho! I think the only pressure around here is coming from the vicinity of you, my friend! You really should learn to relax! I mean, heck, who needs a wing? Not I! Or anything else for that matter. Material possessions are just silly. Let's look at it in a more positive light, like we gave that wing to the world. When you're having a picnic with a friend," *SssssrrrRRRRUNK!* "who needs things? Oh! I almost forgot, there's a message for you! Hmmm. Where did I put it? Gimmie a moment..."

Jud made a low groaning noise. It felt as if the air was trying to grind his body through the carpet. He strained to keep his eyes open and he could no longer breathe under the intense pressure.

"Silly me, here it is. Lemme play it..."

The ship's dampers were working to the breaking point trying to protect the precious human cargo by counteracting the heat and pressures involved with diving directly into the largest gas giant planet in the solar system. As the ship tore apart, it spun wildly, and hopelessly out of control, the one living occupant heard these final two phrases as his body succumbed to the blackness and was crushed into the flooring, as it disintegrated beneath him:

"Trust me, we will find out who it was and deal with them appropriately."

The ship was facing the full-brunt of punishment handed out by Jupiter's forces and could no longer stay intact. The last thing Benedict managed to play as it was torn, crushed, and ripped apart, came across in a sped-up, high-pitch, almost mockingly accusatory tone: "You saved Bryn St-"

Happy Birthday

"I think you should take a break," said Crane. "You've been researching and plotting for most of the day."

Bryn looked around, "Why, what time is it? I'm not wearing my glasses."

"You haven't worn your glasses much at all in the past two months. That's why you're so behind on things."

"I know, I know. Just tell me what time it is."

"It's 11:58pm. You have two minutes until your birthday."

"Ooh! What'd you get me?"

Crane shrugged, "Apart from pulling you out of a bout of severe depression and giving your life back? Nothing."

"Thanks. I'll remember that for when your birthday rolls around."

"Not so fast, young Struse. There is one present for you."

Bryn perked up. "There is? Where? Wait a second, if you didn't get me anything, who's it from?"

Crane said, "It's not your birthday yet, so you need to wait."

"What? Oh come on. I've only got a minute and a half left. Can't I open it a little early?"

"I'm sorry, but you're going to have to wait. You should find your glasses first. You might want them before getting your present."

"Why, so I can spoil the surprise by looking through the wrapping?"

Crane laughed. This made Bryn even more curious since he hardly ever laughs. "Your glasses are hanging on the railing by your perch."

Bryn sprinted down the hall, did a little jump, and slid on her stocking feet the rest of the way to the stairs. She bounded up to the railing and put on her glasses. It was a normal view for a full second until screens began to pop up across them. Some displayed messages she needed to look at and respond to some showed the news, and the one which read, "Time until Bryn's birthday," with a large 00:57 below it counting down.

"Alright Crane, where is it?"

"It's not time yet. Sorry."

She could tell that not only was he not sorry, but he seemed to be enjoying this. A lot.

Crane said, "You can wait another minute."

"What if I can't? Have you considered the possibility of that?"

"I have and I have also considered that you've wasted the last two months being a recluse, so waiting another forty seconds shouldn't be a problem."

Hmm. They've got me there.

Crane suggested, "How about this. You follow the arrows and you'll get there in time to see your present. Does that sound good?"

"Yes! Oh please give me a sign!"

A brightly colored cartoony arrow shimmered into the air in front of her face pointing back down to the first floor. She turned, ran, and jumped down the flight of stairs without touching a single one. There she found a different, but equally wacky arrow pointing to the left. She tore off in that direction. At the end of the hall, a holographic balloon hovered with, *The birthday surprise for the terribly impatient birthday girl is…* written on it. A floating arrow above it spun rapidly. It slowed down until it pointed at the door at the end of the hall.

Bryn paused and pointed to her parents' workshop. "Crane? Are you sure it's in there?"

"Positive."

Bryn stood there for a moment, her joyous smile was replaced by a seemingly emotionless face. She had gotten pretty good at that face which completely masked the deep swell of turbulent emotions that she was experiencing.

"Bryn? In case you hadn't noticed, it's now well past your birthday."

Bryn glanced at the birthday countdown in her glasses which was now a bright red, blinking *+00:00:38+* and spraying confetti all over the rest of the info boxes in her glasses.

Crane continued, "and your present has gone away. Most sorry."

She rolled her eyes, said, "Shut it, you," and walked through the door to her parents' workshop.

Bryn had visited this room a scant few times in the years since her parents went missing. There were just too many memories, good and bad, associated with this place. The lights went on as soon as she walked in and a large, cluttered room lay before her. The table closest to the door had been the one Bryn used to make her fake sun sword handle earlier in the year. Otherwise, various projects and experiments sat undisturbed, as if they were waiting for their owners to return, on the large tables scattered around the room. As she walked down an aisle, it felt like each table was a tombstone, with each experiment acting as a reminder in Bryn's mind of a particular moment in her and her parents' life. It was like walking through a huge cemetery with a different stone for a different period in their lives.

"Hey, Crane? Where's this present at? You know how I feel about this room."

Silence.

She glanced at something on a nearby table for a second before asking again, "Crane, come on. This isn't funny. Where's the present?"

"Hello Bryn, happy birthday."

Bryn froze. A deep chill ran down her back and her eyes started to well up with tears. A second voice added, "Yes! Happy birthday Bryn!"

She spun around to see the source of the voices and was instantly emotionally devastated by what she saw.

There they were: her mom and dad. Alva and Amelia Struse were standing by the doorway, looking exactly as she had remembered them. Alive! They were right there, wishing her a happy birthday, and they were…

"If you are getting this message, then obviously you know we're gone."

…a holographic message. She exhaled to the point of deflation and had to lean on a table for support. The message could sense she wasn't paying attention so it paused until it knew she was really listening.

"We know this message could be a little disturbing, but today is a very big day and we needed to go over some things with you.

"First off, happy, happy, *happy* eighteenth birthday! We've got a big birthday surprise for you in the next room," Bryn's moist eyes got huge at this and quickly scanned the room for whatever the 'next room' they were referring to was. She didn't know of any, but this was a big house after all with lots of nooks and crannies. She was sure she had explored every last centimeter of the house, but then again, when it came to her parents, you never knew. "…but first, the mushy stuff."

Amelia stepped forward. Her long red hair swaying slightly. "Bryn, we love you so much. I hope you realize that. I know it may not have always seemed like it with both your father and I working so hard on our projects, but you were the part of our lives that gave us the most joy."

Alva followed, "Yes, and we hope that you never have to see this message, that we'll be together as a happy family for a very long time but, at the same time, it would be irresponsible of us as parents to not have everything in place to cover for every contingency."

As Amelia spoke, Bryn just stared at her mother and thinking how wonderful it was to see her again, even if her view was partially obstructed by the stream of tears running down her face. "This is a fake decoy room meant to throw off curious visitors. Our real workshop is through a well-concealed doorway in the wall behind you. Anytime someone came down to this end of the hallway, we'd be alerted to it and quickly come to this room and pretend to be working on things.

A fake room? What? Wait a minute, even me? But, every time I saw them working, they were in this room.

"And yes, that also included you."

Bryn made a little *yup-there-it-is* kind of face.

Alva said, "When my father passed away, I felt so overwhelmed that the entire burden of running the company was dumped on me. If that was something you were worried about, please don't. We have very competent and intelligent people who know what they are doing taking care of the day to day operations."

Amelia added: "Yes, please don't feel like you need to step into the business side of things. You do whatever you want with your life, just don't feel any silly obligations to run the company or anything. It's being taken care of."

"But what ab-" Bryn tried to say but was interrupted by the message, while it was wonderful to see a hologram of her parents that she hadn't watched thousands of times already, what she wanted most was to actually be able to speak to them.

"Now, onto the fun stuff," Bryn's mother said. "Crane makes sure that everything in the real workshop continues to keep busy with making all of our ideas and experiments become reality when we're not around. Is it cheating?" Amelia and Alva looked at each other for a shrugged moment of, "ehhhh?" and then finished, "Maybe technically, but in reality Crane is just doing what we've instructed them to do. That way we can be considerably more efficient; whenever we're away we can still keep working on things.

"Now, to get to the real workshop, you need to come over to this table here," Amelia gestured to a table over to the left wall, "and find the old broken keypad under the pile of junk used parts, and press six, eight, four, enter twice, and then the period button three times. Go ahead and try it."

The hologram of her parents froze while it was waiting for the code to be entered. Bryn walked over to the table, rooted around through the substantial pile of parts, and discovered a stained, broken, keypad with old wires dangling from its charred back. She was doubtful that this old piece of equipment could be useful for anything in its current, seemingly unrepairable state, but still pressed the buttons in the same sequence her mother had said. On the wall to the far right of the room, a cluttered shelving unit disappeared and was replaced by a doorway. She went over to it and jumped back slightly when a booming voice commanded, "State your name!"

"Uh, Bryn Struse."

After a moment of silence, the doorway responded, "I do not know of any 'Uh, Bryn Struses.' State your name!"

"Bryn Struse!"

"That's better. Welcome, Bryn. We've been expecting you."

Bryn stepped through the doorway and into a dark room. Her glasses were just kicking on to show the night vision view when the lights snapped on amid a bellowing chorus of, "HAPPY BIRTHDAY!!"

Bryn was very surprised by holograms of years-missing parents throwing a surprise party for her. If there was anything she'd be expecting for her birthday, this would not be it.

The holograms of her parents, along with some small helper robots, all decked out in party hats and noisemakers, were hootin' and hollerin' in front of a huge banner that said, *Happy birthday Bryn!* She was so touched that her parents would have the foresight to throw her a party from the grave. Even though they were right there, she missed them terribly.

They beckoned her over to a table where a freshly made cupcake sat with a single candle cast dancing shadows over the nooks and crannies of the buttercream frosting. "Make a wish!" her father said. She took one long look at them and blew it out. More robot noisemakers sounded in celebration. The robots then lost interest and zoomed off to resume whatever chores they were engrossed in before they were told to throw a party.

That was when she was finally able to full take in the scope of their workshop.

They were in a very large open office with two very tidy desks that faced each other in the middle of the room. The walls were covered with art that she recognized that she and her brothers painted when they were younger. As she ate the cupcake, she walked over to the desks and saw (now) old pictures of the entire family together, as well as some just of Alva and Amelia together.

"Bryn, your surprise is out there," Alva spoke pointing towards the giant floor-to-ceiling window that overlooked a monstrous hangar-sized room. "Happy birthday, Bryn." And with that, her parents disappeared.

She went over to the window, looked out, and thought, *Oh WOW!* She sprinted toward the lift and was impatient as it lowered her down. If it wasn't so far down to the floor of the giant room, she would have just jumped, but this view gave her an interesting vantage point with which to more fully appreciate the room and its contents.

Judging by the measurements her glasses took, the room was a kilometer wide by two and a half kilometers long. *That's crazy. The asteroid the house is on isn't nearly this large. How did they do it?*

There were scores of stations of different shapes and sizes spread throughout the "room," each with robots working hard on various projects. The one that caught her eye was at the far end of the room.

A trumpet sounded and a loud voice boomed, "Hey everyone, guess who's here? Bryn Struse, and it's her eighteenth birthday!"

All of the robots stopped, turned to face her and started singing the birthday song:
Have a hap-hap-happy birthday
Because today's your special day

All of us here wanted to say
Have a hap-happy day today!

Bryn was very touched, but at the same time slightly bemused because she noticed that all of the robots here were wearing pointy birthday hats as well.

A hovering robot came over and greeted her, "Hello Bryn! I'm Boxy. I heard today's your birthday."

She smiled, "Hello, Boxy. Yes, it would appear that way."

"Would you like a tour of your new workshop? Oh, don't tell me you're still wearing the old version of the Tracelet?"

"I would thank you…um, wait…*old version?* This is a spare set I made last month to replace the ones I blew up."

"Yes, while I understand you're probably holding onto it for sentimental reasons, we've made some notable upgrades to your basic design."

Basic design?

Boxy waived her on. "Follow me and I'll show you what we've done to it."

Bryn followed the little flying robot, past testing areas that were in various stages of erupting in color, noise, and heat, as experiments were being tried out in this gigantic factory-like setting. They made their way over to a section where nothing was happening. There was a clean desk, a twenty-meter long range of some sort, and a few tidy shelves.

Boxy took a set of Tracelets off a shelf and handed them to Bryn. "Ok, try these out."

She took off the Tracelets she made and snapped on the new ones. They gelled slightly and formed smoothly around her wrists. A screen popped up in front of her, which welcomed Bryn to the *Tracelet by Bryn™ (a li'l division of StruseCorp).*

Bryn looked up in disbelief. She knew StruseCorp was going to put it into production, but she realized she hadn't seen the finished product yet. Here it was, looking refined and official.

She turned to the floating robot, "Are these being sold?"

"Yes. We took your basic prototype and researched useful applications in different settings for it. For instance, we have a very toned-down version for commercial use where it's useful to get things off from high shelves. Also, a high-powered option has been made for police and military uses. It's a great, non-lethal tool. This has already been a huge seller for StruseCorp."

"Wow." The possibility of finally pulling herself out from under the gargantuan shadows of her parents with her own popular invention popped into her mind.

She played around with the menu and looked over all the different settings. Everything from turning it invisible and undetectable, to the power settings, and even an enhanced SmartGrab™ option that let you dexterously manipulate things from a distance with each individual finger. She was impressed. Her model basically pulled things towards, or pushed them away from her with rudimentary manipulation options. No menus, no customizable features, none of that fancy stuff. They took her core invention, spiffed it up, and made it perfect.

"Who did all of this? The people at StruseCorp?"

Boxy said, "Oh no. When we saw how they were just going to put your original Tracelet into production, as is, Crane sent it here and we made it better."

"Well, thank you. This is great. Can I take these?" she asked, while admiring how they vanished on her arms.

Boxy said, "Sure. Don't forget that this is your invention, made in your workshop, in your home, after all."

Bryn smiled. "Yeah, I guess you're right."

"I just ask that you leave your old ones here. I'd like to include it in the history archive."

History archive? "Uh, sure. Go ahead." Bryn pointed down the rows to the far end of the workshop. "What's that thing at the far end of the workshop?"

A way-too excited voice boomed from the direction Bryn pointed, "Hey! Someone asked about me! Who's looking for me? I hope it's that birthday girl! Hurry up little floaty robot and bring that Bryn down this way!"

Boxy's big eyes narrowed to small slits of annoyance and whispered, "Thanks, Bryn," and then in a normal voice, "Come on. It's time for you to get the birthday present your parents left you."

Fat Louie

After a bit of walking, they cleared the seemingly endless row of testing rooms and cubicles and were now clearly in a starship hangar staring at something that blew Bryn's mind.

It was difficult to accurately gage the size or shape of the mystery object. It was as wide as a small starship, but, at the same time, had no discernible edges, corners, or windows. It appeared to be completely smooth, to the point that the light from the hangar seemed to be slightly distorted as it hit the ship, slipped, and fell onto the floor. Even the color, for that matter, was impossible to distinguish. It was maybe black, possibly blue, some reddish in there, a hint of dark green, everything about it was perplexing. If it was a ship, Bryn had no idea how someone would get inside. She asked, "What is it? Is that a ship?"

286

Boxy was just starting to respond when the ship boomed out, "You bet yer bottom bippie I am! I'm your birthday present..." and lowered their voice to a loud whisper, "although, I secretly find the whole notion of me being given away as a gift to some kid on her birthday a bit insulting, but don't worry, I'll keep that thought tucked away in my head and you'll be none the wiser." It began to happily hum to itself, "Hmm, hmm, hmmm, hm, hm, hm, hmmm, hmmmmm…"

Bryn exchanged an awkward glance with Boxy, who whispered back, "I didn't get a chance to warn you about him. He's a little – odd."

Bryn asked, "*Him? He?* Really?"

The bot nodded, "Oh yes."

Fat Louie whispered loudly to Bryn, "PSST!! IS THE LITTLE DRONE DONE TALKING ABOUT ME TO YOU?"

Bryn snickered and whispered back, "Yes, I think they're done."

"GOOD…BETWEEN YOU AND ME THEY'RE KINDA BOSSY." And he set aside the yelling whisper and took a normal tone, "So, let's do these introduction things. Hello Bryn, my name is Fat Louie."

Bryn wasn't sure where to look when responding since the voice seemed to come from all around her. "It's nice to meet you Louie, I'm Bryn."

"You might be surprised to find this out, but I actually knew your name was Bryn. Am I good, or what? So, hey, how does it feel to be eighteen?"

"Um, kind of the same as I felt an hour ago."

"Yup, yup, I know what you mean, BrynBryn, I totally hear you. Anyways, enough of the idle chit-chat. Way back when, your parents decided to make themselves the way coolest ship ever made," and then whisper-yelled, "BY THE WAY, THAT'S ME."

"Got it," said Bryn.

"GOOD! Anyway, I was under construction when they went missing, but before they went away, they said I should be given to you when you turned eighteen…"

"Why not earlier?" Bryn interrupted.

"Uh, because you'd probably wrap me around an asteroid or something, silly. I'm just telling you what they told me. Stop interruptin'! I was completed years ago, so I figured, hey, let's just keep upgrading me, so that's what we've been doing."

"So, does that mean you're a super ship or something?"

"Yes! I'm the super-est ship that ever shipped super stuff! Delm's couldn't make something a billionth as good as me. Not only can I do all the stuff that other, non-awesome ships can do, but I can also do much, much more awesome stuff as well."

"Really?"

"Yup. Totally."

Bryn smiled, "That was a very thorough run-down of your qualifications. I have to say that I'm impressed, Fat Louie."

"Oh I knew you would be."

"How did you get your name?"

Fat Louie's voice shrugged. "I dunno, I just kinda found it."

"You found it? Where?"

"You know, lying around here somewhere. It sometimes gets cluttered in the workshop."

"Uh, okay…"

"Hey Bryn, how about you and I go for a test flight so I can show you all the zippy-blammo stuff I can do?"

"That's a great idea!" Boxy eagerly interjected.

Bryn guessed correctly that Fat Louie's colorful personality probably got annoying to the other inhabitants of the workshop, so for the ship to leave for a while would be a welcome break for the rest of the bots.

She nodded, "Sure, that'd be great, thanks."

The ship lowered to the floor and a section of the side turned transparent and became an opening, so she walked through…and into the most comfortable-looking living room she had ever seen.

Oversized plush comfy chairs were all about the room, hovering slightly above the ground, each with a matching ottoman, as well as a tastefully inviting couch. Nice paintings, that looked like real oil on canvas, hung around the room, the walls of which were a strange color that could only be described as "soothing." The several windows looked out onto a lushly green grassy field on a beautiful sunny day seemed out of place, yet quite welcome. All of the furniture was arranged facing the wall to the right, where a chair sat whose comfiness overshadowed the comfy-factor of all of the other chairs in the room by a stunning margin. Bryn started in awe at that one chair and thought that if she were to sit in it, she would become lost, and then melt into nothingness within the deep folds of the luxurious purple material.

Bryn was so entranced by the chair that it was a few seconds before she noticed that someone was sitting in it. She was startled by the figure. It was a man of an undeterminable age. He was well dressed; wearing a bright blue patterned suit that was as equally drenched in the grotesquely garish as it was simultaneously sitting on the shore of amazing taste. Bryn had never seen an outfit that caused her to think, *Ugh!* and *Wow!* to this degree at the same time…but yet, it worked.

"It's so nice to finally meet you Miss Bryn. Welcome aboard the good ship *Fat Louie*. I'm your host, pilot, and new friend, Fat Louie, but you can call me Fat Louie. *Mr.* Fat Louie, if you're feeling formal."

It took Bryn a moment to drag her eyes away from the suit to the person, but when she did, her first thought was, *Wow, those are the craziest eyes I've ever seen. They seem to be every shade of every color all at once.* Her second thought was, *I don't think I've ever encountered a computer which identifies as a specific gender before. This is weird.* She replied awkwardly, "Uh, hi. I'm Bryn," and then immediately cringed at how stupid that must have sounded.

Fat Louie laughed. "Wow, you sounded really stupid there. Have a seat and let's chat."

She sat down in one of the oversized arm chairs and sunk in. "Wow, this is really comfortable."

"It's ok. Nowhere near as comfortable as mine, of course, but it'll do for you." He saw her eying his seat and cut off her thought, "Oh no, no, no, missy. Don't be getting any crazy human thoughts about sitting your bony butt down in my chair. This seat is for me only. Sorry. You'll have to make do with what you've got."

"Well, since you're just a holographic projection, you don't really need a seat…"

"Yeah, that's a dangerous line of thinking there, so just start thinking about other stuff. Some suggestions might include butterflies, ice cream, or the social, political, and economic ramifications of the Oort Act upon a post solar-centric human civilization. Please noodle those for a while."

Bryn was confused for a moment and managed, "Uh…I don't see what any of those has to do with you not needing your chair."

Louie pleaded, "Please. Think of the butterflies. Who will think of the poor butterflies?"

"You're weird."

"Nope nope. I'm just me. Ok, stop coveting my chair long enough to focus on things. What day is today?"

"My birthday."

"Right! Happy birthday again, by the way."

"Thanks."

"And for your birthday, your parents have left you me, the most wonderful ship in the known human-known."

"No offense, but this seems more like a living room than a starship."

"None taken. Actually, I will take that as a compliment and place it lovingly in the 'Compliment' bin." A breadbox-sized metal bin appeared and Louie gestured inside. "As you can see, it's pretty empty in there right now, but I'm hoping that you'll fill it in no time."

Bryn giggled.

Louie continued, "Anyway, I tried to make me as comfortable as possible so the occupants would think, 'Hey! I'm just hanging out in my living room, having a grand ol' time.' And then I'm all like, 'Hey there party people, we've just arrived at our amazingly awesome destination,' and they're like, 'Whoa! We didn't know we were in a starship! We thought we were just in the living room!' And then everyone is happy and dances for a bit."

"Are you actually capable of flying?"

"*Capable* of flying, or *allowed* to fly. Those are two *verrry* different things. I'm very much capable of flying, and I can do it faster and with oodles and poodles of more style than anyone else can. Am I *allowed* to fly? Absolutely!...not."

"What? Why not?"

"Because I was built here in the laboratory, instead of a proper shipyard, I'm not registered with the Solar Union, which, for some reason, requires registration for all ships. Personally, I think they're against competition."

"Can't you just get registered?"

"Sure. But I won't."

"Why not?" Bryn asked. "Don't you want to be legal?"

"I'm loaded to the brim's rim, and then some, with all sorts of recently invented, wondrously wonderful technology that that Solar Union does not have. If I were to register myself, I would first have to register all of the new inventions that I'm chock full of. That would A: take a long time, Two: raise a lot of questions as to how some of these things came to be, and C: be annoying. Besides, they can't make me."

"If they catch you, they could."

"Ah ha!" Louie exclaimed. "Therein lies their impossible dream. I have the element of surprise since I have never been outside of this hangar before, so no one has seen me but you, plus I can mask my appearance. I'm not concerned and neither should you be."

Bryn was taken aback, "What? You've never been outside the lab? How do you even know if you can fly? What do you mean you can change your appearance?"

"In all of the simulations, everything about me runs perfectly. Actually more than perfectly, so there." He stuck his tongue out in a mocking manner. "Just like I said, I can change my appearance. Here, look at this."

A monitor appeared in front of Bryn, which showed a picture of a smooth black oval. "This is an above shot of me. I have the ability to change my shape to whatever my little metal heart desires. If I want to look like a Jovian freighter, I just do it." The oval stretched out in all directions, the edges filled out and squared off. She was now looking at a picture of a mid-sized Jovian freighter ship.

She shrugged. "Big deal, you can project a freighter around you to make it look like you're a different ship."

Louie smiled, "You're so cute when you're so wrong." The door to the hangar opened. "Why don't you go outside and have a look-see for yourself."

"Sure. I think I'll do that."

Bryn walked to the doorway and immediately noticed how much higher up in the air they were. The ramp looked different. It had a rough edge with dings, scrapes, and was caked with rough yellow dirt. She backed down the ramp and was astonished to see that the perfectly shaped oval ship had transformed itself into a big freighter, complete with re-entry burns around the bottom and front, along with all the other nicks and knocks that come with a ship that has worked a hard, harsh life mining the moons of Jupiter. Bryn used her glasses to scan the ship, and everything said that it was a freighter: from the ship's identification beacon, to the license markings on the side showing which moons and planets it was registered with. When she was satisfied, she hustled up the ramp and sat back in her seat.

Fat Louie was still sitting in his chair, but now he was dressed in old-time nautical gear from Earth, all mismatched from different eras. A skipper's cap was smartly perched on his head which stood in odd contrast with the knee-length, oversized admiral's jacket with big bristling epaulets that looked like small yellow mops hanging from his shoulders, all above the rubber knee-high wading boots. A parrot appeared out of thin air and landed on one of the shoulder-mop things. It looked strange, but yet, once again, it worked, and he looked damn good in it.

"Talking about my capabilities is boring. Eventually, you'll get to see what I can do. Want to go for a ride?"

"Sure!"

"Now, if I remember correctly, you've got the StruseCorp annual meeting to attend tonight, right?"

"Yes."

Great, that gives us eighteen hours. Let's go on a quick trip out of the solar system before then."

"Wait, how can you use the Lightway when you're not registered? Ships that aren't registered can't go through it."

Louie yawned. "Easy. We're not taking the Lightway."

She looked puzzled, "How can we get anywhere, that's not suborbital, without taking the lightway? Ships can't hit near-light speeds unless they're in the lightway. It's very illegal."

"Oh, Bryn, don't be such a worrier. It'll be fine." Then he shouted over his shoulder to a screen marked, *Crane*. "Hey, Crane, we're taking off for a bit. I don't think she'll be back before she has to go to the meeting."

Crane waived, "Great, have fun you two."

Louie saluted, causing his parrot to squawk and fly down the hall. "Thanks!"

With that, the far wall opened up and it revealed a rocky tunnel beyond. All of the worker robots stopped their experiments for a moment and watched as *Fat Louie* noiselessly lifted up and slipped through in the blink of an eye. The wall closed behind them leaving a large empty area in the lab where the ship had sat for the past several years.

Bryn watched the forward-facing monitor as they cleared the tunnel and the wide expanse of space lay before them. She looked to her right and saw another monitor that grew from floor-to-ceiling to give her a better view of the large, half-full, red crescent of Mars. Bryn's eyes shifted from the contrast of the bright red and green colors on the daytime side versus the peppered specks and swaths of light littering the night.

Louie broke the silence, "You're one popular chickie today."

"What? What are you talking about?"

"Here, have a look." A screen popped up in front of Bryn with a map of the immediate area. "These six ships are pretty much parked in place, just watching your house," circles wrapped around the ships in question. "These three are invisible. Also, this freighter," another circle appeared much further away, "is observing your house as well."

Bryn looked surprised, "What? That's not right. Why are they doing that?"

"I kinda sorta doubt they're well-wishers. It might have something to do with the string of attempts on your life earlier this year, but I really don't know. None of the names coming up on their registrations match any person of known nefariousness. That's still weird though for those three invisible ships as civilian-type-people aren't allowed to have a cloaking device."

"Wait, won't they see us leaving?"

"No, because I'm invisible."

"Well, if you can see them, can't they see us?"

"Heh, no. That's one of those nice things about your parents' private lab…well, *your* private lab now. Where other people are content with making an invention and calling it a day, we are constantly looking for ways to improve, improve, improve. The only way we can be seen is if we're too close to the Birkeland current at the poles of a large star, and even then we'd only be visible for a fraction of a second. Well, there's a few other ways as well, but that's a boring conversation left for a more boring time, which is most definitely not now."

Bryn seemed concerned. "Should we investigate as to why they're there?"

"I'm guessing it has something to do with your birthday and you taking over at StruseCorp. Those ships weren't there yesterday. Plus, I just ran the identification info for each of the ship's owners…they're all bogus registrations. My guess is that they're here to either just watch, or make sure you don't leave. We're going to keep on course."

"Wait, you never told me where we're going."

"Right-o, birthday girl. And I won't until we get there."

Bryn made a tiny disappointed noise at this.

"We're going to be traveling for a few hours, so why not get some sleep. You must be pretty tired."

She yawned. "Yeah, sort of, now that you mention it."

"If you go through the doorway behind you, it leads to the rest of the ship. Find the door marked *Bryn's Bedroom* and there you go."

Bryn got up out of the chair and walked to the doorway, which opened to reveal a nice bright hallway lined with pictures. She paused and said, "Thank you Fat Louie, it's been a great birthday."

He blushed, "Aw shucks Miss Bryn, it wasn't nothing. Just wait, the best has yet to come. Goodnight."

"Goodnight Louie."

Louie was right as Bryn realized how tired she was all of a sudden. Normally she would have poked around to explore the other rooms, but she walked until she found the door with the tastefully ornate sign that read *Bryn's Room*. There was also a colorful holographic banner draped across the doorway proclaiming *Happy Birthday Bryn!* with mini explosive fireworks and colored lights shining. She smiled and went in.

The room was good-sized and it was decorated so nicely that Bryn was a little surprised, and even a little weirded out since if she had a chance to decorate it herself, it would have looked almost exactly like this. She walked over to the large window and saw large boulders streaking by. Two thoughts went through her head at once: *Wow, that's really dangerous to be flying directly through the asteroid belt. That's why all ships are supposed to take the Lightway.* And, *Wait a nan...we're at the asteroid belt already? We only just left Deimos orbit. We must be going really fast to wherever we're going.*

"Hey, Louie?"

A crudely-made cardboard cutout of a screen materialized in front of Bryn, along with the entire holographic body of Fat Louie standing behind it. He peered his face through the "screen" and answered, "Yes? You called?"

"Uh…" Bryn gave him an odd glance, which continued downward to the rest of him.

Louie acted like everything was normal. "Yes?" he repeated sincerely. "Can I help you?"

"Are those bunny slippers?"

Louie's face wrinkled up in a distasteful look. "What are you talking about? No, I am not wearing bunny slippers," he said as he quickly kicked them off.

Bryn looked down at the holographic bunny slippers. The one that was lying sideways, shot the floor an annoyed look, used an ear to push itself back upright and then smiled proudly at Bryn.

"Those bunny slippers right there!" She pointed at them and one of the slippers hopped back a step.

Louie sighed melodramatically. "My goodness. *Here.* Want me to prove to you that I'm not wearing bunny slippers? Here you go." He grabbed the cardboard screen by its sides and pulled it down to his feet, as if Bryn could only see what the screen showed. When his feet came into view, she was surprised to see bright yellow cowboy boots.

Bryn scratched her head and looked around the side of the screen at his feet. They were shod in tube socks and one of the bunny slippers looked like it was trying repeatedly to hop over the other, but not getting anywhere.

Bryn started laughing and thought, *He is totally messing with my head.*

Why yes, yes I am. Replied Louie's voice inside her head.

Hey! Get out of here! And then after a stern look, *Wait, you can read thoughts?*

I'm just doing the same stuff that you and Amory use to secretly chat with each other. I happen to be privy to your frequencies because I helped to create that technology.

Does that mean anyone can pick up on our thoughts?

No, just me, Crane, and Amory...oh, and your parents, if they were around. And besides, it only works for loud, or forefront thoughts, not for the little secret thoughts, you dirty, dirty girl.

"Good to know."

Louie stood up and held the cardboard screen in front of his face again. "So, what did you call me for? I've got a ship to pilot, a birthday spectacular to plan, and I'm a very busy, busy man."

"Oh, I was just wondering where we're going."

"I told you that I'm not going to tell you that. Not until we get to where we're going. I will say that we're going to go a lot faster in a minute, when I darkline, so you may feel that delightful faster-than-light, 'Wave of Wonder.'"

Bryn asked, "We're going to be going faster than light?"

"Oh yes. In fact I need to go now and make sure we're all set for the trip. Do you need anything else?"

"No, I don't think so."

"Great, you get in bed and get some sleep, and when you wake, we'll be there. Wherever that is."

298

"Thanks." She glanced down and started laughing uncontrollably at the knee-deep pile of bunny slippers Louie was standing in.

"Yeah, that's right. You just yuk it up, Struse," and with that, he disappeared.

A few minutes later Bryn finally stopped laughing just in time to see the pinpricks of light from the visible stars elongate, rotate, and wrap up around the ship. The strands stretched wider until once they touched and the entire view was bright white, there was a brighter flash that momentarily blinded Bryn despite the best efforts of her glasses to block as much of the light as possible. When she blinked the blindness out, she entire view outside her window was black. In space there is a lot of blackness, but this was something that Bryn just never got used to. It was a complete and utter lack of light. No stars, no specks, no nothing. Only the purest of darkness can only be "seen" when traveling faster than light. It's the kind of thing that can suck someone in as they try to see something in the darkness, but never succeed. People have come back changed, or even gone mad from staring at the blackness too much while going faster-than-light.

Bryn changed into bedclothes, fresh from the StruseCreator, and climbed into bed.

Ten seconds later she was asleep.

Presents

When Bryn awoke, she sat upright and looked out the window. Thousands of pinpricks of light sat still.

Hm, we must have stopped. Bryn got out of bed, changed clothes and padded down to the bridge. Fat Louie was sitting in a chair facing some screens with his back to her. "Good morning, Louie," she said.

He spun his chair around quickly, and it rotated in place another two and three-quarters times until it faced over to one side. He frowned, put a foot on the floor and awkwardly pushed himself to face Bryn. "Good morning, although I do have a bad bit of news for you."

"Sorry, it's my birthday, bad news isn't allowed."

"Well, you'll find out anyway later today, so you can just be surprised..."

"No, just tell me now. I don't wanna be surprised by bad news."

Louie asked, "You remember Jud Astrid, right?"

"Um, yeah. He's the president of StruseCorp. What happened?"

"He kinda sorta flew his ship into Jupiter."

Bryn was confused, "Is he ok?"

Louie looked around, as if trying to think of a better way to say it, but couldn't. "Um...*yes...?*"

Bryn relaxed, "Oh good, I thought you were going to say he was d..."

Louie continued, "...if being dead is ok with you."

"What? How did it happen?"

"He flew his ship straight into Jupiter and was crushed. It had to have been a suicide because no ship would allow itself to be destroyed like that, so I'm guessing he disabled the ship computer."

Bryn sat down and stared ahead. "Wow. Why would he do that?"

"I'm sorry. I have no idea. I know he was very good friends with your parents, but I gather that you two weren't buddies."

"Yeah. I didn't know him all that well. He would check on me a few times a year, but he was really close with my parents. Wow."

Louie said, "I know you won't want to think about this now, but this means StruseCorp will need to pick a new president."

"Yeah, you're right. I don't want to think about that now." She looked out the window. "I see that we're stopped, but where are we?"

Louie was happy to have changed the subject and smiled, "Guess."

"Earth?"

"Nope, try a little closer to Saybia."

Bryn looked at him in disbelief. "We're at Saybia Station? But that's a..."

A dinging bell sounded. "And we have a winner! Yes, we're at scenic Saybia Station because we have to get your next birthday present. A door on one side of the room opened. "Oh, wait, here it is now!"

A large box measuring two meters in height, wrapped in bright green paper floated in and the door closed behind it. It came to a soft landing in front of Bryn.

Louie smiled, "Any idea what's inside?"

"Uh, no. No idea at all."

"Great!" He stared at her staring at the huge package. "Well, are you going to open it, or look at it?"

"Oh! Sorry." Bryn stepped forward and yanked on the bow. The box folded open by itself as it shot out spools of ribbon and clouds of confetti obscuring her view. When she could see the package again Amory was standing knee-deep in a pile of ribbon and confetti.

"Bryn!" Amory yelled.

"Amory!" Bryn yelled and hugged her best friend.

Louie cautioned, "Hey, be careful not to hug too tightly and break your gift. I lost the receipt so I don't think I can return her."

Amory pulled back and said, "And, I brought you a present!" She handed Bryn a festively wrapped box.

Bryn gushed, "A present within a present! This is the best day EVER!" She opened it and said, "Oh boy, half a cupcake! A big box that holds just half of a small cupcake!"

Amory smiled sheepishly, "Sorry, I ate the rest."

Bryn said, "That's ok. I bet this'll be the best cupcake ever."

Amory nodded, "They were. That's why there's only part of one left."

Louie hopped to his feet and said, "Ok, enough chatter, we've got a schedule to keep and light-years to go before we sleep."

Fat Louie lifted off from the dock at Saybia Station, turned around and sped off.

Bryn said, "Oh hey, Amory, let me introduce you to Fat Louie."

"We've actually already met, sort of."

"You have?"

Amory continued, "Yeah, he and I have been talking here and there for the past couple of months to prepare this surprise for your birthday. We picked Saybia station because it's a good stopping point between Mars and Lossia where I've been on a school field trip." She whispered, "I think he was really lonely in whatever hanger he was sitting in, because he kept going on about how annoying the other robots were."

Bryn whispered back, "I met the other robots and I can say the feeling was more than mutual."

Amory sat down in a comfy couch and asked, "So. We've got a few hours to kill. What've you been up to for the past few months?"

Fat Louie interjected, "Actually, if you don't mind, I have a better suggestion. If you'd like, I can go over the information Crane dug up about your pesky cyborg problem."

"That's putting it mildly," Bryn said. "Wait, I thought I killed it."

"Nope! You just pissed it off."

Bryn deflated, "Crap. Yeah, any information you have would be great."

Outside, the ship's darkliner extended, focused an incredible amount of energy, and pierced through the fabric of space, mainlining the incredibly potent dark energy from subspace directly into *Fat Louie's* engines. The pinpricks of starlight stretched, twisted, and they jumped to faster-than-light speed.

Fat Louie said, "We need to make a stop to Earth on the way home."

Bryn said, "Wait, that's not on the way home."

"It'll be a quick stop, I promise. I just have to destroy a certain pesky cyborg."

Amory said, "I thought no one knew where it was from."

Louie nodded, "We didn't. All year, Crane's been sending trackers out to find and follow our determined friend, but it kept either destroying, or taking control of them. Just today, Crane was finally successful in getting the location at the remains of an ancient factory in rural England but the trackers were destroyed before they could get into the computers. The thing is that the ruins of the factory have been searched several times before because that's where we knew it would have been built, but there's never been any sign of it having been there, until now."

Bryn piped up, "Maybe it just moved in?"

Louie agreed. "That's what we think. If we're lucky, it'll be home and we can end this." Fat Louie looked at Bryn, "Not unless you enjoy being kidnapped by a 200-year old cyborg, in which case I'll just leave it be."

"No, no, no, no! Please, go ahead and destroy it. I'd rather my excitement in life came from the trainer and not from a real-life killer robot."

Amory added, "Heh, or Aver."

Bryn replied, "What about Aver?"

"The trainer or Aver."

"What are you talking about?" Bryn asked.

Exasperated, Amory said, "You said, 'I'd rather the excitement in my life came from the trainer,' and I said, 'or Aver.' It was really funny when I first said it, but now, not so much."

"Oh. Yeah, that is funny."

"Speaking of the boy, what's up with him?"

"Not much. I've been about as communicative with him as I have with you."

Amory nodded.

"Hey, A, I'm really sorry. I really haven't been myself lately and I kind of retreated…"

"Bryn, you have nothing to apologize for. I knew that stuff really freaked you out and I know you had to deal with it in your own way so I gave you the space you needed and was here for you whenever you were ready."

"Thanks. You're the best."

"I know. Now let's catch up." Amory's eyes got huge, "Oh, wow! I've been dying to tell you about…"

Edition D-1.E

Hours later, they dropped out of light speed, approached Earth and entered the atmosphere

A screen opened with Crane addressing them. "You're getting close to the location. If it's there, just destroy the place, but I'm almost certain that it's in one of the cloaked ships watching the house at the moment."

Bryn asked, "It's outside our house? That's scary!"

Crane replied, "If it's here, that means it's not near you. As I was saying, if you scan the building and you don't see it, send in probes and get information. Most likely it will be alerted, so Louie, destroy the cyborg when it returns."

"Got it!"

They flew over the ruins of a long-abandoned factory that poked out from the midst of a dense forest. Fat Louie said, "No life signs, bigger than a squirrel, but

306

the building definitely has power; check out that small energy absorber on the corner of the roof. That had to have been installed recently."

Bryn said, "This place looks like a mini-NoGo."

"It kind of is. No one lives within a dozens of kilometers. This used to be a cyborg factory called Umbridge Cybernetics" A moment later he added, "There isn't a good place to land, so I'm going to put me down on the roof."

Without warning, dozens of blaster cannons fired out from among the forest. *Fat Louie*'s absorber field easily took the hits, and in a single instant, returned fire with dozens of shots, each one destroying a blaster cannon. Smoke rose from the forest.

Amory said, "I think it might know we're here."

Crane's screen re-appeared, "There it goes. It was one of the cloaked ships watching the house. I can see the energy signature, and wow, it just jumped into light speed. It doesn't seem to be trying to cover its tracks anymore, so watch out, it's coming for you. It'll take it a few minutes to get there from here."

Louie released several probes, which approached the roof and emitted a black beam of energy, creating a hole that allowed them to pass through, and sealed up behind them.

"That was awesome! What is that?" Amory asked.

"Something new developed in the workshop called a portable hole," Louie said. "I just downloaded the ability to your Tracelets."

"Thanks!" Bryn said.

Amory said, "Wow, upgradable Tracelets! That's great! We should go in and check the place out. You know, to help the probes."

Bryn was reluctant, "Oh, I don't know about that, A. I doubt they need help."

"You know, that's not a bad idea," Louie said. "The probes are reporting nothing dangerous or unusual inside. The most recent previous heat signature matching the cyborg is at least two days old, so yeah, it's safe there. And besides, I'll blast that two-bit baddie out of the sky before he's within fifty kilometers from here. Go on, you crazy kids. Have fun."

A doorway opened and Bryn and Amory stepped onto the roof. With a smidgen of apprehension, they activated the new portable hole feature just added to their Tracelets. Small, personal-sized wormholes opened, and they jumped down into the building.

The girls landed in an abandoned office, uniformly coated with several inches of dust, dirt, cobwebs, and rat nests. Disgusted, they headed out to the hallway and saw one of Louie's probes, which beeped a green light, giving them the all-clear. A probe down the hall reported that it found a room full of paper and computer files. When they got there, one probe was already connected to the ancient, long-dead computer, and downloading the information contained inside.

Amory looked bored. "Want to see what's in the other rooms?"

Bryn said, "Yeah, sure. We're not helping the probes any."

They look in another office and find a lot of nothing. It was clear that whatever happened here two hundred years ago caused the workers to leave quickly. Bryn thought it was weird that that nothing had been disturbed in the centuries that have since passed. Here and there, reddish-brown flecks radiated out like a crazy painting with the walls playing the canvas. Amory asked, "Louie? What are these spatter marks?"

He matter-of-factly replied, "Blood."

"That's gross," she said and they quickly left the room and continued in a more cautious manner.

Down the hall, the girls went into an office off of a lab room. Even though Fat Louie was sitting cloaked on the roof, he was looking through Bryn's glasses to survey each room. He said, "Whoa there Bryn. Look back to your left. Stop. Right there."

"What? What am I supposed to be looking at?"

"That folder right there. Open it. The tab on that folder said *Edition D-1.E*. The probes told me that this factory never made a cyborg model after the D-1.D."

Bryn opened the folder and took out a memory chip marked, *Edition D-1.E - Top Secret*. Her screen scanned the chip and summed up the contents: how Umbridge Cybernetics was impressed by another company's research on teleportation and how it proved the existence of the human soul because humans who were teleported essentially had their soul stripped from their relocated and reconstructed body. Umbridge Cybernetics wanted to go further by taking Teleportrex's technology and remove the consciousness (or soul) out of a person and implant it into a cyborg. They contacted a nearby prison and paid to "borrow" a death row inmate who was scheduled to die. The inmate selected was an ideal subject; physically fit, very intelligent, and a brutal killer. The trouble was that he was due to be executed before his cyborg body was completed. This is where the information files stopped and the rest was in the form of recorded voice memos and notes from the scientists who discussed what was to happen: The prison was scheduled to hold a fake execution where they would inject him with something to knock him out and make him appear dead. Umbridge then would take his body to their labs, connect him to the cyborg, and kill him. They were sixty percent sure that they would be successful in drawing the prisoner's soul into the cyborg. Their reasoning in wanting a death row inmate was because if they were wrong, it would be, "no big loss."

Amory said, "Well, that would certainly explain why it has that unfinished look."

Louie said, "There's got to be video footage of this happening. Check the labs."

The girls went down the hall and into a small room with a wide window that probably looked into a large laboratory, but the window was covered up so they couldn't see inside. They saw an old memory chip still inside the equipment and pressed play. The old screens lit up and they watched as the unconscious man was wheeled in on a gurney and parked beside an eight-foot tall cyborg with pink muscles, cords, wires, and yellow skeletal frame all visible. The voice of a scientist in a lab coat made a notation that the skin was still being grown in the vat and should be ready in another week. They spent a few minutes connecting the human to the robot and injected him with a needle. The rhythmic beeping from the life monitoring equipment attached to him slowed, stopped, and flatlined.

The scientists checked their cyborg monitoring equipment, again, and again...and again. Some were shaking their heads, one muttered "Better luck next time," and someone whispered to a co-worker on ways they could try to improve for the next trial when the red light of the cyborg's left eye blinked on. The astonished scientists crowded around the table as the right eye lit up, burst with a shower of glass, and crackled to life with electricity.

One of the scientists said, "Amazing. The neural cortex is lit up like a city, but it's not using any of the life support organs we installed. It's as if they're not needed. Odd."

Another scientist leaned over the cyborg and asked, "Hello? Are you there?"

The cyborg moved its head and surveyed the room and sat up.

The scientist pleaded, "No, don't try to get up yet."

Sitting on the edge of the table, the cyborg's large frame dwarfed the scientists, despite being slumped over. It stared down at the metal tubes and wires weaving between the exposed muscle of its arms and going into the large human-like hand. Its eyes burned brighter as one of its arms shot out and grabbed the nearest scientist by the throat, crushed it instantly with a single flex, it tossed the body across the room, smashing through a shelf, like an unwanted toy, cast aside by a giant angry toddler.

Pandemonium erupted as the rest of the scientists screamed in fear and began to run away. The cyborg stood up, and let out a deep, guttural roar; the power of which frightened Bryn and Amory enough to make them jump slightly.

One of the scientists shot the cyborg with a stun gun, to no effect. With a super-human leap, the cyborg was on top of him, did something unseen from the vantage of the camera, and then sprung onto its next kill just as quickly. Within a minute after first sitting up, the cyborg had killed a dozen scientists. Within five minutes, everyone in the complex was dead. Within an hour, the entire town.

A screen popped up in front of the girls. Fat Louie said, "It's home."

Slipped Past

The small starship dropped from light-speed in the upper atmosphere, causing a gigantic sonic boom, rolling through the countryside like a terrible thunder clap from an approaching storm. Even though *Fat Louie* was cloaked and sitting on the roof, he came under fire from the cyborg's ship even before it was within visual range. Each jagged energy beam connected, but was rendered inert by Louie's energy absorber. Annoyed, *Fat Louie* sprung up and let loose with an intense volley of blaster fire with every shot connecting on the attacking ship, which de-cloaked as it blurred by, almost as if to show that it was undamaged from *Fat Louie*'s shots.

Louie said to the girls, "It's here, and wow, it's mad. I didn't expect it to get here this quickly. Stay there in the building. I'll make quick work of this guy." To the cyborg's ship, "Oh, no, no, no. You don't impress me one bit," Louie said as he launched into pursuit, immediately catching up to the cyborg's ship fifty kilometers away.

The wedge-like ship, flipped in mid-air and shot back towards Umbridge Cybernetics. When it was above the complex, it slowed down, banked hard to the left, momentarily blocking out Louie's view of the former factory, and a row of blasters on the ship's roof fired at *Fat Louie*.

Fat Louie said, "Sorry, Mister Cyborg. This isn't getting either one of us anywhere. We both have energy absorbers, so I have to use something else a little more interesting that will actually hurt you, like this..."

Before Louie could open the wormhole he planned on using to redirect the cyborg's ship into the ground, it jumped to light speed causing a huge thunderclap rolling in its wake.

"Aw, nuts!" Louie exclaimed. "Bryn, it just flew the coop, heading directly for our house. I'm in pursuit. You guys stay put."

"Will do," Bryn replied.

Fat Louie swooped up and blurred into light speed, sending a second deafening roar across the valley.

Amory said, "Well, I guess we've got some time to explore this place some more."

Bryn swiped a finger across the top of a table and came up with a thick layer of dirt. "Or, we could clean."

They both laughed.

Amory looked down and pointed, "Hey, those look like fresh footprints. A clue! Let's follow them."

"I don't know about that," Bryn hesitated.

"Oh come on, there's nothing here. We've got probes flying all around this place and we know we're alone. Let's see where they go."

They walked down a hallway with windows on one side that looked out onto the nearby forest and the gray, drizzly afternoon beyond.

A screen popped up and Louie said, "FYI, it changed course and it's heading toward Eris. It's fast but

I'm faster so I'll be waiting for it by the time it arrives. I'm going to have George go and pick you up."

"Thanks Louie."

Amory said, "Well, that's nice of them...*him*. Ugh, I'm not used to a computer having a gender."

"*I know*, right? Oh, hey, these tracks go into this room."

They walked through a huge set of double doors and into a cavernous room filled with piles of junk.

Amory looked around and said, "You know what this place needs is a Recycler."

"I think I know someone who knows someone who might be able to make that happen." Something at the far end of the room caught Bryn's attention. "Actually, never mind. Coincidentally, there happens to be a...*really old* Recycler over there." When they got closer she said, "Holy shuck, this is one of the first commercial Struse Recyclers."

A display on Bryn's glasses showed the history of the machine, which she relayed to Amory. "This unit is supposed to be in New Mumbai...and was as recently as two weeks ago. How did it get here of all places?"

"Maybe creepy cyborg-thing brought it here for something?"

Bryn remembered something from her private tour of the Struse Museum. "Uh oh."

"What oh?"

Bryn said, "These old Recyclers..." and trailed off.

"Are what?" Amory asked. "Old?"

"No. They were a favorite of mobsters because they were made before the human protections were built into them so people couldn't be recycled into their core elements."

"What? You mean your family didn't think of adding that in *before* they created the Recycler? Geez. I'm picturing Tilden and Triton as toddlers trying to push one another into a Recycler and your grandfather saying, 'Huh, you know, we really should put a baby gate on that thing.'"

A screen from George popped up. "Bryn, Amory, I am on the roof ready to bring you home."

"Great, thanks. We're on our way." As they walked back through the building and up a stairwell, Bryn asked Amory, "What do you want to do tonight before we go to StruseCorp?"

With a grunt, they pushed open the rusted door to the roof.

"I dunno. Maybe play hide and seek with Waggles?"

"Yeah, that sounds..." Bryn looked up at *The Bryn* hovering erratically fifty meters up. "Hey George, it's going to be hard for us to get to you unless you..."

An explosion ripped half of the ship apart, sending out a powerful shockwave, which knocked Bryn and Amory off their feet.

At the same moment, a screen from Louie opened. "Get inside now! It tricked me! I'm on my way back to you!"

Bryn shook off the compression blast and leapt to her feet just in time to see the flaming wreckage of her ship crash into the forest, setting it ablaze. "NO! GEORGE!"

A nearby digitized voice croaked, "Bryn Struse, you are coming with me."

Fight

Amory swung a hand out, fingers splayed, activating the portable hole device on her new Tractlet, and opened a temporary wormhole beneath the cyborg, dropping it to the floor below. She closed her hand and the hole disappeared, leaving only the gravel and grass-covered roof of the abandoned factory looking the same as it had before its physics had been violated.

Both girls got up and looked over the edge at the wreckage of Bryn's ship.

"How?" Bryn asked. "How did it..."

The section of floor they had been standing on liquefied and drained down inside the building with both Bryn and Amory falling down. Instinct kicked in and both girls locked their Tracelets on the next floor and wormholed their way past the cyborg's level and down to the first floor. When they hit solid ground, they ran.

316

The cyborg leapt down through the hole, landed, and followed in pursuit.

Bryn's glasses showed her the view behind her where the cyborg was following. "Shuck, it's still behind us!" She ran at full speed down the long corridor and used her Tracelets to rip the wide door at the end off its hinges so she wouldn't have to stop.

The cyborg walked at a steady pace and was halfway down the hallway when Amory spun around, used her Tracelets to lift it off the ground and slammed it up and down, into the ceiling and the floor. "You...shucking...leave...her...alone...you...shucking... shuck!" She crushed it against the floor with all of her Tracelet-powered, super-nano-enhanced might.

It didn't move.

I did it! She thought. *I stopped it!*

Dropped

Amory slowly walked toward the trench coat-covered sprawled-out body on the floor.

When she was five meters away, the hand on its outstretched arm flexed, and a wave of invisible energy enveloped and lifted her off the ground.

"Shuuuuckk!"

Holding that one arm up, the cyborg rose to its feet, pulled the other arm back and swung its fist at the empty air. The Tracelet it was wearing amplified the energy of its mighty swing aimed at Amory hovering helpless in the air. The blast of energy was partially absorbed by her personal energy absorber, but it was only meant to withstand small amounts of energy, not the amplified Tracelet punch of a powerful cyborg. Amory soared backward, smashing through the large glass window, across the courtyard, and crumpled into a tree near the now raging blaze.

In the flickering fiery light, the cyborg snatched its dusty hat from the floor, put it on, and strode toward the large room at the end of the hallway to get Bryn Struse.

One Down, One to Go

Dazed, Amory thought to herself, *Oh shuck. That really hurt.* She sat up and leaned against the tree. *Oof. I never thought to use the Tracelets in that way. What a good idea. Thanks ugly cyborg guy.* She took the Tracelet off her left wrist and wrapped it to her right ankle. With pained effort, she got to her feet and, using the Tracelet on her foot, she leapt across the courtyard, through the broken window, and limped fast after the cyborg.

Ed.D1E was almost to the doorway when it heard Amory, and was turning to face her when she jumped.

Amory aimed a perfectly-placed Tracelet-powered kick at the center of its chest. The energy wave caught it in the torso and blasted it backward, through the room's open entrance, and it skidded across the floor.

Bryn, working on the controls for the Recycler, looked over in time to see the cyborg hit the far wall, and then Amory using her Tracelets to kick and punch it. "Holy shuck Amory, no! Get away from it!"

With her eyes locked on the trench-coated monster, Amory grabbed a four-meter length of solid pipe attached to the wall, and pulled it free with a strong yank. In a blur of movement, Amory vaulted high in the air, and thrust the pipe downward to impale the cyborg.

Its computer brain instantly did the math. It waited until the precise moment, rotated with her thrust, grabbed the leading end of the pipe, and swung it around like a bat, throwing Amory off, and slammed her into the wall with enough force to make the entire structure shake, creak, and release centuries-old dust clouds, which slowly lowered and enveloped them.

The cyborg hefted the pipe and threw it, like a javelin, piercing Amory's stomach, like wet paper, and pinned her body to the concrete wall. Her bulging eyes went from the cyborg to staring down in surprise and shock at the red spot spreading out from the pipe in her shirt. Amory's body convulsed with death throes.

A screen in Bryn's glasses lit up with an alert that Amory would be dead within seconds.

It turned away from Amory and walked towards Bryn.

"Bryn Struse. You are coming with me."

Raging Red

"*NNNOOOOOOO!*" Bryn screamed as the cyborg turned towards her with a smirk on its face.

Bryn ignored the cyborg and ran over to her friend, "Amory! Are you ok?"

Amory breathing was labored, "I-I'm going now buh-Bryn." She painfully coughed up a wad of blood.

Bryn, looked at the wound said, "No, you can't go!"

Amory gestured to the pipe pinning her to the wall like a butterfly to a corkboard and said. "I - I think so. Wuh-why, does it hurt so much?"

Helplessly, Bryn replied, "I don't know. Your nanos…"

"I d-don't think they're w-working. I've never felt puh-pain like this." Her knees buckled, putting stress on the pipe, which tore the hole in her torso slightly larger. Blood poured out of her body like a faucet.

322

"No. NO! AMORY! *AMORY!*"

A section of the wall near where Amory was pinned blasted inward as *Fat Louie* smashed through, sending chunks of concrete cascading across the rubble-strewn floor.

The cyborg spun around and raised a blaster when *Fat Louie* let loose with a barrage of blaster fire that flung its body a hundred yards across the length of the room, and slammed it into the far wall.

Bryn reached out to Amory but Louie warned her off. "Stay back! She's dying and I need to get her to a trauma center as quickly as possible."

The wall Amory was attached to was teleported away, along with both long ends of the pipe. For a brief moment, Amory hung in mid-air before tilting back and being pulled quickly by a tractor beam into the ship, which zipped up and out of view instantly. A fraction of a second later, while still in the atmosphere, *Louie* darklined causing a liquid ripple of sound to thunder through reality and hammer the ground. Bryn toppled over and landed in a puddle of Amory's blood.

Outside, several drones flew past in pursuit, blasters firing.

She curled up and cried. Her best friend was, for real, dying and it was so bad Louie didn't even waste the time to grab her too. *That's how bad she is.*

"AMMMOORRRRYYY!" Every muscle in Bryn's entire body strained to the tearing point with adrenaline-fueled rage.

Louie's voice appeared in Bryn's mind, *Hold out your hands, right now.*

She was still screaming. She wanted nothing more than for this *thing* to die, and didn't realize that she had obeyed Louie and was now holding her hands out. Why, she didn't know. Only that her best friend is probably dying this very moment because of this monster. The hatred overflowed just as a bright light, accompanied by a light breeze whooshed in her hands. When the light dimmed, she was holding a bulbous, rifle-looking weapon.

Concrete clattered by the far wall as the battle-scarred Ed-D1.E rose from the rubble and strode towards her; its skinless face contorting into a growing smile.

She didn't know what this weapon was, or how it got to her, but a gun has only a single purpose: destruction. Bryn pulled back on the trigger as hard as she could.

"Die! Just shucking die!"

The SunGun

The SunGun was the most complex and catastrophically dangerous weapon ever devised by humans. Amelia Struse theorized that if a heavily shielded, teleportation-equipped satellite were placed close enough to the surface of the Sun, or any star, it could teleport magnetically-charged plasma to an equally heavily shielded weapon. This weapon would be a portable mini-teleport-receiver, which would focus the plasma into a tightly woven beam with a centrifuging magnetic amplifier, and release it, to annihilate any target in front of the wielder…as well as everything behind the target for several kilometers. This gun had been the most closely guarded secret in the Struses' private laboratory with Amelia and Alva being the only people who knew of its existence, as this was the kind of ultimate personal weapon that people and governments would kill for.

When Alva asked his wife why she came up with the idea, Amelia replied that, "When considering the troubles and suffering we have previously experienced at the hands of those who wished to do us harm, I wanted to be able to not only kill, but so totally annihilate any enemy that dared to threaten our family there would be nothing left save for the nightmarish legends of what would happen when you shuck with the Struses." She never had a chance to finish the SunGun before their disappearance, but in their absence, Crane directed the Workshop to complete her vision for the most destructive personal weapon ever. A weapon that had never been tested.

Until now.

When Bryn's finger activated the gun, it verified her DNA, cross-checked to see if her nanos were present and in good health, fired up an intensely powerful multi-fielded force shield/energy absorber around Bryn, and sent a compressed, faster than light, message to the satellite in close orbit around the Sun. The satellite verified the information, the intensity setting and flow rate of the weapon, and measured the temperature, radiation, magnetic imbalance, pressure differential, and other pertinent conditions of the Sun. The teleportation gate opened and beamed the stream of solar plasma to the SunGun's chamber, which amplified, focused, torqued, and released the star's energy.

For half a second, Bryn though something was wrong, that this gun-thing didn't work apart from the crazy force field that radiated around her. She could tell that the cyborg was thinking the same thing as it paused slightly when the protective aura surrounded her.

The barrel of the gun glowed with an intensity and fury never before witnessed by human eyes. The cyborg started to leap to one side as the eternally burning, hellish fire of the Sun erupted out of the gun, spraying the magnetically-charged, screaming plasmatic braids of pure, hot, blinding death across the room.

326

The gun kicked hard and the deafening magnetic roar of solar wrath shook the ground with the energy transference, causing Bryn to momentarily lose control, shooting the stream of the Sun's surface up and to the right. She had to fight hard to pull the stream to the left, back where she remembered the cyborg being last. After what seemed like a forever moment later, she released the trigger.

The shock of the instant muffled silence was just as jarring as the blasting sound of the Sun. Despite her glasses darkening to block the Sun's light, she fought to blink away the white blobs that floated in her vision. Soon, she was able to see the damage that the SunGun wrought. The floor in the center of the large room had been transformed into a molten trench and what remained was either burning or melting. The wall to the right was missing, as was the roof, the nearby hill, and kilometers of nearby forest, which had exploded into a raging wall of flame.

A scraping noise grabbed her attention.

She sniffed and lifted her head out of the debris. *What was that?*

Nothing.

Shuck, now I'm hearing things…

Movement. Her eyes caught something crawling on the floor, under a pile of molten rubble.

Terrified that it was somehow *still* alive, she raised the gun.

A nearby pile of debris burst upward as the charred legless body of the cyborg floated free, rising from the ash. The SunGun had vaporized everything from the waist down as it had leapt to try and avoid the blast, leaving a melted metal spinal column and ribcage.

"Bryn Struse. You are coming with me."

Bryn let the SunGun decline its offer for her and hit the trigger.

She swung the Sun's energy blast back at the cyborg for a half a second. It dropped at the first indication that she would be firing again and this time only the top part of its head was skimmed with the lowest edge of the beam. Its hat was vaporized, along with the top dome of its head and another section of the building. The electro-tissue of its brain inside burst into flames, but there it was, somehow still alive, laughing a hideous evil laugh at them like a mad, partially melted, unfinished, beat-to-hell phantom.

Bryn dropped the SunGun and swung out her fist, engaging her Tracelets, and sent out a powerfully angry, and fear-fueled blast of nano-fueled super strength Tracelet energy.

The flaming remains of the cyborg was blown back, spinning through the air, where it slammed hard into the edge of the Struse Recycler. It swung out an arm, catching the side, and clawed desperately at the metal frame. Its other arm and remnants of its spine hit the consuming vortex of the Recycler and began to vaporize.

It struggled to hold on as it croaked, "Must bring Bryn Struse to Wrathwoo-"

Its metallic voice was cut short as it was torn to shreds, with those shreds being molecularly separated into its component elements. Its severed, and finally dead, arm could no longer fight the pull of gravity and fell with a clunk to the floor.

Bryn activated her Tracelet and flicked the arm into the Recycler where it was destroyed.

She stared at the Recycler, almost out of fear that it would somehow find a way to climb out and come after her. But a minute later, it was still gone and the only sound, apart from the whirring of the Recycler, was the occasional clunking of debris falling from the destroyed building.

Bryn immediately opened a screen, "Louie…" She braced herself for the worst, "What's going on? Is Amory…"

"Alive? Yes."

Bryn's knees buckled and she sat heavily on a chunk of concrete. "Oh, thank Source. Oh wow."

Louie said, "It was close. Another few seconds and she would have died. She has been stabilized and is recovering quickly. I'm on my way to pick you up now. Oh, and Bryn?"

"Yes?"

"Good job. You did it."

"Is all of this really over?"

"Yes. It's over."

"Thank you." Bryn slashed out the screen and all of the emotions hit her at once. She sat there sobbing with gratitude until Louie arrived.

What the Watcher Sees

DoopDoop

Bonna was sitting at a desk with her chin resting in her hand when the screen popped up. She thought about not answering it, until she saw the call was coming from one of her cloaked ships stationed outside the Struse house. She stabbed a finger at the screen to answer it. "Calling with news?"

A short bearded man nodded and said, "Yes, indeed. See this clip I just got. It's a good one."

The screen split and showed Bryn's house as it sat on the large asteroid. One side was bathed in light, while the other was shrouded in darkness. A moment later, a ship entered the scene and went into the asteroid through an opening that appeared and closed after the ship was inside. A few minutes later, the camera zoomed in on the large living room window and two girls were now visible on the upper level.

The man said, "It looks like she has a female visitor. I'm guessing they'll be there for a while, at least."

Bonna smiled. "Thank you, Nestor. Good work. Keep an eye on them and let me know if they try to leave.

"Yes, sir," and the connection ended.

Good, good, good. If that's her friend, Amory, that means they're probably not going anywhere since they haven't seen each other in months, especially not to some boring general meeting for StruseCorp. Her smile grew. *It looks like we're in the clear.*

She whistled a happy ditty as she thumbed open a new screen.

Follow Up

StruseCorp Executive Vice President, Dave Dagenham walked down the hallway with a serious look on his face. He stopped outside a door marked *Lig Fallo - Director of Interns*, made sure his expensive suit was perfect, as always, and entered.

Lig knew someone had walked in, but didn't know who yet. "Yeah, what d'ya want?" he said from behind the wall of screens.

Dagenham just stood there, not saying anything.

Lig, annoyed, pushed some of the screens over and started to yell, "Do I need to repeat my-" he saw the Executive Vice President of the company standing in his office and immediately shrunk back. "Oh! I-I'm sorry Mr. Dagenham. I didn't know it was you." He thought, *What's he doing here? He never leaves the executive offices and he has never been down here once. Ever. Oh, this can't be good.*

Dagenham's steel gray eyes seemed to burrow straight through Lig. "Mr. Fallo, I need to know about one of your interns, Linna Meekins. Is she here today?"

Lig was surprised. "Uh, yeah, of course she's here." His hands fumbled with the screens and a few of them floated off in different directions. "Here she is, right here. She hasn't missed a day in nearly two years." He spun a screen around showing an average-looking girl taking a stack of screens and pushing them into a larger screen."

The Vice President asked, "What is she doing?"

"Hm, let's see...she's getting the company reports ready for tonight's company meeting. Did she do something wrong?"

Dagenham looked at Lig with an unreadable look. "As far as I can tell, not yet." He started for the door. "Thank you for your time," and left.

Lig breathed a heavy sigh of relief. He stabbed at the screen for Linna and barked, "Linna, call me."

DoopDoop

A new screen appeared with Linna's face on it. "You rang?"

"What did you do to Vice President Dagenham?"

She looked surprised. "Uh, nothing. Why?"

"He was just here asking about you and I assumed you did something to anger him."

"No sir. I don't think I've ever met the guy."

Lig said, "Well, today's your lucky day because I think he's on his way down there to see you."

Linna looked excited, "Does this mean I'm getting a promotion?"

"Doubtful. This guy never promotes, only fires, so watch out. I don't want to lose an intern an hour before the graduation ceremony."

"Good to know. Thanks."

Lig slashed out a finger, shook his head, and hunkered down again behind his wall of screens.

False Lead

Dagenham went to his office, paused to wipe a mote of dust off his nameplate (*Dr. Dave Dagenham - Executive Vice President*), and closed the door. He opened a screen and a moment later a weaseled-looking man appeared. "Oh! Hello, Dr. D. Yer prob'ly wonderin' 'bout the girl."

"Yes I am. Is she still there?"

"Yup, she's still there. Al'do there's a'nudder girl there now. She arriv'd early'r t'day."

"Good. Let me know immediately if anything changes."

"You k'n bet on that, sir."

Dagenham slashed out the screen and held his hands over a small sonic purifier, as if to clean any perceived dirt from dealing with such a filthy individual.

A screen popped up with a pleasant chime. It was a reminder that the annual StruseCorp meeting started in twenty minutes.

He sighed heavily. *Maybe we were wrong about Linna. If Bryn is still at her house, and Linna is here, there's no way it can be her. I don't know who else it could be...unless that rumor was false to begin with.* His anger started to build up. *Which means we wasted a lot of time trailing a false lead.* He breathed deeply, exhaled, and left his office, heading down to the amphitheater.

Come Back to Wrathwood

An hour after the last of the Solar Union Navy's investigation ships departed, the Sun's final rays of the evening radiated a pretty pinkly hue on the abandoned factory that once housed the Umbridge Cybernetics complex. The nondescript starship circled over the nearby hillside, which still glowed as the bedrock, exposed and liquefied by the SunGun, started to slowly solidify, and landed by the melted ruins of the factory.

Minutes later, a standard-height man, in average clothing, wearing a noticeably serious look, stepped from the ship and walked toward the rubble. A fist-sized ball of light hovered silently over his head, illuminating his path as he maneuvered through a huge hole in the wall.

After spending an hour in the main computer room reviewing camera feeds of the day's action from different angles, he visited each site where the girls battled, pointed out scuffs in the floors, holes and burns in the walls, and

337

other damage. The light orb duly noted and recorded everything.

Armed with the information of what took place, he thumbed open a screen, and tapped a name. A secure transmission screen popped up and he spoke his name, "Kale Maggen." A light flashed green and he was connected with a red-headed man in his thirties who also wore a serious look.

"Give me the news, Kale. It's bad isn't it."

Kale nodded, "Yes, sir. The cyborg is gone. It was hit with some kind of crazy powerful weapon, which also blasted through nearby mountaintops going about ten kilometers out. The cyborg was still alive and trying to carry out the mission, but she finally killed it by pushing it into a Recycler."

The red-headed man, clearly upset, chuckled briefly to himself as if he somehow knew that would be the outcome. "*Of course* she did." He stared off-camera for a moment. "Kale, why don't you come back to Wrathwood."

"But sir, shouldn't I try and complete the mission?"

"Be realistic. If the cyborg, with over two hundred years of bounty hunting experience, never once failing, until now, couldn't get her, I don't think you'll be able to. No offense."

"None taken."

"No, come back to Wrathwood, I need you here. I've got a good back-up idea, which has already been set into motion. I'm going to need your help with it. If getting Bryn by force didn't work, let's try luring her with something that I know she can't possibly resist."

Kale said, "I can't wait to hear it, Tilden. I'm on my way back now."

"Good," he nodded. "Struse out."

Surprise

Vice President Dagenham arrived at the amphitheater and saw the interns passing out company reports at the door. He made sure to get in line where Linna was. A moment later she handed him a screen and said, "Here you go, sir," with a smile, just like she did for everyone else. He nodded, entered the mostly full auditorium, and went through a side door to bring him backstage where he chatted quietly with Schanna Fife.

At exactly the right time, Dagenham stepped onto the stage and the light music that had been playing quieted down along with the conversational hum of the audience and the house lights.

"Hello and thank you for coming to the annual StruseCorp company meeting. Before we begin, I'd like to first talk about the tragic event that happened yesterday. I know you all received my memo this morning regarding the death of StruseCorp President, Jud Astrid, but I wanted to say a few words about him. Jud was not only a good friend to the Struse family, and myself, but also to many of you as well. He was well-known for his generosity. He was a man would crush you with kindness, and was helpful to a fault. His smiling face will be deeply missed around these halls. Let's have a moment of silence in his memory."

He bowed his head and everyone was silent. A few seconds later, he raised his head and looked at the crowd. "Again, welcome to the annual StruseCorp company meeting. Every year, the Struse family would have the company meeting on the same night as the holiday party, probably so there would be something fun to balance out the boring meeting part. Let's face it, talking about numbers and figures can be a little dry. However, on this night eighteen years ago, the meeting was a little more lively than usual as Amelia Struse, demonstrating her consistent fortitude and dedication, brought her newborn daughter, only hours old, to the company meeting." On the screen behind him, it showed a woman with long, red hair holding a bundle with a tiny face poking out.

Dagenham turned to look at the screen. "What a trooper Amelia was." He turned back to the thousands of employees before him. "She made it to the meeting, and so did little Bryn. Well, Bryn's all grown up now, and she turned eighteen today." The crowd clapped and he smiled until it died down. "Yes, yes, it seems just like yesterday when baby Bryn was first introduced here and as of today, she is now the owner of StruseCorp. Unfortunately, in light of recent events, Bryn is unable to make it tonight, but she can be rest assured that no matter what, her company, the largest and best in the Solar Union, is being run smoothly and I will take it into the 26th century and beyond at faster than light speed."

The crowd clapped loudly, which quickly turned to a standing ovation with whistling, hooting, and the audience just going crazy.

Dagenham was taken aback. *Wow, I knew I'd get some claps there, but everyone seems so happy. Wow. Things just got a whole lot easier for us. This is great!*

As he raised his arms triumphantly, he noticed that the crowd's attention was not directed at him, but at something behind him. He turned and his smile dropped like lead.

Bryn Struse walked on stage.

The anger billowed up inside Dagenham as he stared at her. *She's supposed to be at home right now. No, no, NO. I was told she was at home right now. What the shuck is going on? Someone's going to pay for this.*

Bryn stepped forward and her words boomed through the speaker system. "Sorry, I'm late, did I miss anything?"

The crowd went wild.

The group of interns, including Linna, came out from the other side of the stage pushing a huge floating birthday cake that said *Happy 18th birthday Bryn!* while singing,

Have a hap-hap-happy birthday
Because today's your special day
All of us here wanted to say
Have a happy Bryn-day today!

Bryn looked a little embarrassed and blushed. "Aw, come on. You shouldn't have." She ate the cake and said, "This looks good. Please, dig in. There's plenty for everyone." The interns began to distribute slices to everyone in the audience.

Dagenham was trying to be careful not to betray any emotions, but his eyes told a different story as they glared and burned with a deep rage. *This was all pre-planned. The cake, the singing, the lighting...all of this. I should have known about this. My people should have discovered and shut it down before it got anywhere. Why didn't I know?*

Linna walked up to him, standing at the side of the stage, and said, "Mr. Dagenham, would you like some cake?"

He mustered as much pleasantries as possible and accepted the cake. "Thank you, Linna."

"Thank you. You really are too much. Thank you." Bryn said. She cut the cake, and the interns used Tracelets to send pieces flying off to everyone in the crowd. Peppy music started up while the cake was being distributed. After a few minutes Bryn looked around. "Does everyone have a piece? Yes? No? Ok, my turn." and she took a piece from the decimated sheet cake. "This is really good, thank you."

After a couple of bites, she sat down on the edge of a table and said, "I hope you don't mind, but I'm going to talk a bit while I'm eating. I know its technically bad etiquette, but I've had a hell of a day."

The crowd settled down and all eyes remained stuck to the new owner of StruseCorp.

"Actually, it's been a hell of a year, but the past day or two really takes the cake." She laughed and held up her piece of cake. "No pun intended." She became serious and continued, "First, I am heartbroken over the death of Jud. He did a great job of running things in the years since my parents went missing. I know I can't be the only one who finds it suspicious that his ship crashed into Jupiter and I will do everything in my power to press the Solar Union to investigate the circumstances of what happened. It's not normal and we will find out what really caused his death."

Dagenham's eyes narrowed at Bryn.

Bryn took a bite of cake, thought for a moment, and said, "Along the same vein, I am not naïve when it comes to the responsibility that now rests on my shoulders. Yes, I now own the largest company in the Solar Union, which means that at the next election in 2494, I alone have the ability to appoint the majority of politicians. While Jud did a good job with our company, I feel that his political choices have strayed too far from what my parents and myself would have voted for. Needless to say, there will be big changes starting in 2495 when the new politicians take office."

Dagenham's fists clenched.

Bryn set down her empty plate and said, "That was a great cake. Thank you again. Where was I? Oh, yes, changes. I know change can be scary, but I think some of the ideas I've come up with will be best not only for you and I, StruseCorp in general, but for all of society. I want to work on lowering prices of elements for everyone, and to help increase monthly element allowances for all Basics."

A big round of applause swept the amphitheater.

"There will be more changes, most of which will be presented to the employees so I can get your feedback. I'm just one person with ideas, but there are over ten thousand of you who work here who also have ideas that will be even better than mine. Together, we're going to make things better."

Bryn looked over and caught a glimpse of the horror on Dagenham's face. She chuckled to herself before saying, "You may be sitting there and wondering to yourself, 'Who does this kid think she is? She doesn't know what we do here. She hasn't worked a day in her life. Just because her name is on the building doesn't give her the automatic right to step in and change things.' Well, if you're thinking that, you're wrong. Truth, finally, be told, I've worked at StruseCorp almost every day for the past two years."

A murmur ran through the auditorium.

"I've worked along-side each and every one of you. I've talked with all of you about your fears, your dreams, your frustrations, what you love about working here, what you hate, and what needs to be changed to make our company run better. I've shared those tough workdays; the good, the bad, the everything with all of you. Instead of being compartmentalized, I've worked in every department. I've done work that no one wants to do. The kind of stuff that we normally have drones do. Why? Well, I've always thought that many of you must have seen through my disguise and purposely enjoyed giving me the crap jobs, but mostly because I can't run this company from the top, if I haven't experienced it from the bottom. I can tell you that I've worked hard. I've proven myself time and time again. And, I am the one person in this room who can do anything at StruseCorp, so I believe that gives me the right to say, 'Hey, let's make some changes for the better.' So, I hope you're all on board as I put my experiences, combined with your input, into action as we inject this company with new life and ideas. Thank you for your time, and goodness, please thank whichever StruseCreator made this cake!"

She stood up to a cheering crowd that was on its feet, applauding loudly.

Unexpected Appointment

After spending an hour greeting people in the lobby outside the auditorium, a screen opened up with an incoming message for Bryn. Olympia, the executive assistant said, "Bryn, you have a video call appointment in your office."

She asked, "Really? I didn't think I had any appointments yet."

Olympia looked worried. "Yes you do. This, 'gentleman' made his appointment to see you exactly five years ago today."

It was like someone threw a bucket of ice water over Bryn's head. Apart from being her birthday, it was also the anniversary of the most tragic day in her life. Five years ago today, her parents disappeared.

"Bryn? What should I tell him?"

"I, uh...I'll be right up."

She wove her way through the remainder of the crowd, through the smiles and pats on the back, and headed up to the executive offices. In the outer office, Olympia was standing there still wearing the worried look. "I'm sorry, I thought it must have been a joke or something. I mean, who makes an appointment five years in advance with a kid?"

Bryn asked, "Who is it?"

Olympia gestured toward Amelia' old office. "Danny Incubo."

Bryn stopped, "You mean Incubo as in the Incubo crime family?"

"I don't know, do you want me to ask him?" Her worried look intensified. "Oh, please don't ask me to ask him that."

"No, but please just keep an eye on things."

Nervously, Bryn walked into the office belonging to her mother. A hologram of a tall man with slicked-back black hair, and an expensive, but slightly-too-large suit, stood when she entered the room and nodded at her. "Good evening, Bryn. It's nice to meet you. I'm Danny Incubo."

Bryn sat down. *This is so weird to be sitting at my mom's desk. It's so big.* "How can I help you, Danny?"

"I sure hope you can help, Bryn. You see, we've got some important things that need straightening out between your company and my family."

Bryn asked, "If these things are important, then why didn't you discuss them with our president?"

He smiled, "Mr. Astrid? I'm sorry, but it's somewhat difficult to talk to the dead. That's why we wanted to talk to you."

"You made this appointment five years ago. Why would you do that?"

He shrugged and his large shoulders moved like the rolling pistons of a machine under his large suit jacket. "Because your parents were dead. Once again, it's awfully hard to talk to the dead, so we chose to make an appointment with the next most important person, and that's you."

Bryn wanted this over as soon as possible so she cut straight to the point. "What do you want?"

"Simple. We want the landfills back that your grandfather swindled from us, plus a fair share of any profits derived from the use of those landfills."

Bryn's anger leapt out of her. "What? Are you nuts? First of all, any deal our ancestors engaged in is between them and has nothing to do with either you or I. Secondly, the sale of your family's landfills was perfectly legal and I believe I've even seen a clip where someone in your family said the Struses were 'suckers' for buying the landfills. And now you want the land back and the money we made from cleaning them up with our recyclers? No way."

Incubo frowned, smoothed a crease on his pants and shrugged. "You know, that's a shame. A real shame. Because you're new around here, I'll give you a month to think about my offer." He stood up.

"What offer? You demanded I give you money and land in exchange for nothing. What kind of offer is that?"

"One that a wise person would take. It would be terrible if we had to make an appointment with someone else because you were...*difficult* to talk to." He tipped his hat at her. "Good day, Bryn. It was nice to meet you," and vanished.

Staring down the hall, Olympia came into the room. "What'd he want?"

Bryn shook her head. "Everything."

Ready To Go

After wishing Olympia a goodnight, Bryn thumbed open a screen and Crane appeared. "How's Amory? Is she doing better?"

"Since your last call ten minutes ago? Yes, actually."

"Is she going to be ok?"

Crane smiled, "Do you mean ok in general, or ok enough to go to your birthday party at home tonight?"

Bryn laughed, "Mostly the latter."

"Yes. She will be there. Louie picked her up from the hospital and dropped her off here a few minutes ago. The extra healing nanos they gave her are doing their job and she'll be back to normal within a day or two. He's on his way out to pick you and Aver up, so be ready."

"Let him know I might be a few minutes late, wait a second. Aver? He's not here, is he?"

Crane said, "Really? Who do you think has been pretending to be Linna while you were depressed and not going to StruseCorp for all those months? We had to keep up appearances somehow and Aver was wonderful to volunteer and help out."

Shocked, Bryn managed to say, "Whaaaaaaaaaaaat?" to Crane. "I...I saw Linna earlier and wondered how you did that. Wow."

"And I've also been putting holograms of you and Amory in the window so the people watching the house would think you're home when you're not."

"That's such a great idea."

Just then, Linna walked into the executive offices, closed the door, swiped a screen, and changed into Aver.

Bryn continued, "Whaaaaat?" to Aver and gave him a big hug.

"Hi, Bryn."

"Thank you so, so, so much for what you've done. That was a huge help, thank you."

"No problem. It's been fun, actually. I learned a lot, but I am pretty happy about not having to do it again and get a chance to just be myself."

"You're a hero to me."

"Uh, *you're* the hero. Crane showed me footage of what happened today. That was insane."

"It was super scary and I was terrified for most of the time."

"Well, you killed that thing for good. You are one scary shucker when you're pissed off. You're also one really brave woman. Ready to go?"

Bryn said, "Thank you and yes, but I need to kill one last monster first."

She opened a screen and called up Dave Dagenham.

"This is Dr. Dagenham. Hello, Bryn, what can I do for you?"

"Hi, Dave. You can resign."

"Uh, excuse me? *What?*"

"You asked what you can do for me. I want you to resign."

"You spoiled brat, how dare you? I will do no such thing," he spat.

"Well, Dave, you have two choices. You can resign and save face while collecting your large severance package, or you can stay and be investigated for the exceedingly long list of violations against our corporate code of conduct you've racked up while here." She smiled. "Your choice."

He glared at her. "Fine. Bryn Goddamn Shucking Struse, I hereby resign my position at StruseCorp effective immediately. I hope you're happy, you little witch."

"Very. Thank you, goodbye, and goodnight." Bryn swiped off the screen and turned to Aver, "Done!"

As they walked to the shiplot, Aver asked, "Oh, wow! What did Dagenham do?"

Bryn shrugged, "Nothing that I'm aware of, but I assumed a total jerk like that would have been up to no good for years, and it turns out I was right. Anyway, enough about him. It's my birthday, it's New Year's Eve, the cyborg's gone, and Amory is alive and healing nicely. We've got a lot of reasons to celebrate."

"Yeah!" Aver said. "Let's get out of here and have fun!"

End of the Year

Two hours later, Bryn, Amory, Teb, and Aver were having a festive gathering in Bryn's two-story living room. Waggles happily galloped around with a holographic banner saying, *2493* on one side, and *Happy New Year!* on the other. Music was playing in the background while the friends, hanging out in the upper and lower living rooms, tried to decide where to be at midnight; a louder, public New Year's celebration in the tube room – someplace like Mount Olympus, or if they should go with a quieter backyard party and shoot off fireworks and have a light show with help from Crane.

    Doopdoop

    Aver pointed to the screen which popped up in front of Bryn. "Hey, Bryn, you've got a call there."

    She hit the ignore button and said, "Ha! No I don't."

A minute later another screen popped up along with another incoming call. On the side screen, it was Crane. They said, "Bryn, I think you need to take this one, and I'd suggest privacy when you do."

Bryn gave a sigh of annoyance and said, "Sorry, I've got to take this one. I'll be right back. You guys vote on what you want to do at midnight without me." She leaned over the balcony she was sitting on and mouthed, *Be back in a minute* to a heavily-bandaged Amory who responded with a sympathetic look and a thumbs-up.

Amory thought back, *Don't worry, I'll have the guys get our celebration stuff ready while you're gone.*

As Bryn headed to the quiet and sanctity of the library, she pulled up the screen and hit the *Please Hold* button. After entering, she closed the oversized doors, walked across the shelf-filled room, and leaned against a long wooden table. With a deep breath and a nervous finger, she swiped open the screen and poked the *Answer* button.

The sketchy-looking, blond-haired man on the screen smiled. His sharp facial features were almost weasel-like in appearance and from behind squinted eyes said, "Bryn Struse. You're a hard girl to get in touch with. Are you finally able to talk now? I've been playing message tag quite a bit today with your butler, and...oh hey, are those actual books? Heh, of course they are. You're the richest girl ever. Of course you own real books, probably the paper kind too."

She glared at him with zero expression on her face and said nothing.

"Oh, what's wrong? Isn't tonight a night of celebration? You should be so happy that I've dropped into your realm of existence. What I know will completely change your life."

Impatient and wanting to be done with this guy as soon as possible, Bryn said, "You said you had information on my parents. What do you know?"

His face contorted to a slick smile. "A whole lot more than you do, which is why my fee is so steep. Good knowledge like this don't come cheap."

"How would someone like you know anything about what happened to them? They didn't even know you."

"True that. Not me directly, but let's say I work for someone who knew them very well. So well, in fact, that this person was there when their experiment went down, or, should I say, went wrong. There's even a video. It's the very last video of your parents before they disappeared. That's gotta be worth a whole lot, to you. Heh, it'd be worth a lot to most anyone. I bet Turdox News would make me super rich for it and they don't even have nearly the vested interest that you do in the subject."

Exasperated, Bryn said, "Why can't you tell me right now? I'll forward the money to your account when you give me the information?"

He laughed. "No, no, no, no. It doesn't work that way. I'm sure you'd have the authorities all over me in minutes. Besides, I'm willing to sell you this information at considerable risk to my own life. If my boss knew about this? Forget it. Myself, and everyone I know would be killed straight away. This is big stuff. This is how it'll happen. You meet me in person, on a nice middle ground, let's say Wrathwood, you give me the money, and I give you everything you've been wanting to know."

She thought, *Wrathwood, what the shuck is it with that place?* "No," Bryn said firmly. "I don't even know your name. And besides, I won't go to the Fringe. It's entirely too far. I mean, it would take weeks to get there."

"Well, I won't go to the Central Solar Union, so we've got ourselves a dilemma. You see, I don't need your money so much, since I can sell it to just about anyone and still be rich beyond my wildest dreams. But you, on the other hand, desperately need this. It's the kind of thing that'll gnaw at your heart like a starving rat for the rest of your life if you don't go through with it."

Bryn stoically stared at him with her arms folded across her chest and said nothing.

"Suit yourself." He leaned forward to shut off the connection. "Have a good life not knowing."

"Wait."

He paused with his arm still outstretched, smiling widely.

Bryn acquiesced. "Ok. Fine. Give me the details for when and where we're meeting."

He leaned back and his big mouth broadened into a smile so big it looked like it would almost touch the wrinkles at the edges of his eyes if it were stretched any further. "I'm glad you've decided to do the rational thing. Many questions will be answered."

"They'd better be."

"I'll contact you with the exact time and location later. I'm doing this with great personal risk to myself and I want this settled as soon as possible, so keep your calendar open for the first part of the year. Plus, you've been waiting five years for this, so I figured you would want your answers right away."

"Fine, whatever."

"I'll be in touch. Have a happy New Year. It'll be an interesting one for you, that much I know. Oh, and the name is Glim." He leaned in and ended the connection.

Bryn stared at the blank screen. "Thanks."

The mix of emotions was hard for Bryn. This was something she needed to know, but at the same time, she didn't trust this guy; and 50 billion credits was an extraordinary amount of money, especially for information that could be fake.

I'd give anything to see my parents again. A billion, a trillion. I don't care. It's just money. It doesn't mean anything…not like a hug, or to have family to feel close to once again. This emptiness has gone on too long in my life and I'll take this tiny chance, no matter how rickety it may seem, just for the slimmest of possibilities that I'll see them alive again. Or dead. They could be dead, but if they are, I need to know that so I can move on. Who just disappears? No one. They're either alive, and if so I need to find them, or they're dead and I need to bury them, physically and emotionally. Whichever way, I just need an answer.

One thing that kept nagging the back of her mind was Wrathwood. *Why that planet again? First with the cyborg, and now this guy? What a shucking day.*

Bryn wiped away a tear that was crawling down her cheek, sniffed, and composed herself before turning around and heading out of the library. When she got to the upper living room Teb said, "Hey, Bryn, we, I mean Amory, made a decision on what to do for the New Year...are you ok?"

Bryn's sleeve caught the last stray tear that had sneaked out since she thought she was all set. "Oh yeah, I'm great," she lied. "What're we doing?"

From downstairs, Aver said, "We're gonna do the backyard thing. Crane said that Dr. Waggles loves catching snowballs, and we really want to see that."

Amory said, "Good thing, since there's only half an hour left!"

Waggles jumped up, "Bak! Bak!"

Everyone laughed, and Bryn felt relief flooding back in which pushed out the worries on her mind. *Tonight I can feel normal again.*

From downstairs, Amory thought to Bryn, *Hey, B. You ok?*

Yeah. I'll tell you about it later. Let's have some fun and enjoy what's left of the year.

Agreed.

Bryn peered over the railing to smile at her best friend and was greeted with a pillow hitting her squarely in the face.

"Oof!"

"Pillow fight!"

In between volleys, Amory protested, "Don't hit my bandages! I'm still healing!" and "Go easy on me, I nearly died today!"

Everyone started tossing pillows at each other, but soon it devolved into people using their Tracelets and flinging the pillows at each other at much higher speeds.

They went outside and threw snowballs for Waggles and watched as Crane set up a big countdown clock projected on a large sheet strung between two trees. Little white lights were strung everywhere as flakes of snow gently swayed down the cloudy night sky above.

Teb said, "Wow, this looks magical."

The group of them got together and said things like, "Goodbye 2492!" and "Make a wish for 2493!"

"Four!"

"Three!"

"Two!"

"One!"

As the last seconds dripped out of 2492, the light and fireworks show started into motion. Just as this memorable year started with a single moment, so it ended. For a short time, all of the problems of the past and the future were left in their respective places as the group of smiling friends were firmly in the present and joyously yelled, "HAPPY NEW YEAR!"

2492: Attack Of The Ancient Cyborg

Afterward

Holy wow. Wow, wow, wow.

For a very long time it seemed like I would never be *here*, at the end of this book. *2492* has been the BIG THING in my life and it has occupied a huge portion of my daily thinking space and time since I came up with this story back when I was 13 years old. I've spent the ensuing 30 years tinkering around with it in one form or another. The story itself ballooned up to over 500 pages and that's when it started to feel like my albatross – the impossible project that I would always be re-writing and re-editing until the day I died.

It was so unwieldy that I even conceptualized, wrote, edited, and published another novel, *Emily Dickinson, Superhero – Vol. 1* (as well as seven poetry collections) while working on this book. For the longest time it seemed like *2492* would never see the light of day. In my mind it was (to borrow a phrase), "too much tuna," and had turned from something I loved to dive into, to a huge monster I dreaded to confront.

The Universe, however, would not let me forget *2492*. Several times a week (at least), I would see the numbers 2492 in some way, shape, or form; whether they be in license plates, addresses, or financial reports at work. I honestly could not escape *2492*. Those numbers kept popping up *everywhere*. One day, while driving home from work, I was trying to decide what my writing project would be: if I wanted to continue slogging through editing *2492* or start writing my unpublished chick-lit series. In my mind it would be easier to just start something new than go back and try to chip away at *2492*.

I was in a weird mood, so I said aloud, "Ok, Universe, send me some kind of a sign as to which writing project I should be working on," not seriously expecting any kind real sign.

Scouts honor, *at that very same moment*, a car passed me on the left with the license plate of 492ENX – basically "2492 Eric Nixon" but crammed into six characters. That was too much of a coincidence and it wasn't the only one. Those four numbers, in that order, have appeared constantly and consistently in my life as a repeated reminder from the Universe to get working on this book.

In late 2016 I looked over the seemingly endless *Stuff I Need To Do In 2492*-Word document and thought, *Huh. If I spent a good solid week doing nothing but editing the book full-time, it would be in good enough shape to send to test readers.* As luck would have it, I had one week of vacation I needed to use before the end of the year, so I blocked a week off on the calendar and got to work. At the end of that week, *2492* was in great shape. A few weeks later my test readers sent me their suggestions, I made some edits, and *poof* the albatross had been captured, tamed, and transmogrified into a sassy-assed peacock.

Seeing the physical proof edition of *2492* for the first time totally blew my mind. It was the culmination of my creative life's work there in my hands. I wished I could have gone back thirty years to my newly teenaged self, shown the book to me, and said, "We did it."

Reading the physical book also did something else for me – it reinvigorated my love for writing. It showed me the end result of my thousands of hours of lonely, solitary work; that the effort is totally worth it.

I'm sure I'll be writing many more novels since I've been blessed with the ability to come up with story ideas faster than I can write them, but this one, the one you just read, will always hold the most special place in my heart. Thank you for reading it and sharing in my joy.

Onward to *2493*!

August 29, 2017
Galena, Illinois

Acknowledgements and Thanks

I would like to thank the following people for their help in making this book a reality:

Kari Chapin – my wife and biggest source of encouragement. Writing is an intensely solitary endeavor and I sincerely thank you for the thousands of hours of loneliness you endured while I wrote. Then again, you spent most of it watching all the iterations of the *Housewives* so you would probably classify it as a win-win. Anyway, thank you.

Todd Nixon – my brother, test-reader, and proof-reader. Writing a novel is like building an intricate walkway through the forest; you spend 99% of your time focused on the tiny details and tend to lose sight of the bigger picture. You helped me to focus in on the big stuff while also catching typos like a boss. Thank you!

Sharon Jandrow and (the late) Robert Nixon – my parents who helped foster my love of all things related to space by taking me to places like the planetarium at Williams College nearly every year, the Boston Museum of Science, and that side trip to NASA when we went to Florida. I wish I had paid more attention when my father spent all that time with me in the backyard pointing out stars, constellations, and comets. Big hugs to my mom who helped type, edit, and encourage me with my original *2492* story I wrote way back when I was in middle school. I may not know the names of all the stars above, but thanks to you, I am creating my own universe.

David Fugate for reading an early draft of this novel. Your suggestions were very helpful, thank you.

Also thanks to: Janis McWayne, Ron Chapin, Robyn Chapin, Euretta Chapin, NASA/JPL-Caltech, Abraham Hicks, Michael Newton, the nice people on my favorite Team Fortress 2 server, and Ben Karis-Nix.

A special thanks to Iron Maiden for providing the majority of the music I listened to while writing this book as well as for the inspiration for the character Ed-D.1E from the cover of your "Stranger In A Strange Land" single. Writing action scenes is so much easier with your music pounding through my headphones. Thanks.

Written by Eric Nixon

You Are A Poet: A Guided Poetry Journal
The Little Hierophant – 2019 poetry collection
Equidistant – 2018 poetry collection
The Cupcake – 2017 poetry collection
2492: Attack Of The Ancient Cyborg – science fiction novel
The Ocean Above – 2016 poetry collection
Cascadia's Fault – 2015 poetry collection
The Taborist – 2014 poetry collection
The Entire Universe – 2013 poetry collection
Trying Not To Blink – 2012 poetry collection
Lost In Thought – poetry collection
Emily Dickinson – Superhero: Vol. 1 – historical fiction novel
Anything But Dreams – poetry collection

Available at Amazon.com/author/ericnixon

Support Independent Authors...

...like me! If you enjoyed this book, please let others know by writing a review on Amazon, Powells, Goodreads, or your favorite place to say kind words about good books. As an independent author, reviews of my books are critical in getting the word out so more people can enjoy these stories. A few words in a review would be a huge help and can really make a difference.

Thank you! I greatly appreciate it.

www.ingramcontent.com/pod-product-compliance
Lightning Source LLC
Chambersburg PA
CBHW071211250626
47159CB00001B/275